Praise for the Ca

"A high-speed chase of a mystery, filled with very likable characters, a timely plot, and writing so compelling that readers will be unable to turn away from the page."

– Kings River Life Magazine

"Will keep you turning pages late into the night and make you think twice about the dark side of the Hollywood Dream."

– Paul D. Marks,
Shamus Award-Winning Author of *Vortex*

"Radio host Carol Childs meets her match in this page-turner. Her opponent is everyone's good guy but she knows the truth about the man behind the mask. Now Carol must reveal a supremely clever enemy before he gets the chance to silence her for good."

– Laurie Stevens,
Award-Winning Author of the Gabriel McRay Series

"A story of suspense, raw emotion, and peril which builds up to a satisfying climax...Silverman has given us another book where we can sit down and get our teeth into, and I look forward to the next in the series. Highly recommended."

– Any Good Book

"Fast paced and cleverly plotted, an edgy cozy with undertones of noir."

– Sue McGinty,
Author of the Bella Kowalski Central Coast Mysteries

"A thoroughly satisfying crime novel with fascinating, authentic glimpses into the world of talk radio and some of its nastier stars...The writing is compelling and the settings ring true thanks to the author's background as a newscaster herself."

– Jill Amadio,
Author of *Digging Too Deep*

"The author gives us a terrific story building up to a climax that will please the reader. The old saying regarding 'people are not always what they seem' fits perfectly in this case...Readers will be waiting impatiently for the next installment."

– Suspense Magazine

"Silverman provides us with inside look into the world of talk radio as Carol Childs, an investigative reporter, finds herself in the middle of a Hollywood murder mystery...A hunky FBI Agent and a wacky psychic will keep readers guessing from beginning to end."

– Annette Dashofy,
USA Today Bestselling Author of Lost Legacy

"Silverman creates a trip through Hollywood filled with aging hippies, greedy agents, and a deadly case of product tampering. Forget the shower scene in *Psycho*; *Shadow of Doubt* will make you scared to take a bath!"

– Diane Vallere,
National Bestselling Author of Pillow Stalk

"Carol is a smart, savvy heroine that will appeal to readers. This is a cozy with a bite."

– Books for Avid Readers

"Crackles with memorable characters, Hollywood legends, and as much action behind the mic as investigative reporter Carol Childs finds in the field."

– Mar Preston,
Author of A Very Private High School

"I loved the tone, the pace, and the drama which pulled me in immediately...All the while I suspected something was amiss, and when it came to fruition, I knew the author was going to pull a fast one, and yes, she did, and bravo because now I must read the next book to see how it all plays out."

– Dru's Book Musings

REAS⊙N TO DOUBT

To Linda,
Enjoy,

Nancy Cole

Copyright

REASON TO DOUBT
A Carol Childs Mystery
Part of the Henery Press Mystery Collection

First Edition | November 2018

Henery Press
www.henerypress.com

Copyright © 2018 by Nancy Cole Silverman
Cover art by Stephanie Savage

Trade Paperback ISBN-13: 978-1-63511-422-5
Digital epub ISBN-13: 978-1-63511-423-2
Kindle ISBN-13: 978-1-63511-424-9
Hardcover ISBN-13: 978-1-63511-425-6

Printed in the United States of America

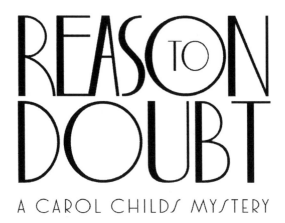

REASON TO DOUBT

A CAROL CHILDS MYSTERY

NANCY COLE SILVERMAN

HENERY PRESS

**The Carol Childs Mystery Series
by Nancy Cole Silverman**

SHADOW OF DOUBT (#1)
BEYOND A DOUBT (#2)
WITHOUT A DOUBT (#3)
ROOM FOR DOUBT (#4)
REASON TO DOUBT (#5)

To Mothers and Daughters

ACKNOWLEDGMENTS

While writing may be a solitary occupation, requiring long spells of isolation in front of a keyboard and a blank page, bringing a book to fruition is not. And for that I'm thankful.

I have a wonderful team of cheerleaders and support, and once a manuscript is completed, they are like angels and help me in so many ways to get it out the door. For that, I would like to thank my husband Bruce and my family, who put up with my double life. My good friend and hiking partner Rhona Robbie, who reads all my initial drafts and provides a much-needed sounding board. My author friends Ellen Byron and Rochelle Staab, who understand the importance of story-therapy and are always there for me.

And for this book, a fabulous reader, Joan Ames in San Diego who enthusiastically stepped forward and volunteered her keen eyes to proofread some early drafts. Without her, my tired eyes would never catch everything.

And to my publisher, Kendel Lynn and her entire staff at Henery Press. They make the Carol Childs Mysteries possible. And finally, and most importantly, my readers. I continue to be inspired by your support. Thank you.

CHAPTER 1

"Say Cheeeese."

The photographer stood barefoot in the sand with his jeans rolled up around his ankles and looked out from behind his black Nikon, winked at my daughter, and snapped off a series of shots while Cate, Charlie and I did our best not to squint into the California sun.

"Come on people, work with me. You too, Mom. Big smile."

I gritted my teeth. I had been wearing the same pasted grin on my face since my daughter had returned home from college with an aspiring young fashion photographer in tow. In Cate's eyes, Pete Pompidou was handsome, talented and destined to be the next Richard Avedon.

And, at the time, she had no reason to believe otherwise.

My name is Carol Childs. I'm a forty-year-old investigative reporter for KTLK, a talk radio station in Los Angeles, and for the last seven months, I've been investigating the deaths of three young fashion models. Victims of a serial killer, who we in the press had tagged the Model Slayer. The Model Slayer is my story, a story I broke after finding the first victim tied to a tree with her hands strung up above her head. News of the murders has terrorized the city and been the top story on every news outlet in town. And, up until my phone rang in my office two weeks after our little beachside photo shoot, a story I had no idea was about to become personal or that my daughter might be involved.

"Mom." The angst in Cate's voice was palpable. "I need your help. The police arrested Pete. They think he's the Model Slayer."

"What?" My stomach knotted. I glanced at the digital clock on my desk. Tuesday, June 12th. 10:43 a.m. At this hour Cate should have been at work, not at the beach. "Where are you?"

"Pete's place. Venice Beach. The police had a search warrant. They banged on the door, came in, and...and they...they–"

"Slow down." Cate was hyperventilating, her breathing unusually fast. "Are you alright?"

"I'm...I'm fine, Mom. But, but Pete's not."

"What happened?"

Cate explained she and Pete were in bed–a vision I quickly blotted from my mind–enjoying a morning latte when the cops broke down the front door.

"They burst in and tore the place apart. Like they were looking for something."

"What?" I asked.

"I don't know, pictures maybe? Pete had photos of all those models who were murdered. The cops took everything. His laptop. Photographs. Notebooks. Mom, they even took his shoes. You've got to help. This is all some horrible mistake."

I glanced at the picture of Cate, her younger brother, Charlie, and me on my desk. Much as I didn't like the idea of Cate cozying up with a young man I barely knew, I could hardly envision Pete a serial killer.

"Catie, I need you to stay where you are. Text me the address and don't say anything. Not a word, not to anybody."

I grabbed my reporter's bag and headed down the hall to Tyler Hunt's office. Tyler's my boss, the station's news and programming director. A redheaded boy wonder, who on any given day, was either my best advocate or my worst nightmare. I'm never certain which, and for good reason. The station had once again gone through a format change, the third in as many years, and Tyler was feeling the pressure of new management to prove himself.

I tapped on the door.

"Tyler?"

Tyler didn't look up. His fingers clicked away on the computer keyboard like a woodpecker, non-stop. His eyes locked on his screen. "What do you need, Childs?"

"Cate called. The police have arrested the Model Slayer."

Tyler tilted his head in my direction, his fingers momentarily paused. "Your daughter?"

"She's in Venice, with a friend. She said the police showed up with a warrant, pulled her friend out of his apartment. Then charged him with the murders."

"What are you waiting for? If she's right, you better get down there. And now. I want that story."

I was halfway out the door, my hand still on the jamb when Tyler hollered back.

"And, Carol—"

I paused, my heart pounding. "Be careful, if Cate's right and she knows this guy—"

"I know," I said.

I didn't wait for Tyler to finish the sentence. If Pete Pompidou was the Model Slayer, I didn't want to think what trouble my daughter had gotten herself into.

It was impossible to find parking in Venice, particularly for those close-knit bungalows along the bike path facing the beach. The closest street is Speedway, which is more like an alley that runs behind the houses with beachfront property. The area is littered with No Parking signs boasting fines more than the monthly payment on my car. Finally, I found metered parking off Washington Boulevard, about three blocks from the address Cate had given me. Kicking off my heels, I grabbed a pair of tennis shoes from my reporter's go-to bag, then jogged, or at least walked as fast as I could in a pencil skirt, down the boardwalk. By the time I reached Pete's bungalow I was panting and out of breath.

I spotted Cate with her back to me, her arms wrapped around herself, staring at the ocean. She was dressed in a pair of short denim cutoffs that showed off her slim, tanned legs, sandals and a gray hoodie she had pulled up over her head. As I approached, she turned and glanced at me, then looked down at the sand. I didn't know whether to be angry or happy to see her.

"What's going on, Catie? You care to explain to me why you're here and not at work this morning?"

Cate's a pre-med major at UC San Diego and had been lucky enough to secure a summer position with UCLA in their pathology department, a rare opportunity for an undergrad.

"Mom. Please, don't lecture me, okay? Not now." Without another word she grabbed me and pulled me to her and buried her head in my shoulder.

I steadied myself, put my arms around her and then took her chin in my hands and turned her face to mine. "Cate, what happened? You need to tell me everything."

"Pete and I...we were...we were having coffee when there's a banging at the front door, and suddenly there's this SWAT team in the house. They started yelling at us to stay put while they went through everything. They pulled Pete's photos from the wall and went through his drawers. Then one of them grabbed me and told me to get dressed. Next thing I knew Pete's in handcuffs and they're dragging him away. I asked what was going on and they told me they were arresting him for the model slayings. That's all they would say."

"Did they ask you anything?"

"They wanted to know if I was okay. They asked me my name and where I lived. Finally, one of the officers told me to get out of there. They'd be in touch."

"Did you get the officer's name?"

"I got a card." Cate took a business card from her back pocket and handed it to me.

Detective Ryan, LAPD Robbery-Homicide.

"Did Pete say anything?"

Cate rolled her eyes.

"What could he say? Other than what he's heard and read in the news, Pete doesn't know anything about the murders. Just 'cause he's a photographer and took a couple of these models' pictures, doesn't mean he's guilty. Mom, you've got to do something."

I didn't have the first idea what I could do to help Pete. But I knew once the news broke about the Model Slayer's arrest, the area would be swarming with reporters. Some would canvas the neighborhood, go door-to-door and talk to neighbors about Pete. While overhead, news choppers, like locusts, would film the location for televised news reports. It was bad enough Cate had been there when Pete was arrested, and if I was going to keep my daughter out of it, we needed to leave right away before someone recognized her.

I hugged Cate, kissed her on the cheek and told her my Jeep was parked at the end of the boardwalk and to go on ahead of me. I'd be along in a minute. Once Cate was out of earshot, I took my iPhone from my bag and called Tyler.

"Newsroom," Tyler's quick staccato voice sounded almost mechanical.

"Tyler, it's Carol. It's Cate's boyfriend alright. The police picked him up this morning."

"For the model slayings? You got verification?"

"They had a warrant, and I've got the detective's card."

Even though Cate was an eyewitness to Pete's arrest, as a reporter, I couldn't risk breaking a story—particularly a story as big as the Model Slayer—and finding out later Cate had been mistaken. She had been frightened when the cops had entered his bungalow and arrested Pete. What I needed was a third party to confirm what Cate had seen.

"Call him, Carol. See if you can get a statement. If the police made an arrest, we'll break into the morning show with the news."

I hung up with Tyler and dialed Detective Ryan's cell and introduced myself. Well, kind of introduced myself. I left out the part about Cate being my daughter.

"Detective Ryan, my name's Carol Childs. I'm a reporter with KTLK Talk Radio. I was talking with a young woman who said she witnessed an arrest this morning in Venice Beach. She believes you arrested the Model Slayer."

"What are you people, ambulance chasers? You know I'm not going to comment on a suspect in custody." The detective's voice was gruff, and I feared he was about to hang up.

I volleyed back good-naturedly. "Hey, we're on the same side here, Detective. You've got a nervous public, and I've got a talk radio station that reaches more than a million listeners. Word of the Model Slayer's arrest would go a long way in calming those nerves."

Ryan barked back. "Central Booking, Miss. That's who you need to call. Until this guy's processed, I've got no comment."

I glanced at my watch. If I wanted the first crack at the story, I needed something fast. An hour from now, Pete would be processed and his name everywhere. I had one chance to be the first to report the Model Slayer's arrest, and I needed to take it.

"Then how about we do this?" I suggested an old reporter's trick, a standby I'd used before to secure information from sources who didn't want to be identified. "I'll ask if you believe the man you picked up in Venice this morning is the Model Slayer. When I do, I'll give you to the count of five to answer. If you don't, I'll assume he is, and you never told me. You good with that?"

"Fire away Ms. Childs."

I asked again, then counted backward. "Five. Four. Three. Two. One."

No answer.

"Detective?"

"Yes?"

"Just wanted to make sure you heard me," I said.

"I heard you, Miss. You got any other questions?"

"No, sir. I've got everything I need. Thank you."

I was elated. I had what no other reporter in town had. Not only news of the arrest of a possible suspect in the model slayings, but a name as well. A name my daughter would probably never forgive me for broadcasting, but I couldn't stop to think about that now.

My cell buzzed. Tyler was waiting. I glanced back up at the boardwalk where Cate was waiting in my Jeep and answered.

"What do you know, Carol? We got a story or not?"

"I got confirmation a few minutes ago the police arrested a suspect in the Model Slayings. Cate was right. It's her friend, Pete Pompidou."

Tyler put me on hold. One thing about talk radio, when news breaks, stations like KTLK are all over it. Like a vulture, once listeners got news of an arrest, it would be non-stop talk all day.

Through the phone, I could hear Tyler set up my report. "We interrupt this broadcast with news from Venice Beach where KTLK reporter Carol Childs says police have arrested a suspect in the Model Slayings. Carol, can you fill us in?"

"Thank you, Tyler. Neighbors along the Venice boardwalk this morning were alarmed when SWAT officers swarmed a beach residence and arrested a man police suspect may be the Model Slayer. A witness, who asked we not use her name, identified the man arrested as Pete Pompidou, a twenty-three-year-old freelance photographer."

CHAPTER 2

When I got back to the car, Cate was huddled in the passenger seat, up against the door with her arms wrapped around herself.

"You want to tell me what's going on? When I left for work this morning, your car was parked in the garage next to mine."

"Pete picked me up." Cate's eyes avoided mine.

"When?"

"Last night."

I looked out at the window at the ocean and bit my bottom lip. Cate had snuck out of the house, and I hadn't even noticed. What kind of mother am I?

"Okay, Cate, let's start at the beginning. Tell me everything you know about Pete Pompidou and how you met."

I would have liked to have the time alone with Cate to go over exactly what she knew about Pete Pompidou. To date, all I had was he was twenty-three, a freelance photographer, in love with my daughter, and liked burritos. My daughter wasn't big on sharing details, and getting anything more was going to take time. But I wasn't about to get any. I hadn't even backed out of the parking space when my cell phone rang. It was Tyler.

"How is she?" Tyler sounded anxious. The only time I'd ever seen Tyler express anything even close to human emotion was when it came to my kids. Cate in particular. Tyler had been raised by a single working mom, too, and I often thought he either related to Cate or maybe had some kind of schoolboy crush on her. The age difference wasn't much. Cate was eighteen and Tyler barely twenty-three. Although somewhere between the bowties, the stovepipe pants, and the high-top tennis shoes, I doubted Tyler had much experience or interest in girls.

"She's with me now," I said. "I'm taking her home."

"Can she hear me?"

"You're on speaker."

"Good. Because, Cate, I need to talk to you. I know this is a shock, but you're going to need to keep your mouth shut. Not a word to anyone, you got that?" Tyler paused.

Cate nodded, and I answered for her. "She understands."

"If the police haven't talked to you already, they will. And you don't want to say anything that will draw you into their investigation. At least not until you've talked to an attorney."

"An attorney!" I couldn't believe what Tyler was saying. "Why would she need an attorney? She doesn't have anything to do with the murders."

"Maybe not."

"Maybe?" My voice cracked. "Tyler, this is Cate we're talking about. Not some perp."

"Slow down, Carol. Your daughter was just found alone in the home of the man the police arrested as a possible suspect in a major crime, and thanks to her we broke the story of his arrest. In the next hour, this story's going to be the lead on every station in town. And Pete Pompidou could be one of the biggest suspected serial killers we've seen in the city since the Hillside Strangler. Believe me, the cops, the District Attorney, and the FBI are going to be all over this case."

"Yes, but she isn't involved, Tyler, she's—"

"Listen to me. I've put in calls to the station's attorney, Mr. King, and Gerhardt Chasen. He's familiar with things like—"

"Chase?" Mr. King didn't worry me, but Chase—a former Army Ranger who had returned from Afghanistan and hung up his PI shingle—he and I had a history. Last year, while Cate was away at school, we worked a case together. I was convinced the only reason Chase was still working as a PI was that he had the goods on some of L.A.'s more powerful players in town and knew where certain bodies were buried. Unfortunately, that list included me, and parts of my body. "Tyler, please tell me you didn't call Chase."

Cate looked over at me. "Mom, who's Chase?"

CHAPTER 3

Maybe it was because I gave Cate the sterilized version of my relationship with Chase that she clammed up. But what could I say? I couldn't explain my feelings about Chase to my daughter any more than I could rationalize them to myself. The truth was, I was still mourning my breakup with Eric, my long-time steady. I missed him, or the thought of him anyway. And Chase? Well, he was a mistake. A weak moment when he was there and I needed him. But I wasn't about to tell my teenage daughter that. As far as Cate was concerned, Chase was a work friend and nothing more. But when I tried to explain it to Cate, it got me an immediate eye roll followed by a heavy sigh and the old, unmerciful silent treatment.

I've never been good with silence.

Finally, when I couldn't take the chill between us any longer, I pulled the mother card from my deck of tricks, and said, "I think you need to tell me how it is you know this Pete Pompidou. I'm your mother. I deserve to know."

"Look. Mom. I know you want to know what's going on. I do, too. But I don't. Okay? And I don't want to talk about it. Not right now." Cate snapped her hoodie up over her head then huddled back in the corner of the passenger seat with her arms wrapped around herself and looked out the window.

The message was clear. Any Q&A on my part would only drive Cate deeper into her shell. I turned on the radio, found her favorite top 40's pop station, and hoped the music might do something to warm things up. It didn't. The silence got stonier and by the time we got home, Cate got out of the car, slammed the Jeep door shut, and followed me up the steps from the garage without saying a word.

It wasn't until I put my key in the front door that things changed.

The door swung open, and my best friend, Sheri, flung her arms wide and hugged me like an Italian mother. "You're home."

Then going to Cate, Sheri threw both arms around her as though Cate was her own daughter. "Cate, you had us so worried. How are you?"

Cate didn't answer

I stepped into the foyer and watched as Sheri kissed Cate's cheek and brushed the hair from her face. I was about to ask how she knew anything when I heard a noise coming from the kitchen.

Misty, my rescue, live-in housekeeper, was bent over a pot of something on the stove and next to her, with an apron tied around his waist and a wooden spoon in his hand, was Chase. The musky smell of mint wafted from the kitchen to the front door.

"You!" My voice hit like a dart across the room. "What are *you* doing here?"

It wasn't like I had been avoiding Chase since our *encounter*– or whatever the proper term for a one-night stand might be–or that I had left things up in the air between us. The fact was, I just wasn't ready to deal with a day-to-day boyfriend. Particularly, one who stopped by unannounced.

"Tyler called." Chase smiled at me and winked.

I rolled my eyes back to Sheri. *Did you know this?*

Sheri shrugged, and by way of an excuse, said, "And then Chase called Misty and Misty called me, and well, here we are."

"Just like one big happy family," Chase said.

Cate, with her arms still about Sheri, looked over at me. "Mom? Who's that?"

"Gerhardt Chasen," I said, "He's a– "

"Friend?" Cate gave Chase a quick once over and from the look on her face, I could tell she liked what she saw. Mid-thirties, tall, dark wavy hair, blue eyes, with a short stubble beard and dressed in a T-shirt and jeans. "Yeah, right, Mom."

Chase walked away from the stove, handed me the spoon, and extended his hand to Cate. "People call me Chase. Your mom and I work together."

"Sometimes," I said firmly. I slapped the spoon back into Chase's hand and went into the kitchen to get a drink of water.

"You a reporter?" Cate asked.

"No," Chase answered.

"Cop then?"

"Neither. Private Investigator. The difference is we don't arrest people. Instead, we dig around for things the cops sometimes miss. Your mom's boss thought I might be able to help, and the station's attorney, Mr. King, hired me to look around."

Chase took a sucker from inside his shirt pocket, unwrapped it, and offered it to Cate.

Cate smiled. The first smile I'd seen all day. "And you carry these instead of a gun?"

"No, but it beats smoking. It's my vice."

Cate took the candy from his hand like a baby and I glanced back at Misty. *Do you believe this?*

Misty is a flashback to the sixties, a former Hollywood psychic who came to California in a flower painted VW camper selling love potions. I've never been one to believe in any of that stuff. Although, throughout her career, she was a favorite with the Hollywood set and had consulted with the FBI on some pretty big cases. Several years ago, we worked a case together. But that was before she fell out of favor with her agent and her eyesight and memory started to fail. Last year, she showed up on my doorstep and suggested I might need a housekeeper. She keeps saying she's going to move out, but for the time being she's a welcome relief to my busy schedule.

Misty put the lid back on the pot and shuffled over to the kitchen table. "Well, don't just stand there, child, come in and sit down. You must be starving. I've made some nettle soup. It'll clear your head and calm your nerves. And, Carol, it wouldn't hurt you either."

I'll never understand the effect some men have on women. But whatever magic Chase had, it was working wonders with my daughter. She sat next to him at the table, and within minutes she was not only sucking on the lollipop he had given her, but also explaining everything she hadn't shared with me about Pete Pompidou and his roving photography business.

I interrupted. "So, Pete Pompidou isn't a student at UC San Diego?"

Cate took the sucker out of her mouth and exhaled like she didn't believe I didn't know.

"No, Mom. How many times do I have to tell you? Pete's an artist. He's not interested in school. He doesn't think it has anything to offer him. He wants to take pictures and share his vision with the world."

I glanced over at Sheri. Nothing Cate said about Pete was making me feel any better about him.

"He travels up and down the state taking photographs," Cate said. "Kind of like Ansel Adams."

"I thought he wanted to be a fashion photographer like Richard Avedon?" I said.

"He prefers nature, but he can't make a living just shooting pictures of mountains and rivers right now, so he makes his money taking pictures of models. They pay him for headshots and such. You know how models and actors are. They always have to have their photos updated. It's not much, but it pays."

"And when he's on the road, where does he sleep? In his car?" I sounded like a snob, but I couldn't help myself. This vagabond drifter was sleeping with my daughter.

"Mom, don't be so judgmental. He's got a van. Like Misty's, only a little newer. And when he's here in town, he shacks up with a friend at the beach."

"That's the place in Venice where the police arrested him?" Chase asked.

"It belongs to his friend or his friend's parents anyway. His roommate's away right now. That's why Pete asked me down last night."

I clenched my jaw. The news wasn't getting any better.

"His friend got a name?" Chase asked.

"Billy Tyson. His father's some big shot investment banker. The house is his. I don't know anything more than that. But Pete's not the Model Slayer, and neither is his friend. This whole thing's ridiculous."

"I'll tell you what's ridiculous, Cate. You sneaking out of here in the middle of the night and going to the beach. How could you do that?"

Sheri bumped shoulders with me and whispered. "Careful, Mom. The girl's in love. Patience."

Sheri didn't need to remind me to be patient. I wasn't much older than Cate when I married her dad. Patience wasn't part of my vocabulary back then and neither was Cate who was born barely nine months later.

"I'm not doing anything different than I would at school, Mom. You just have to get used to it."

"I'll tell you what I'll get used to. You going to work every day, coming home every night and staying in. That's what I'll get used to. And you will too."

"Are you grounding me? I'm a little old for that don't you think?" Cate stood up, took the sucker from her mouth, and slammed her hand on the table. "I'm in college now, Mom, I know what I'm doing. And I don't have to ask permission."

I looked over at Misty then back at Sheri. I could use a little help here. Sheri raised an eyebrow, an indication for me to dial it back a bit.

Then in a final outburst, Cate announced she was going upstairs. "I need to be alone."

"We're not done here," I said.

I wanted to follow her, but Sheri grabbed my hand and shook her head. "Let her go. She needs some time."

CHAPTER 4

The next day the headlines in the *LA Times* read, "Suspect in Model Slayings Arrested." Beneath the story, front and center, above the fold, a photo of Pete Pompidou with his hands cuffed behind his back stared out at me. From the slack look on his face and the blond hair hanging in his eyes, he looked like a fugitive on the lam. A two-page jump story included details of the murders along with headshots of the three young models: Shana Walters, Kara Stieffers, and Eileen Kim.

According to the story in the paper, the police believed all three girls had been lured to their deaths thinking they were meeting with a photographer for a photo shoot. Blood from victims and traces from the killer had been used to paint smiles on their faces. The coroner said stab wounds had been inflicted post-mortem. He theorized the killer must have stabbed himself as well when he cut the girls. Investigators described each scene similarly. The bodies of the women all appeared as though they had been posed like centerfolds. Their hands were tied above their heads, secured with plastic ties. A twelve-inch piece of white nylon rope had been wrapped around their necks, like a choker collar. Cause of death had been strangulation.

The arrest of the suspected Model Slayer made for a big news day. Reports about Pete's arrest were everywhere, including on KTLK.

KTLK's morning talk team, Kit and Carson, began fielding questions from listeners as soon as I finished my own ripped-from-the-headlines version of the latest news. Not wanting to take part in any freewheeling conversation about Pete or his arrest, I packed up my gear and was about to head back to my own small office when Tyler poked his head in the news booth.

"My office. Now."

I followed Tyler back through the newsroom to his office, a cramped ten-by-ten square room stacked with old newspapers. I waited until he sat down.

"What's up?" I asked.

"Cate say anything more to you last night about this guy the police arrested?"

"You mean other than she's convinced they've got the wrong guy? No." I shook my head. "She says the only possible connection Pete Pompidou has to any of the slain models was that he took their pictures...before they were murdered. She thinks this whole thing is just some crazy coincidence and that the police are jumping to conclusions."

Tyler hesitated, then picked up a pink call-slip. "She may be right."

"Why?" I felt my heart quicken. Tyler wasn't one to jump to conclusions. "What do you know?"

"I got a call this morning from a woman who said her name was Xstacy."

"Xstacy?" I repeated the name with a question in my voice. The name sounded made up. But in Hollywood, lots of people have stage names. With talk radio, it's not unusual for people to call-in using a pseudonym, afraid of being recognized. "Really?"

"That's what she said. Told me she works as a cocktail waitress at the Sky High Club, a topless bar by the airport. I suppose for somebody in that line of work, the name works. You know it?"

"It's not quite my style, Tyler, but I've seen the billboard." It didn't take much imagination to know what went on in a place like the Sky High Club. Outside, the club had a neon sign, an illuminated statue of a partially nude girl raising a whiskey glass to her mouth as she winked at passersby. "Why?" I asked.

"Because Xstacy agrees with your daughter. She thinks the

police have the wrong man in custody."

"And she knows this how?" I asked.

"She says the Model Slayer's dead. Because she killed him."

"What?" I sat down in front of Tyler's desk. "When?"

"Last week. She said she ran him over with her van behind the club."

"Was this some type of hit-and-run?"

"On the contrary. She claims she reported it to the police. And, according to her, the cops wrote it up as an accident."

That much didn't surprise me. Between the city's growing homeless population and the number of people staring at their cell phones as they stepped into traffic, L.A. was quickly becoming the pedestrian death capital of the nation.

"And what now? She wants to confess on the air maybe?" I asked.

"No. She says there's more to it than that. She wants to talk to a reporter. It may be nothing, Carol, and I'm hesitant to pass this off to you, seeing as you're somewhat involved, but—"

"But, since it's Cate and you're understaffed, you're going to give it to me." I stood up and snatched the call slip from Tyler's hand. "Besides, if she is just some nut case, it's no big deal. And if she's not, and we uncover information the police don't have—and aren't likely to go looking for since they already have Pete Pompidou in their custody—then you're helping me help my daughter."

Tyler held his hands up as though to surrender, then pointed to the door. "Just go. Check it out and keep me posted."

I called the number Tyler had scribbled on the call slip and suggested Xstacy meet me at Dupar's, a diner located next to the Farmer's Market off Third and Fairfax, not far from the station. We agreed to a late lunch at two p.m.

I had no idea what to expect, but with a name like Xstacy and knowing she worked at a gentlemen's club, I figured I would know her when I saw her. I took a seat in one of the restaurant's red vinyl booths, next to the windows facing the parking lot, and grabbed a menu. From the looks of things, not much had changed at Dupar's since the day the place opened in 1938. The waitstaff wore the same old-fashioned white uniforms with aprons and little caps. It was still possible to order a mile-high stack of pancakes or a Monte Cristo sandwich. The only difference was a much more modern price.

I ordered an ice tea and waited. Xstacy was running late. Finally, about 2:20, I noticed a dirty, white utility van mounted on giant oversized truck tires pulling into a parking space directly behind the window where I was seated. It was obvious the van had been in an accident. The chassis was sprung, the front fender dented, and the right headlight had been patched with duct tape.

The windows of the van were tinted black, so I couldn't see the driver. But when the door on the driver's side opened and a pair of short, very pale legs in combat boots shimmied out from behind the wheel, I knew, given the car, this had to be Xstacy. She wasn't at all what I expected from a waitress working at a strip club. Xstacy was plump, a good twenty pounds overweight and dressed in a plaid mini-skirt and an Annie Oakley-style fringed vest with a black halter top beneath it. She had tats running up and down her arms and her hair, short and boy-cut, was dyed a kind of red-magenta with purple streaks.

I stood up when she entered the restaurant. I had described myself on the phone as a tall blonde person. I'm six feet in heels and hard to miss. Xstacy noticed me right away.

"You must be Carol Childs?"

I nodded and pointed to an empty seat in the booth and sat down. "And you must be Xstacy."

Without saying another word, Xstacy slid into the booth, picked up the menu on the table, and started to flip through it. In addition to the tats up and down her arms, Xstacy had silver rings on every finger, and the nails on her hands had been polished black and were chipped and bitten to the quick.

"Mind if I order?" Xstacy's brown eyes flashed at me from above the menu. "I'm starving."

"Order whatever you like," I said. "It's on me. I'm not hungry."

The waitress came and Xstacy ordered a double cheeseburger with onion rings, plus fries and an extra-large slice of cherry pie a la mode with a soda.

"Bet you don't get many calls like mine." Xstacy played with her napkin, twisting it between her hands as she spoke.

"You'd be surprised," I said. Talk radio gets a lot of crazies. People calling in to confess to all kinds of things. Some in hopes of clearing their conscience, others seeking fame or maybe just a free meal. Judging from the size of Xstacy's order, this was the latter. "But you're right, you're the only one to call and confess to killing the Model Slayer."

"You don't believe me, do ya?"

"I didn't say that. But I am curious as to why you called."

"Maybe it's 'cause I got a conscience and I don't wanna see Pete Pompidou take the wrap for somethin' he didn't do."

"You know Pete?" I pushed my ice tea away and reached into my reporter's bag for my notepad. If Xstacy knew Pete, I wanted to know how and why and exactly when they'd met.

"A little. Pete and me, we met when I was still on the street. He was taking pictures for some news story about homeless kids like I used to be. That article's what got me off the street. Some ways I guess I owe him."

"How long ago?" I asked.

"Not long. A year. Maybe more."

The waitress arrived with Xstacy's order and placed it on the table. Without waiting, Xstacy reached for her burger with both hands and took a bite. Then, grabbing her napkin like she was suddenly self-conscious of her table manners, she dabbed the side of her mouth. "But you gotta promise me somethin' 'fore I tell you anymore."

"What's that?"

"You don't go tellin' the cops 'bout me. It's the reason I called the radio station, you being a reporter and all. I thought you could find a way to convince the cops Pete's not their guy without telling 'em 'bout me. Like they do in the movies. So the cops don't come back after me and wanna talk."

"You mean off the record?" I put my pen down.

"If that's what ya call it, yeah. Off the record. I just don't want nobody knowing it was me who told you the guy I hit was the Model Slayer."

I looked away. If Xstacy was on the level, she was going to have to tell me something about the murders I didn't already know.

"Okay, but before I agree to that. Tell me something that'll prove to me why you're convinced this man you hit was the Model Slayer."

Xstacy took another bite of her burger and started talking. "Those girls, the models he killed, he painted smiles on their faces with his own blood."

I pushed myself away from the table. If this was an excuse for a free lunch, I'd pay the server and leave now. I didn't have time to be drawn into some made-up story she was peddling.

"Nice try, Xstacy. That was reported in the paper."

"Wait." Xstacy held her hand up. "He took their pictures with one of those Polaroid cameras right before he killed them."

Now she had my interest. I put my elbows on the table and leaned closer to her. "How do you know that? Did he show you a photo?"

"No. And I didn't ask. I'm not some freak." Xstacy took a sip of her cola and put the glass back down on the table. "But I heard him talkin' about it plenty. So you gonna promise me or what?"

None of the news reports had mentioned anything about Polaroid photos being left at the crime scene. But I knew it was true. I had seen the photos myself when I had reported on Shana Walters' murder, the first of the Model Slayer's victims. They had been scattered at her feet and were the kind I'd seen Pete use to test for composition before taking a final shot. When I questioned one of the detectives about them, he asked me not to mention them in my report. Which I didn't. In high profile cases, it's not unusual for cops to ask the press to hold back certain details. But the fact Xstacy knew about the photos was.

"Okay," I said. "I promise." I had no idea what to expect, but as far as the rules for confidentiality go, as long as Xstacy wasn't about to tell me she was planning to murder someone else, there was no reason I couldn't keep her name out of it. "But first, I need you to start by telling me what you know about the Model Slayer."

"I know for sure it's not Pete. 'Cause like I told your boss when I called the station, I killed the Model Slayer. I ran him over with my van a couple weeks ago outside the Sky High Club where I worked."

"And then you reported it to the police?"

"I did. Just like you're supposed to. Told the cops it was an accident." Xstacy put her napkin down and started to bite the side of her thumb. "But—"

"But what?"

"It didn't really happen that way. I mean like how I told the cops."

I glanced at the room around us. The restaurant was nearly empty. Midday slow. A couple of regulars at the counter, but nobody close enough to hear our conversation. All the same, I lowered my voice, "Then how did it happen, Xstacy?"

"I knew he'd be there. He had been coming to the club for months. Always sittin' at my table, up front by the stage. When I'd bring him drinks, I'd hear him talkin' 'bout the girls on stage."

"Was he talking to himself?"

"No. There was another man sittin' at the table with him. Don't ask me who, I couldn't tell you. The club's dark and with the strobe lights, I can't always see the faces. Anyway, one night I have this tray full of drinks, and I'm waitin' to get paid by the table next to him, and I hear him talkin'. He's super drunk and talkin' to the guy at the table with him, and I realize he's sayin' somethin' about those models. How they had all been stabbed and their blood used to paint smiles on their faces. At first, I thought he must have read somethin' 'bout it in the news. But then he kept talking 'bout how they all deserved what they got. Little temptresses, he called them. Said he was taking their pictures so other young women wouldn't follow them into temptation."

"He said this in a public place?"

"It's a bar, a strip club. It's not like anybody's paying attention to him. Everybody's drunk, know what I mean?"

"And he used the word temptress and the phrase, 'into temptation'? You're sure?"

"Swear to God." Xstacy crossed herself with the sign of the cross. "And he started talkin' 'bout the pictures, too. Said he left some Polaroids at the foot of each girl. Like a shrine, only to shame them."

"I assume you told your management?"

"They thought I was makin' it up. Said nobody would be stupid enough to take pictures of a dead body and 'sides, there was nothin' in the paper about photos being found with the girls."

I nodded. I could understand the club, particularly a strip club with a questionable clientele, not wanting to support a whistle-blower. And Xstacy didn't exactly look like a reliable witness.

"Plus, the guy was a big tipper," Xstacy said. "The bouncers, they looked out for the girls. But when there's money on the table, what are they gonna do? Throw him out? Besides, the last thing a club like the Sky High wants is a bunch of undercover cops hanging 'round."

"And you never told the cops?"

"I figured I'd done my job. And if the club knew I'd said anything, by the time the cops got 'round to lookin' into it, I'd be out of a job."

"So what did you do?"

"That night?" Xstacy paused and took the last bite of her burger and wiped her hands on her legs. "I spilled my drink tray on him. That good enough for you?"

I squelched a smiled. "I take it that didn't work?"

"Hardly. I nearly lost my job. But it was worth it. I told you, the man was disgusting. He used to make all kinds of hand signals to the girls when they were dancing. You know what I mean." Xstacy put her hand to her mouth and spread her middle and ring finger, then started to pantomime an obscene gesture with her tongue. "And when he started harassing my girlfriend–"

"Your girlfriend?"

"Yeah, Jewels. She's one of the dancers. I call her that 'cause the club calls her their 'Crown Jewel'. Best dancer they got. He kept following her around. Showing up backstage, and out back when she'd go for a cigarette break. Kept telling her how pretty he thought she was and how much he could help, and that he wanted to take her picture all professional like."

"And?"

"And then, Jewels and me, we came up with a plan. If the club wouldn't get rid of him, we would. So we waited 'til it was almost closing time and Jewels went out back for a smoke. Like she usually did. Meanwhile, I closed out my drink tab, told everybody I was going home for the night, then went out back and got in my car and waited. Few minutes later, this creep shows up and starts hitting on Jewels, just like we knew he'd do. That's when I gunned it. Mowed him down like the miserable piece of sh–"

"Whoa! Hang on a minute." I put my hands up and took a deep breath. This was a very different story from what I expected to hear. "You deliberately ran him over? Planned it out and waited for him to come out of the club and then hit him?"

"Yep. And I'd do it again if I had to."

My head was spinning. "No regrets? No remorse?"

"He dented my van. But other than that, I figured I did the world a favor."

I steadied myself with both hands on the side of the table and took a deep breath, then exhaled slowly. If what Xstacy had just told me was true, she had just confessed to first-degree murder. "Okay, so this man you hit, the man you think was the Model Slayer, you got his name?"

"Ely Wade. But I didn't know it until after the accident. The guy always paid cash. Never used a credit card. It wasn't until the cops checked for his wallet that I got a name."

"And the cops just assumed he was some derelict?"

"I don't know what the cops thought. By the time they got there, he smelled of alcohol and cigarettes, and his clothes were all messed up from the accident. I may have helped a bit. You know, poured a little extra scotch on him. I think the cops figured he had tied one on and gone out back to sober up 'fore driving home. Cops said he was in the wrong place at the wrong time and I wasn't about to say any different. I just wanted to get out of there."

Xstacy stared at the empty soda glass in front of her and started playing with it, turning it around between her fingers. She had been careful throughout our conversation not to make eye contact. If I've learned one thing as a reporter, it's a fallacy to think eye contact made a Jack's-worth of difference. I had been looked straight in the eye by some pretty good con artists, while some of the most oppressed victims I'd interviewed refused to make any eye contact at all. I put my hands on top of hers to stop her fidgeting. I thought there might be something more she wanted to say.

"You want something else to drink?"

"Why not? I got time." Xstacy shrugged and looked out the window at her van. "It's not like I got anywhere to be."

I signaled the waiter and waited for him to refill her glass. "How long have you been working at the club?"

"Depends on what you mean by long." Xstacy took a sip of her drink then put the glass down. "I've never been anywhere for long if you know what I mean. I move around a lot."

"You have a last name?"

"My real name's Stacy Minor, but nobody needs to know that. 'Sides like I told you, I need you to keep my story about Jewels and me running that Ely Wade guy down on purpose a secret. I don't want no cops or anybody else coming back at me or Jewels 'bout it."

"What do mean coming back at you?" I took a sip of my ice tea. I couldn't help but feel there was something more to Xstacy's story than she was telling me. "You ever been in trouble with the law?"

"I'm not a prostitute if that's what you're asking. Not that I haven't lived the life. Got arrested once, but I was underage and the record's sealed. Turned out to be a good thing, or as good as those things can be. Got me into a shelter, and later I lived with a foster family who helped me turn my life around. I was with them 'til I aged out of the system at eighteen."

"How old are you now?"

"Nineteen. But my driver's license says I'm twenty-one. Which I need to be to serve liquor. So that's 'tween you and me, too."

Xstacy's age surprised me. I would have pegged her much older.

"Where do you live?"

"Different places. Right now I got a place in Venice Beach with a bunch of other kids like me. All trying to stay clean. Look, I didn't come here to talk about me, but if it helps, you can call Jewels." Xstacy reached across the table for my notepad and wrote Jewels' number down. "She's better at this kind of thing than I am. Tell her we talked. Long as you promise to keep her name out of it, she'll tell you all about Ely and what went down. The rest is up to you."

I called Tyler from the car as I left Dupar's. The phone rang through to his office. He answered and put me on speaker.

"What ya got, Childs? I'm on deadline."

In the background, I could hear the sound of the newsroom, the clacking of Tyler's keyboard, and the broadcast of the midday team piped through the office on the intercom. At best I had only half of Tyler's attention and not much time to get more. I led with news of Xstacy's confession.

"Xstacy's convinced she killed the Model Slayer. And get this— she claims she and her girlfriend, a dancer from the club named Jewels, did it together. Planned it out, step-by-step."

"You believe her?"

"She knew about the Polaroids. Said this guy they killed was a regular at the club and bragged about the murders."

Tyler picked up the phone.

"Xstacy give you her real name?"

"She did, but it wouldn't make any difference if she didn't." I gripped the steering wheel tighter. Tyler wasn't going to like this. "She'd only speak to me if I agreed to keep both her name and that of her girlfriend off the record."

"Undisclosed source confesses to the murder?" Tyler chuckled. "I've heard that before." I expected Tyler to say as much. Talk radio had more than its share of people who called to hype conspiracy theories or confess to things they hadn't done. "We're going to need more than that for a story, Carol."

"Let me chase it, Tyler. There's something there. Xstacy gave me her girlfriend's number. She said Jewels could back up her story and I think there's more to it than she'd say. Until I've talked with her friend and verified this so-called 'accident', I don't know how on the level this all is. But if there's anything there at all, I'm going to pursue it."

"Sorry. No can do. You're too close to this case. I need you to hand it off to–"

"Forget it, Tyler. No way am I passing this off. Not to anyone. If I uncover something to prove the police arrested Pete Pompidou by mistake, it'll go a long way to healing my relationship with my daughter, which right now needs a lot of salvaging."

Tyler paused. "You sure you want to do this, Carol? Might not work out as well for your daughter as you think. I mean if you find he's guilty." My stomach knotted. "Just sayin'."

"I'll do two weeks of traffic reports if you give it to me."

"Make it a month, and you got a deal."

I wasn't surprised Tyler agreed. KTLK's news department operated with a staff of five. Tyler, Eddie, a retired tower engineer, a part-time Sportscaster who filled in on the weekend, and me. Finding someone to sub in for a story I was already working on would be tough. Volunteering to do traffic reports virtually guaranteed Tyler would give me the story.

"And don't tell anyone what you're up to. I mean no one. Not

Chase. Not your family. No one. Close as you are to this case with your daughter dating the prime suspect, the cops are going to be watching and listening to everything you do and report on. If the cops learn you're sitting on the confession of a suspected first-degree murderer, they're going to want to talk to you. In fact, they'll probably subpoena you and threaten to throw you in jail if you don't reveal your source."

Tyler didn't have to explain to me the importance of not revealing the name of a confidential informant. News operations, particularly those investigating stories behind the scenes, needed insider information. Without people willing to talk off the record, KTLK didn't have leads on stories that were the station's lifeblood. As a reporter, it was my job to take what a confidential informant gave me, verify that information with a second and third source, and report it. If word got out a reporter had rolled over and given up to the police what information had been given to us in confidence, that reporter would be burned and the station toast.

CHAPTER 5

The first thing I noticed when I got home Wednesday night was Cate's car. I considered it a good sign since we'd argued the night before about her being grounded. The second thing I noticed was Chase. He was standing in the courtyard outside my front door when I came up the stairs from the parking garage.

"I hope you're not planning on making this a habit," I said.

"Nice to see you too, Blondie." Chase took a sucker from inside his jacket and smiled. He hadn't shaved and there was just enough of a shadowed beard to remind me of how it had tickled against my face. "Cate here?"

I brushed the thought of our previous close encounter from my mind and placed the key in the lock. "Should be. Her car's parked downstairs."

"Good, because I thought as a *friend*," he emphasized the word, "this deserved a face-to-face."

"Friend, huh?" I glanced over my shoulder, the smell of his cologne distracting. "You talked to the police?"

"I did. And I've got some news about Pete, I think the both of you should hear."

I shoved the front door open. Misty and Cate were seated at the kitchen table, a copy of the morning paper in front of them. The smell of homemade lasagna wafted from the oven.

Cate looked up and, seeing Chase behind me, smiled. "He's back."

"He is." I dropped my bag on the counter and joined Misty and Cate at the table. "And he's got news concerning Pete."

"You talked to Pete?" Cate sounded hopeful.

"No. But I did talk to a couple of buddies of mine in Robbery-Homicide. They agreed to share with me a little of what they knew in exchange for my help on another case." Chase pulled a chair up to the table. "Word around the unit is they started tracking Pete after Shana Walters was killed. They're pretty sure they got their guy."

"Why?" Cate's eyes narrowed, and she looked anxiously at Chase, then back at Misty.

"They didn't tell me everything, but when they found Shana's car, they also found one of Pete's business cards in the glove box. He mention anything to you about when they last worked together?"

"No." Cate shook her head.

Chase locked eyes with me. I wasn't going to like this.

"Pete's name was on the cell phones for the other two models he's suspected of killing. Each of them had called him prior to their deaths. And when homicide detectives learned Pete was in Venice and had a girl with him—alone in his apartment—they got nervous." Chase paused and looked at me. "They were afraid Cate might be his next victim."

"What?" I put my hand to my heart and looked at Cate. "Did the cops say anything to you about that?"

"No. And that's ridiculous. They asked my name and if I was okay. Then they told me I should get out of there. Why would they think—"

"Hold on," Chase held his hand up. "The good news here is that because Cate's okay and doesn't appear to have been a victim, the cops may have overreached. I'll get to that in a minute, but first, Cate, how well do you know Pete's roommate, Billy Tyson?"

"Billy?" Cate shook her head and gestured with her hands up. "I've never met him in person if that's what you mean. Pete said he worked with him a couple times. He liked to tell people he was a photographer, but he's not."

"I did a little checking around on my own. Pete's roommate's a registered sex offender. He was charged and convicted of having sex with a minor when he was eighteen. Turns out, Tyson had a rich daddy and paid some expensive defense attorney who advised him to plead guilty to avoid jail time. He was released on probation. But the registry jacket as a sex offender follows him the rest of his life. He's required by law to notify the officials where he's living, and if he moves or leaves the state, he has to let them know. The place at the beach belongs to his family, and it looks like he's been there for at least ten years."

"Oh, come on. It's not like Pete knew that." Cate shook her head. "He didn't even know Billy before he found an ad on Craig's List. And they didn't exactly hang out together. The beach house is a place for Pete to crash between jobs. He's not there that often."

Chase rubbed his hands together.

"Are you aware Pete never listed the Venice address on his driver's license?"

"So?" Cate shrugged. "Paperwork's not Pete's thing. Maybe he forgot."

"Maybe. But he also forgot the registration on his van. It's past due, along with a couple outstanding traffic tickets. In fact, there was a bench warrant out for his arrest."

"Arrest?" I looked at Cate and shook my head.

"And that's not all. Pete's last tax return was three years ago when he claimed moving expenses from Seattle to L.A. His real name's not Pete Pompidou. It's Peter Phillips. Born June first, 1989. Vancouver, Canada."

"Is he even legal?" My voice cracked.

"Mom!" Cate snapped at me and crossed her arms.

Chase continued. "He has a green card. But his tax return back then showed he worked briefly for Lenny Marx Photography. Maybe you heard of him?" Chase looked at me and raised a brow. I shook my head. The name meant nothing. "Big-time photographer. Does a lot of high-end celebrity portrait stuff. Mostly black and white. Museum quality. Like Annie Leibovitz. But according to his former employer, Pete didn't last too long. Lenny said he used him mostly for setting lights and stuff, but thought the kid was getting antsy. Didn't like putting in the time to learn the trade. After a couple months, Pete told Lenny he was moving on. If it hadn't been for Pete's website, my buddies in Robbery-Homicide might not be so interested."

"What about his website?" I asked.

"PompidouPhotography.com. It was a virtual cash box of information for the cops."

"Why? Because he's got photos of each of those girls on his website?" Cate's tone was sarcastic. "It's not exactly like he's the only photographer in L.A."

"Cate!" I scolded.

"Oh come on, Mom, you know how it is with actors and models in this town. They need new headshots and photos all the time. The photos Pete took were all the girl-next-door type of shots. The paper said all those girls were posed like centerfolds. Pete never took nude shots. That's not his style."

I glanced over at Chase. It sounded reasonable.

"Which, if Cate's right," Chase said, "might work in Pete's favor. That and the fact the site didn't have the best security. An amateur hack could have downloaded the models' photos with their contact information right from the site."

"See. It could be anyone," Cate said.

"Maybe, but in addition to the photos on the website, the cops had a search warrant for his apartment."

Cate rolled her eyes. "Yeah, I was there. Remember?"

Chase laid out what investigators had found. A pair of tan work boots. Size ten. The tread matching footprints from the sites where the girls had been murdered. "Forensics is checking soil samples now to see if there's a connection. Plus, Cate, they found a silver lunchbox tucked away in the back of a closet at the house. Detectives think Pete may have been keeping souvenirs."

Cate bit her lips and looked up at the ceiling. I wasn't sure if she were about to cry or scream. I reached for her hand, and she pulled away and crossed her arms .

"Inside," Chase said, "were a pair of earrings, a couple of barrettes and a hairbrush with long strands of dark hair in it. Investigators are pretty sure the hair may be that of Eilene Kim."

"Did they find a tube of lipstick as well? Gloss anyway. And don't bother checking for DNA. I'm sure they'll find it. That lunchbox was Pete's toolkit. He wasn't keeping souvenirs. The brush? The barrettes? The lip gloss? They were there if the girls needed something for a shoot."

"Detectives have also been talking to a friend of Shana Walters. She remembers the last time she saw Shana. She told her she was going on a photo shoot with Pete Pompidou."

"Look, I don't care how much so-called 'evidence' the cops think they found or who says what about Shana Walters going to meet Pete for a photo shoot. Pete didn't kill that girl or anyone else. And I can prove it."

"Wha–" I was ready to explode.

Chase held his hand up to keep me quiet.

"You may have to do that, Cate. The cops are going to want to talk to you. And, Carol, if I were you, I'd get Mr. King's number on speed dial."

"If I need a lawyer," Cate said, "I'll call my dad. He's an attorney."

"Cate," I put my hand on her arm and held it firmly. "Your dad's a corporate lawyer. He doesn't handle criminal cases, not like this."

Cate shook my hand free. "Yeah, well it won't matter. If the cops ask me, I was with Pete the day Shana Walters was murdered. I remember because I saw her picture in the paper the next day."

"Do you remember where you were when you saw it?" I asked.

"Big Bear. We drove up for the weekend and stopped for gas and supplies at a convenience store."

"You remember the name?" Chase asked.

"Big Bear something. I forget. But we were there twice. We went back the next day for some canned chili. It was cold and Pete loves chili. We cooked it over a small Bunsen burner because we couldn't get a fire going."

"You get a receipt? Anything to prove you were there?" I asked.

"I don't know. Pete paid for everything. If he got a receipt, it's probably in the glove box in the van. And just so you know, since the cops have Pete's van, there were shovels and ropes in the back because we were camping."

I raised my brows and looked back at Chase. If Cate could prove they had been there, if there had been cameras or if we could find the receipt, it might be enough to explain why Pete was in the same area where Shana was murdered. And if Cate could retrace their steps, we might be able to convince the cops they had the wrong guy.

Misty stood up and brushed a section of Cate's hair behind her ear. "It's going to be okay, Catie."

"I hope you're right, Misty. Pete doesn't deserve any of this." Cate pushed Misty's hand away and stood up. "I'm sorry, I can't listen to this anymore. I'm going upstairs."

Misty went back to the kitchen to check on dinner.

I waited until Cate was out of earshot. "I don't see any hard evidence here. If all the cops have on Pete is a pair of shoes that are maybe the same size and type worn by the killer and a–"

"Not so fast," Chase said. "Investigators don't think Pete acted alone."

"They certainly don't think Cate–"

"No. But they do think someone else may have helped him. Kenneth Bianchi, the Hillside Strangler, didn't act alone. He had his cousin, Angelo Buono. Together they killed ten women. It's likely whoever's killing these girls isn't working alone either."

"And now that Pete's roommate is missing, and has a record, you think there're two of them? That they're in on this together?"

"I'm not thinking anything at all. Not yet. All I know is your daughter's no fool, Carol. I seriously doubt if Pete Pompidou was some serial killer she'd be running around with him. But the fact Pete's roommate has a record and is missing doesn't make things any easier for him."

I was tempted to say while I wasn't wild about Pete, I didn't fancy him a serial killer. Even harder, I had to resist the urge to tell Chase about Xstacy. How she had called the station and confessed to killing the Model Slayer. But I didn't dare. I knew better. Tyler had warned me not to say a word to anyone, and I had promised Xstacy I'd leave her name out of it. If I broke my silence and told Chase, not only would I be violating a trust, but if things went south and I was later arrested for withholding evidence in a murder investigation and asked to reveal my source and refused, Chase might be called in to testify and asked what he knew as well. Not a good idea. Besides, I had no proof anything Xstacy had shared with me was true. I still had my research to do concerning the accident and a call to make to Xstacy's friend, a dancer named Jewels. Whoever she was.

Misty returned from the kitchen and placed a casserole dish down in front of us.

"I made your favorite, Chase. Lasagna Bolognese with homemade pasta and some fresh herbs from the garden. Help yourself. I'll take a plate upstairs for Cate and leave you two alone to figure things out."

I waited for Misty to leave, then asked Chase if he had told Misty he was coming over. How else would she have known to make his favorite dish from scratch? Given Misty's age and speed at which she shuffled around the kitchen, it would have taken her several hours.

"No. Absolutely not," he said.

"Then how did she know to make–"

"What? Lasagna Bolognese? Carol, at some point you just have to give yourself over to the fact you're living with a psychic, and like it or not, she knows about us."

"Us?" I got up from the table and took two dishes from the cabinet. "There is no us, Chase. There was just that once and it was a mistake."

"A mistake?" Chase took the dishes from my hands and put them on the table. "I'd like to make a few more mistakes like that in my life."

"Yeah, well, that's not going to happen." I sat down and placed a napkin on my lap. If it weren't for the fact Chase was already plugged into the investigation and had uncovered more information about Pete than I knew, I would have told him to go home right then. Instead, I said, "You need to understand, just because we're working together doesn't mean anything's going to happen between us. I don't care what Misty thinks. We're not an item."

Chase scooped out a large portion of Misty's lasagna onto his plate. Hot gooey stands of stringy cheese clung from the plate to the spoon. My taste buds began to salivate.

"Come on, Carol, it's not like I seduced you. If I recall you were very–"

"Vulnerable," I said. "Besides, I've told you, it's complicated."

Chase broke a long stringy strand of cheese from the plate with his finger and licked it, then let it melt in his mouth. "Hot and messy. Just like I like it."

"I assume you're talking about the lasagna and not our relationship," I said.

"I thought you said we didn't have a relationship."

Chase scooped a smaller portion of lasagna onto my plate.

"I did."

"Good, because I get it, Carol. We're just friends."

I stared at my plate. "I want to make it perfectly clear since we're going to be working together that I intend to keep this thing between us professional."

"Carol, I get it. We're friends."

I sat back in my chair. The hot smell of melted cheese beckoned me.

"But with benefits, right?" Chase winked.

CHAPTER 6

Thursday morning, Pete was arraigned, and I joined a chorus of reporters outside the County Courthouse. All of us were there for the filing of formal charges against Pete Pompidou. Like cattle we were shuttled through security scanners, our pocketbooks examined, and reporters' bags searched. Once cleared, we were directed to the fifth floor. Not since the Night Stalker or the Hillside Strangler had a case raised so much fury and concern among Angelenos.

Inside Judge Petrossian's courtroom, I sat shoulder-to-shoulder in the visitor's section with reporters on either side of me while we waited for this morning's proceedings to begin.

Arraignments are little more than an opportunity for the suspect to enter a plea and the judge to check his schedule with the defense and the prosecution and set a date for trial. Today's proceeding was expected to take no more than ten to fifteen minutes.

In an attempt to make certain KTLK was the first with the news of Pete's plea, Tyler and I had agreed I would text him once the plea had been officially entered into the court's record. Upon receipt of my text, Tyler would then interrupt Kit and Carson's morning show to report the news, which would undoubtedly become the topic for KTLK's court of public opinion.

When Pete entered the courtroom, I was taken back by his appearance. Gone was his youthful, blond, boyish look. Replacing it was a lost soul I barely recognized. He was dressed in an orange prison jumpsuit with his hands cuffed behind his back. Two beefy-looking security guards led him to a seat next to his attorney, a public defender named Melinda Croft. Croft, a heavy-set, middle-aged woman, looked like she hadn't slept or had much time to prep for this morning's proceeding.

Judge Petrossian asked Pete to stand and informed him of the first-degree murder charges against him, then instructed Ms. Croft to advise her client of his choices. Guilty. Not guilty. Or with the consent of the court, Nolo Contendere. Which meant Pete would accept a conviction without pleading guilty.

Croft whispered into Pete's ear, and Pete answered, "Not guilty, Your Honor."

After entering the plea, the court then assigned a trial date for six weeks from today. Not a lot of time for prosecutors to gather evidence and build a case. The entire process took less than ten minutes.

I texted Tyler back with news of Pete's not guilty plea and made a beeline for the elevators. If the prosecution had six weeks to build a case, I had less than that to try to find something to convince the cops they had the wrong guy and drop the charges. If I didn't, Pete would go to trial, and if convicted, would likely face a life sentence or worse. Death by lethal injection. And based upon the cold shoulder Cate had been giving me, she would probably never talk to me again. I had to get busy.

I never thought I'd be so thankful for an earthquake in my life, but I was. At noon, a three-point-eight tumbler hit the San Fernando Valley, and news of Pete's arrest quickly became a secondary story. News is like that. Last week, an eight-point-two earthquake had hit Mexico City and earthquake aficionados feared our smaller quake might be related. As a result, talk of Pete's arrest was back-burnered for talk about shattered dishes and the city's readiness for the Big One. All of which I considered good news. An earthquake meant I was no longer required to hang out in the studio to back up KTLK's station hosts with facts about the Model Slayer as they continued their on-air chatter about this morning's arraignment. Instead, it allowed me time to slip from the news booth so that I might comb through some of the station's archives, where the station stashed old broadcasts and newspapers in hopes of digging up something about Xstacy and Ely Wade.

After doing a quick search through the station's morgue, where anything and everything that had ever run on KTLK's air was kept in a kind of digital heaven, I found nothing concerning a pedestrian fatality behind the Sky High Club or any mention of Ely Wade. I decided to try Tyler's office.

Next to Tyler's desk was a stack of newspapers going back six months or more. Newspapers, particularly the smaller local ones, were better at covering local news. I hoped one of the westside rags might have covered it. I was on my hands and knees sorting through the pile when I noticed a pair of red high tops next to me.

"Looking for this?" Tyler stood over me with a copy of the *LA Argonaut* in his hands. A popular westside newspaper.

"Pedestrian Struck by Car in West L.A." I took the paper from his hand and sat down on the stack of papers behind me. I towered over Tyler, who, at five-two, was more comfortable with eye-to-eye contact. Sitting seemed like a much better idea.

"Story's not much," he said, "but if you're looking for information about Xstacy's accident, this is it. You can thank me later. I pulled a few strings with LAPD's traffic division as well. Got a copy of the accident report. You'll find it in your email."

"How did you—"

"Get a copy of the report? I talked with a Sergeant Lane at LAPD. Told him KTLK was considering doing a town hall meeting on the increasing number of pedestrian accidents in the city. I asked if he might help us out with some actual reports. Of course, I explained we wouldn't be using any names. Just some facts and stats. That kind of thing. I told him you'd be in touch to follow up."

"Me?" I pointed to myself.

"Yes, you, Carol." Tyler walked back to his desk and sat down. "And Sergeant Lane appeared to like the idea. He emailed over a year's worth of files. They're all a matter of public record, but if you had to request them, it'd probably take you six weeks. I forwarded the batch to you. I'm sure you'll find what you're looking for."

I glanced back down at the newspaper in my hand. Tyler was right, the story was barely two column inches. The actual police report would have everything. Time. Date. Responsible parties. Including the names of the responding officers.

"And, Carol, I'm going to need your help on something else. A Town Hall Meeting. Work up a fact sheet for me. Number of accidents. Worst locations in the city. You know what to do." Tyler turned his attention back to his computer screen, and I stood up.

I was about to walk out of the office when Tyler added, "Oh, and write up some promo spots. We need to get something on the air soon as possible. I'll need them by the end of the day. I've scheduled it on the program log for a week from Sunday. Eleven a.m. I'd like you to sit in with me as co-host."

When I got back to my office, I skimmed through my emails looking for what Tyler had forwarded to me and found a zip file from LAPD. Inside was a batch of recent pedestrian accident reports. A quick search of Ely Wade's name brought me to the file I needed.

Everything Xstacy had told me and more was in the report, including her legal name. Stacy Minor. Age nineteen. Birthday date August 18, 1998. The report stated on May 25, at approximately 1:25 a.m., Ms. Minor had placed an emergency call to 911 to report an accident. The dispatcher reported the caller said she had accidentally struck a man in the alleyway behind the Sky High Club on Sepulveda Boulevard. A patrol unit along with an emergency response team was immediately dispatched. LAPD Officers Ross and Evans arrived minutes later and reported finding the victim lying unconscious in the roadway. The attending EMTs declared the victim to be unresponsive. The victim, identified as Ely Wade, forty-two, was later pronounced DOA at Cedars Sinai Hospital.

In the notes section of the report, Sergeant Evans indicated Mr. Wade appeared to have gone outside the club for a cigarette and was standing next to a dumpster when Ms. Minor entered the alleyway off Sepulveda and, not noticing Wade, accidentally struck him with her van. Evans noted the surface street conditions. It had been raining. The alley was dark. There were no street lights. The police performed their usual investigation. Secured the scene, measured for skid marks and found there were none. Ms. Minor was tested for alcohol and since she hadn't been drinking, passed the test without incident. All of which tallied with Xstacy's claim she hadn't seen Wade until it was too late to stop. Xstacy had signed the report with her real name, Stacy Minor, and was sent home. No charges were filed.

Satisfied Xstacy had been telling the truth, I picked up the phone and dialed the number she had given me for Jewels. The phone rang four times. I was prepared to leave a message when a woman's voice answered.

"Hello?" The voice was soft and youthful, almost breathy.

"Jewels?" I wasn't certain I had the right number.

"Who's calling?" Whoever Jewels was, she sounded suspicious.

"My name's Carol Childs. Xstacy asked me to call. I'm a—"

"Is she in trouble?" The voice came back quickly.

"No. Absolutely not. But she said I should talk to you. About Ely Wade and the accident?"

"You a cop?"

"No. I'm a reporter," I said.

There was an uneasy silence and I feared she was about to hang up. "She made me promise I'd keep your names out of it."

"So she really did it then."

"Did what?" I asked.

"Called a reporter. I told her it might be a good idea. But you never know with Xstacy. She does what she does. Tells you later, if at all. So what do you want?"

"I was hoping we might talk."

"You familiar with the campus at UCLA?"

"I'm an alumn," I said.

"You know sorority row off Hilgard?"

"I do," I said.

"Good. Meet me there tonight. The Tri-Delta house. Nine

p.m."

I paused. Did I hear that right? "The sorority house?"

"You have a problem with that?"

"No," I said.

"Ring the bell and tell them you're looking for Sam."

"Sam?"

"I'll explain later. Jewels is a stage name. Keep it to yourself, will you? Nobody there knows me by that name."

I was still trying to figure out how an erotic dancer named Jewels had anything to do with the Tri-Delts at UCLA when my cell phone buzzed. It was Cate, and I took the call before it could ring twice.

"You okay?"

"I don't know, Mom. A Detective Soto just called. He said he's investigating the model murders and wants to talk to me. First thing tomorrow morning." Cate's voice was thin, and she sounded close to tears.

"What did you tell him?"

"What was I supposed to tell him? I told him yes."

"What time?"

"Ten o'clock. LAPD Headquarters. Mom, I'm scared. What's he want? I asked if I could see Pete and he said no."

"Catie, listen to me. You're going to be fine. I'll call Mr. King. We'll get him to come with us."

"I don't want Mr. King, Mom. I want my dad. I'm not going anywhere without him."

"Okay, call your dad." I closed my eyes and wished I could have put my arms around her. She sounded so fragile. "But just to be on the safe side, I'll call Mr. King anyway. He won't care if your dad's with you. But like I said before, Catie, your dad's a civil attorney. You're going to need someone more experienced with criminal law."

Cate sighed. I could picture her rolling her eyes. "Whatever."

"I'm serious, Cate. King knows what he's doing when it comes to criminal cases. He's the best."

"Fine. Call Mr. King. But, Mom, I'm going to Dad's tonight. I know none of this is your fault, but I need to be with Dad right now."

"Catie...I–" I wanted to say I was sorry. I needed her to come home tonight. I understood how confused she was. How she might blame me for breaking the story of Pete's arrest, but I loved her, and we'd work through this.

"I'll meet you at the police station in the morning. And Mom–" Cate paused, and I braced myself for another disappointment.

"Yes?"

"Bring Chase, too. Okay?"

Cate hung up the phone and I stared at my keyboard. I felt like my daughter was angry at me for doing my job. I was in a race against time. The clock had started ticking on the investigation with Pete and I knew it would be a tight race. I had to find something that would cause the cops to slow down and look elsewhere, and unless Jewels could offer me something concrete proving Ely Wade was the Model Slayer, that wasn't going to happen.

CHAPTER 7

Later that night, as I drove to UCLA, I kept thinking how odd it was to be meeting with an erotic dancer named Jewels inside a sorority house. I knew a lot about UCLA. I had graduated from there. What I didn't know about were the inner-workings of a sorority. I had never pledged or gone through rush, and I had no idea about Greek life or the activities that surrounded it. But it mystified me that some fresh-faced college sorority girl, particularly a Tri-Delt, was working in a dive like the Sky High Club. Back when I was in school, the Tri-Delts had a reputation that appealed more to an aloof set of pretty, blonde, serious-minded girls with an eye toward academia, than that of a party girl. I couldn't help but wonder what kind of double life Sam must be living.

I wasn't at all sure what the protocol was for visitors to the Tri-Delt House. Did I knock? Ring the bell or just walk in? Would a house mother answer or some sister open the door and announce me?

The situation rectified itself when two young girls with books in their arms opened the door as I approached.

"Hi, you looking for someone? Your daughter maybe?" A pretty blonde with a ponytail stopped in the doorway and gave me the once-over. It was obvious, despite the fact people frequently told me my daughter and I could pass for sisters, she wasn't confusing me for a college student.

"No, a friend. Her name's Sam. She asked me to meet her here. My name's Carol Childs, I'm a..." I stopped myself before telling them I was a reporter. Sam's warning, asking me not to use her stage name, made me think she wouldn't want anyone to know she was talking to a reporter. I smiled and said, "a family friend. She's expecting me."

"I'm Brita," the girl said. "Sam's finishing up a yoga class in the playroom. If you'd like to come in, I'll tell her you're here."

I'd never been inside a sorority house before, and I was amazed how big and palatial looking it was. From the outside, the house looked like one of the smaller on sorority row, but inside with its sweeping staircase and arched porticos, it possessed all the charm of a southern mansion.

"Sorry, guests aren't allowed to wander around, but you can wait for her here." Brita showed me to a small sitting room to the left of the foyer. The room was furnished with a love seat, coffee table, and three Queen Anne chairs. All the furnishings were covered in Tri Delt's colors, cerulean-blue velvet and accented with gold throw pillows. On the coffee table was a copy of the latest issue of *The Trident*, Tri-Delt's quarterly publication. I picked it up and breezed through it. Lots of pretty girls with big smiles and quotes about what different chapters were doing around the country.

Several minutes later Sam appeared in the doorway. She was small, maybe five three, slim and dressed in a pair of loose-fitting yoga pants and a T-shirt. Her dark hair was pulled back in a ponytail, and she was wearing a pair of large, square-framed eyeglasses, the type that made me think she was trying to hide behind them.

"You must be Carol." She smiled a Pepsodent smile, revealing straight white teeth exactly like those in the magazine, and a face that lit up with an inner glow that radiated confidence. I recognized the stage training immediately. Actresses all have that certain stage presence they can turn on and off at will.

I started to stand.

"Please, don't." She pointed to the couch. "If you don't mind, I'd prefer we meet here. It's quiet this time of night and I've asked that we not be disturbed."

I waited until she took a seat at the other end of the couch.

"You look surprised," she said.

"I wasn't expecting to meet with a college student." I took out my notepad. "You are a student, right?"

"I am. My real name is Samantha Anne Miller. Friends call me Sam for short. But if you're curious as to my part-time job, it's just that. A job. Nothing else." She folded her hands neatly in her lap and looked me in the eye. "I'm not a *working girl* if that's what you're thinking. I'm strictly a dancer. Topless clubs only."

"I'm not here to judge," I said.

"Of course you're not. But just so you know, I've never done totally nude. I don't do lap dances. And I'm not a prostitute. I'm a college student. Around here, nobody knows about my work at the club. Just like nobody at the club knows I'm a college student or that my real name is Sam Miller, and I want to keep it that way."

"I'm not going to say anything," I said.

"It'd be a problem if you did. You see, I'm on a dance scholarship, and I'd be in violation of their moral clause if anyone were to find out what I was doing." She paused and looked over her shoulder as though to make certain no one could hear our conversation and then looked back at me. "But what am I going to do? I've got another year to go until I graduate, and a stack of bills that will keep me in debt until I'm ready for social security. Dancing at the clubs pays more than I could make anywhere else and my scholarship doesn't touch the cost of room and board."

Sam didn't have to explain. Cate's scholarship, probably like Sam's, was for tuition only and didn't begin to cover the ancillary expenses. Between books, room and board, and any extra-curricular activities, I felt like I was cash-strapped at the end of every month.

"Believe me, I get it. I've got a daughter in college, and like I said, I'm not here to judge."

"But you are here to ask about what happened."

"I need to know if what Xstacy told me is true."

"You mean about Pete?"

"You know him?" My heart started to beat a little faster.

"We all do. He's the reason Xstacy called the radio station. When she saw his picture in the paper, she wanted to do something. Xstacy wasn't about to call the cops, and I told her she should call a reporter."

"And you don't think he's the Model Slayer?"

"Pete?" Sam winced her nose and shook her head. "No way. He's one of the good guys. He's taken my picture a couple of times. I don't know how he's gotten himself mixed up in all this. Doesn't deserve it. Not any of it."

I was relieved Sam didn't have any reservations about Pete. As for Xstacy, I still had questions.

"How long have you known Xstacy?"

"Awhile. Maybe a year. I met her after she started working the club and we became friends."

"She says she's your girlfriend."

"Depends on what you mean by girlfriend. Xstacy's a friend. I'm not gay if that's what you're asking. But when Ely Wade started harassing me, I was glad she was around. Never hurts to have an extra set of eyes looking out for you. Xstacy can call me whatever she likes. I really don't care."

"You believed Ely Wade was stalking you."

"He tried to get backstage a couple times. Bouncers wouldn't let him. Then one night he was out back, behind the club where a bunch of us girls go to smoke, waiting for me. He tried to get me off by myself. Kept saying how pretty he thought I was. That he wanted to help me with my career. I told him I didn't need his help and to get lost. After that, management posted another bouncer out back by the door, but it didn't last. They said the girls shouldn't be out there anyway. The door had a lock on it and nobody could get in. That's when Xstacy and I decided if the club wasn't going to do anything, we would."

"It was Xstacy's idea to run Ely down with her van?" I bit the end my pen and waited for Sam to answer.

"More or less." Sam shrugged like she didn't care.

"Meaning what?" I asked.

"Meaning the reason Xstacy doesn't want her name to come up with any investigation concerning Ely Wade's death is because she's afraid of what might happen if it did."

"She's afraid she might be charged with murder?"

"Jail's the least of her worries. What's got Xstacy freaked was that Ely wasn't alone that night. He had a friend with him."

"A witness?"

"She didn't tell you?"

"No. But I got the idea there might be something more."

"I'm not surprised. It's not like she's been thinking clearly since the accident. Nice girl, but not too smart, if you know what I mean. Anyway, right after Xstacy hits Ely with her van, she freaks. There he was lying in the street with blood all over him. Dead as could be. Xstacy had just called the police on her cell, just like we planned, and when I heard the sirens, I got out of there. Only, that's when Xstacy saw this man come running down the alley. He was hollering for Ely like he knew him, and when he saw him lying there in the street, he must have also seen the cop cars coming. Because Xstacy said he stopped, looked straight at her. Told her he'd get her for this and gave her the finger. Then he took off. Xstacy wasn't going to say anything to the cops, and now she's afraid if he finds her, he'll kill her."

"You any idea who this other man was?"

"All I know is that creep Ely never showed up alone. He always had another man with him. Sometimes they'd sit up front together by the stage."

"You remember what this other man looked like?"

"It's hard to see anyone from the stage. Xstacy said he had dark hair. Big shoulders. But I couldn't tell you."

"And you don't have a name?"

"No. Men around bars like the Sky High always pay cash. That's the way it is with strip clubs. The men don't want to leave a trail."

"And since the accident, has he come back?"

Sam shook her head and smiled. "You don't know how these

clubs work, do you? I work one club for a while and then I'm on to another. My last night at the Sky High was the night of the accident. Right now I'm working downtown. As for Xstacy, she was so freaked out she moved out of her apartment and told management she wasn't coming back."

"Where's Xstacy living now?" I asked.

"I was hoping you might tell me," Sam said. "For all I know, she might be living in her van."

CHAPTER 8

Friday morning I met Cate and her dad outside LAPD's new police administration building on the corner of West First Street and North Main. Cate looked pale. She was dressed in a short, sleeveless cotton dress with flats and was shaking like an autumn leaf. In her hands, she was holding a paper cup filled with hot coffee like I do when I need to calm myself. Standing next to her in a blue pinstriped suit was Mr. King, and behind him, Chase. Together, they all looked like a defense team about to face an executioner.

"You ready?" I put my arm around Cate's shoulder and pulled her to me. "You'll be fine," I whispered.

Cate nodded. The look in her eye not so sure.

"She's got nothing to worry about." King stepped between us. "Just remember, Cate, don't say anything unless I tell you to. Just answer what they ask and keep your answers short. Like we rehearsed." Then turning to me, he added, "And Carol, I want you to stay outside with Chase. You can't be in the room when they question her."

"What?" I shook my head and raised my hands in protest. "No. That doesn't work. Not at all. I'm her mother. I need to be there."

"Trust me, Carol, you don't need to be there, and the cops aren't going to want you in the room when they question her. I've already spoken to Cate about it and she's fine with just her dad and me. You and I can talk after. I'll fill you in on what happened."

I was about to make another objection when Chase pulled me aside.

"He's right, Carol. You need to let King do his thing. They're not going to arrest her. They're simply going to ask her a few questions. How she met Pete. How long she's known him. That kind of thing. You've nothing to worry about."

I watched as Cate, her dad, and Mr. King disappeared behind the glass doors to the building. My mind was full of crazy scenarios. I had reported on enough police investigations to know how overworked many LAPD detectives were and how easy it was to coerce a nervous witness. Under the right circumstances, people confessed to all kinds of things.

"I wish I could be as certain of that as you are," I said.

"Relax," Chase said, "The District Attorney told King they already know Cate and Pete were together the night Shana was killed."

"How?"

"How do you think? They checked Pete's van and found a gas receipt for the country store in Big Bear just like she told you. Then they checked the store for security cameras and got both Pete and Cate on tape. All they're going to want from her now is to know how she and Pete hooked up and what she knows about his roommate, Billy Tyson."

An hour later, Cate came bursting out from within the building. She was steps ahead of King and her dad and looked as though she were about to be sick. She stopped at one of the small planters outside the doors and wrapped her arms around her waist and bowed her head.

"Catie?" I walked over to her and put my arms around her shoulders. She was shaking.

Cate looked at me, her eyes filled with tears. "Mom, they won't let me see Pete. He's still in lockup. I can't even talk to him." Her voice was strained.

I pulled her close and held her like I might if she were still a small child and I could fix everything with a kiss and the promise of ice cream.

"It's going to be okay," I said. I stroked the hair away from her eyes and looked into her tearstained face. "I promise."

"I know you think so, Mom, but I want to get out of here. Dad says if we leave now we can take the boat to Catalina. He thinks it'd be a good idea if I came along. I know you want me to come home, but I can't. I need to go. Please?"

I looked back at my ex standing with King in front of the doors to the police station. Were they talking or was he avoiding eye contact with me? How could he take my daughter away now? She needed her mother, or maybe I needed her? I put my hands on the side of Cate's face and looked into her eyes. Perhaps a change of scenery and fresh air might be a good idea.

"If it's what you want, yes. Of course. But you need to be back Sunday night and don't be late. You've got to be at work Monday morning."

Cate bussed me on the cheek. "You don't have to remind me. See you Sunday."

I watched as Cate left me and went to her dad, grabbed his hand like a child, and walked off with him.

King waited until they were out of earshot then approached. "Carol, you got a minute?" With his index finger he motioned for me to follow to a corner of the quad with a small bench and sat down.

"How'd it go?" I asked.

"About what I expected," King said. "They asked her a lot of questions about Pete, their relationship, and Billy Tyson. But that's not what I need to talk to you about right now."

"What's up?" I asked.

"Tyler called me last night. He mentioned we may have an issue concerning a confidential source you interviewed."

"Oh?" I said. My stomach tightened. Whatever King had to tell me I feared wouldn't be good.

"He said this witness confessed to killing the Model Slayer."

"That's how I understand it."

"To be honest, Carol, it's the reason I didn't want you in the room when they questioned Cate. Detective Soto's convinced Pete's good for the murders. And the fact Cate's not only Pete's girlfriend, but your daughter as well puts you in a messy position. You suddenly start quoting anonymous sources and information that pertains to the case, they're going to want to subpoena you." King shook his head. "Dammit, Carol, I hate to say it, but you've gotten yourself into a tight situation."

I couldn't look King in the eye.

"I'm sorry, Carol, but if you're subpoenaed and refuse to reveal your source, you're looking at jail time. And don't go thinking the California Shield Law will protect you. It may have been designed to protect a reporter from revealing his sources, but if the judge orders you to reveal what information you have along with your source and you refuse, there's not much I can do."

I squeezed my eyes shut. "Tell me something I don't already know."

"Find another way. A way to reveal whatever your source shared with you without revealing who they are. And quickly. For everyone's sake."

"Believe me, I'm working on it." In the back of my mind, I was already thinking of ways I could find Xstacy's mystery man without the cops ever knowing anything about Xstacy or Sam. Something that wouldn't cause the cops to reopen their investigation into Xstacy's accident. That would keep Sam's identity a secret and Pete would go free.

"Good, because right now, the less the police know what you're doing, the better."

I left King and started to walk back towards Chase when I heard someone call my name. I turned around and nearly stumbled. I hadn't seen Eric since our breakup six months ago. He jogged over to me. Six foot four and with the body of a long-distance runner.

"I thought I recognized those legs. How you doing?" Eric smiled.

Under any other circumstances Eric's smile would have been disarming.

I steeled my surprise, my stomach bumping up against my heart, and lied. "Fine," I said. "And how about you? What are you doing here?"

"You know how it goes, following up on a case I can't talk about. And you?"

"Same old same old. Reporting on news you guys don't want to talk about." I forced a smile. The moment was awkward for us both.

Eric looked down at his shoes, black polished and spit-shined, then glanced at me from beneath his arched brows. "Always on the case, huh?"

"Hey, there's a deadline somewhere."

"I suppose so. Well, it's good to see you." Eric leaned in and bussed me lightly on the cheek, like an old friend. "You look great by the way."

"You too," I said. Maybe a little grayer around the temples, but still Eric. Always Mr. FBI. Fit, trim, and handsome.

"Stay safe, Carol."

My throat tightened as I watched the man who I once thought could have been my everything walk back inside the building. I refused to think about it. We had closed that door, and I had work to do. A killer to find and a daughter's faith to restore.

"Old friend?" Chase waited on the sidewalk for me and took a sucker from inside his pocket. "Or maybe more of a complication?"

"I don't know what you're talking about." I grabbed the sucker from Chase and started to walk back toward my Jeep. My hand was on the door when Chase stopped me.

"So what's up, Carol? Is it Cate or that complication back there who's got you so uptight?" Chase nodded in the direction of the building.

"I'm not uptight," I snapped.

"Clearly."

"In fact, King assured me Cate's fine."

"He did, huh?"

"Yeah."

"Then where's she going?"

"Her father thought she needed to get away. They're taking the boat to Catalina."

Chase grabbed me by the arm and spun me around. "You're hiding something, Carol. I know when someone's not shooting straight with me. What's up?"

"Nothing," I said.

"That's too bad, because I was going to offer to buy you dinner. See if maybe I could help with your daughter. But based on what I just saw back there," Chase nodded back in the direction of the doors where Eric and I had been talking, "I get the feeling it's not just Cate who's got you upset."

"I'm not upset. Like I told you before, it's—"

"I know. It's complicated."

My cell phone buzzed. I glanced down at the face of my phone. Tyler had texted me. *911. Fire in the North Valley.*

"Sorry, Chase, I've got to go."

CHAPTER 9

Southern Californians like to say they only have two seasons. Earthquake and Fire. Both of them driven by the Santa Anas or the devil wind, known for creating havoc with their dry seasonal temperatures that suck the moisture from the earth with gales of red desert dust that sweep down from the mountains and howl like wounded animals. The Santa Anas can drive a person crazy. I've covered enough stories—everything from suicides to shootings—to know when the winds blow, strange things happen.

The winds had started at dawn and by the time I got to the station, were gusting at speeds up to forty miles an hour. North of the city, a firestorm had started to eat away at the hillsides like Pac-Man and threatened to choke the valley below with a thick blanket of black smoke. Every fire truck, fixed-wing tanker, and water-carrying helicopter within the county had been called into action. The city was on full alert.

Tyler assigned me to the news booth and told me I was hostage to the situation until things died down. It was my job to chat it up with the on-air hosts while keeping our listeners up to date on the road closures, evacuations, and conditions in the field. By the time the sun finally set and my shift ended, the direction of the winds had changed, and the fire—the press had now dubbed the Oh Susana Fire—was 30 percent contained. I had been on the air for better than six hours straight and felt like my voice had dropped an octave. My throat felt as raw and dry as the hills the fire had swept through.

Back in my office I had two messages. The first from Tyler,

reminding me, despite the destruction of the fire and Pete's arraignment this morning, he was still waiting for a list of questions and names for the Town Hall meeting. He needed them before I went home for the day. The second was from Sam. She had tried my cell phone, left a message there and hoped this might be a better number. *Please call.*

I hung up the phone, took my cell from my bag, and searched for Sam's number.

The call went immediately to voicemail. "Sam here. Can't take your call right now. Leave a message. I'll call ya back."

I left my name and number and told Sam to call anytime, then stared back at my computer. If Tyler wanted a list of questions and names, I needed to get busy. I put together a quick list of the usual suspects. The mayor. People from City Hall. LAPD. And Philip Petre, aka Papa Phil, a gay activist, supportive of a number of civil causes, including lobbying City Hall for better crosswalks in the valley. A year ago, Papa Phil's partner had been killed after leaving a nightclub as he crossed Santa Monica Boulevard in West Hollywood. I was in the process of finalizing a list for Tyler when my cell rang. Caller ID identified the caller as Sam Miller.

"Hi, Sam. I got your message. What's up?"

"I've been thinking about the guy Ely used to hang out with. He might still be there, waiting to see if Xstacy or I show up. You want to come to the club with me and check?"

"When?" I asked. While the valley was still smoldering from the fire, the rest of the city, particularly on the other side of the Santa Monica Mountains, was business as usual.

"How about tonight?"

"I thought you weren't working the Sky High anymore?" I was surprised Sam would even think of going back after what she had told me about Ely's friend.

"I'm not, but that doesn't mean we can't go together."

"You're not worried Ely's friend might recognize you?"

"It's not like I'm planning on being on stage. Believe me, the man won't recognize me. Not with clothes on anyway." Sam paused. "That's a joke, Carol."

"Right." I chuckled to myself and saved the Town Hall files I had been working on and attached them to an email to Tyler. Then added a short note. *Following up with Xstacy's friend, Sam. More TK.* That's journalism-speak for "to come." I hit send and stood up.

"Sam, you're sure you're up for this?"

"I've got to do something. I haven't heard from Xstacy and I'm getting worried."

"What time?"

"Ten o'clock. The club'll be busy by then. I'll meet you at the bar. And try not to look too much like a reporter, will you? You don't want to stand out in a place like that."

Sam hung up and I stared down at my black slacks and sensible shoes, something I'd worn to meet with Cate downtown at LAPD's Robbery-Homicide unit. If I didn't want to stand out like a mud hen in my conservative little black and white business suit, I needed a change of outfits, and I knew exactly where to go.

CHAPTER 10

My best friend, Sheri, is a clotheshorse. She has a closet that could rival any wardrobe studio in Hollywood. And it's no wonder, Sheri's father was a former big screen actor and award-winning movie producer. There wasn't a set in Hollywood she hadn't, at one time or another, stepped foot on. As a result, Sheri's closet was like a museum. It ran the entire length of the SoCal manse she had inherited from her father. Situated on the second floor, with its high-gloss wooden floor and inset lighting, it was chock-full of designer wear, vintage clothing in various sizes and celebrity-wear that had once been worn in the movies. Rows of hanging garments. Shelves stuffed with hat boxes filled with wigs, feather boas, decorative masks. And shoes. Dozens upon dozens of shoes. But the *pièce de résistance* and the clue for navigating Sheri's wardrobe was a vintage ladder Sheri's father had modeled after the one Henry Higgins had used in the library scene from the movie *My Fair Lady*. It rolled the entire length of the closet and allowed Sheri, who is barely five foot two, access to shelves beyond her diminutive reach.

As I pulled out of the station's parking lot, I punched up Sheri's number on my cell. In a situation like I was about to face at the Sky High Club, I not only needed the right outfit, I needed my best friend.

"What are you doing tonight?"

I knew before I asked Sheri wouldn't have plans. Her son Clint and my son Charlie are best friends and the two of them were away together at a summer sports camp for two weeks.

"Not much, why?"

"You know anything about pole dancing?"

"Are you thinking we should take a class?"

"Not exactly. I'm working on a story and I could use your help." I explained without divulging the exact reason for my request that I had a lead about college girls working at a couple of strip clubs in town and needed to check it out. It was an innocent enough request and for the time being anyway, close enough to the truth. "Want to go with me?"

"Sounds kinda kinky," Sheri giggled. Then the inevitable question, "What are you gonna wear?"

"I was thinking—"

"Stop. Don't tell me. I've got the perfect thing," Sheri said.

I smiled to myself. Mission accomplished.

"I thought you might. How about I swing by your place about nine?"

"Perfect. I'll pick out a couple of resist-me-nots. What do you want? Dark and decadent or slinky and sexy?"

"Whatever, just not too revealing. I need to blend in. Dark would work best."

Despite our height differences and Sheri's yo-yo dieting, we each managed to fit perfectly into a size six. And in a pinch, as long as I didn't mind wearing Sheri's skirts a little shorter than I might normally, whatever she could pull from her closet would be better than anything I had hanging in mine.

Sheri greeted me at the front door with her long dark hair loose about her shoulders, looking like she was ready to pose for a glamour shot. From her false eyelashes to her stiletto heels, everything about her spelled lady on the prowl. She was dressed in a double-tailed black tuxedo blazer with red cuffs, skin-tight pants, and a low-cut bustier that left nothing to the imagination.

"You planning on auditioning?" I asked.

"You never know who you might meet." Sheri gave me a

wicked smiled, crooked her index finger beneath my nose, did an about-face and cat-walked slowly down the hall and up the stairs to her closet.

I followed.

"Don't worry," she said, "I've got something special for you too."

"Not as special as what you're wearing, I hope." No way was I stepping into a strip club looking like a cigarette girl from a cabaret.

"Not to worry. You asked for something simple and I aim to please. How's this?"

From within her closet, Sheri pulled out a short, sassy black cocktail dress with a low, plunging neckline from the shoulders to the navel. The only difference between the back and the front was a wide rhinestone belt buckle that cinched the waist in the front. The hang tags were still on it.

"You haven't worn this?" I said.

"Wasn't sure if it was right for me, but you? I think it works. Go ahead, try it on."

I'm not big on showing cleavage. Unlike Sheri, I'm built like a stick, but she convinced me to at least give it a try. One look at myself in a full-length mirror, and I stepped back and grabbed a bomber jacket off the clothes rack. Like a life preserver I hugged it to my chest. "With this maybe."

Despite the warmer summer weather, I wasn't going to a bar wearing an outfit that looked more like a jumper with suspenders, than a cocktail dress. With the jacket I was at least covered. Sheri handed me a pair of spiky heels and I glanced back in the mirror. "Not bad."

I should have known the dress code for a strip club was not exactly like one of L.A.'s classier nightclubs. When we walked through the door, we must have looked like a couple of overdressed soccer moms out for a girls' night out. Everyone else was dressed down in black. Jeans. Sweatshirts and variations of the same. But at least I didn't look like a reporter, and with all the activity on the stage, nobody was looking at us, or me anyway. Sheri, on the other hand, with those boobs of hers like milky white headlights, immediately attracted attention. Within minutes a tall, dark-haired man, wearing a sportscoat and looking as out of place as we did, approached and offered to buy her a drink. Sheri gave him a sly smile and did one of those coquettish little shoulder dips then looked at me. *Didn't I have someone I needed to interview?* I took the hint and moved down to the end of the bar.

On stage a trio of near-naked girls had just finished and a standup comedian was struggling to hold the crowd's attention, while many of those seated headed back to the bar for refills.

"What's the matter, you don't want to buy a girl a drink?"

I turned my head, standing next to me at the bar was Sam. She had squeezed herself in between several other customers and I barely recognized her. She had on a slouch beanie cap that hugged her head, and a pair of baggie jeans with suspenders over a checkered shirt.

"You don't come here often, do you?"

"Never," I said.

"That's obvious. The way you're dressed, you're probably the only single, straight girl in the bar." Sam signaled the waiter and with her hand above her head ordered a couple of brewskies. Then leaning closer to me, with her shoulder touching mine, her eyes scanned the room. On stage, a tall, leggy fan dancer had begun performing a striptease, with more tease than strip. "Just keep looking at me," she said. "Pretend we're talking."

My eyes went quickly from the stage and back to hers. "Why, you see anyone?"

"There's a man sitting up front. To the left of the stage. That's where Ely used to sit. There's an empty chair next to him."

"You think that's the same man Ely used to sit with?" I forced myself not to turn and look.

"Maybe. You can't see much from the stage. But I had this routine with a feather boa. I'd drop the boa and drag it behind me while I strutted across the front of the stage. When the light was just right, I could catch the faces in the front row. His wasn't one of the pretty ones. It looked like someone had taken a knife to him."

"Anything else?"

"I haven't heard from Xstacy in a while. I'm worried. This isn't like her."

The music started up again, and I glanced back at the stage. The man Sam had pointed out to me was still there. If I was going to learn anything, I needed to make my move.

"You suppose he might like some company?" I asked.

Sam turned her back to the bar, leaned her elbows up against it and stared at the table by the stage. "You realize he might consider you competition."

"For the girls?" I stood up and reached inside my bomber jacket and threw a couple of bucks on the bar. "Well, I guess we'll just have to see, won't we?"

Sam raised a brow. "You're on your own here, Carol. Just remember, keep my name out of it."

I took a couple steps back from the bar and saluted Sam. Seemed to be an appropriate way to say good night in a place like this. Then I did an about-face, which isn't easy to do in spiked heels, and placing my hands in the pockets of my bomber jacket, did my best John Wayne impersonation as I worked my way through the cocktail tables to an empty seat, next to him.

"You mind?" I asked.

CHAPTER 11

Much as I pretended to be interested in the dancers, I couldn't keep my eyes from wandering from the stage to the man sitting next to me. At one point a red strobe light flashed across the dimly lit room, and I got a glimpse of the side of his face and couldn't turn away. His head was large, which fit his hulk-like frame, and his face was pock-marked and scarred. From his forehead to his jaw, it looked like someone had taken a knife, carved out his eye, and dragged the blade down across his cheek.

In the instant it took for the strobe to pass from his face to mine, I knew he had seen the horror in my eyes and any chance I had of talking with him was gone. He turned his head back towards the stage and focused on the girls and followed their every move like they were his prey. It was as though they were dancing for him alone. And when one came too close to the lip of the stage and dragged her boa in front of him—exactly as Sam had said she had done—I noticed his hands. Workmen's hands. Hard and calloused. His fat fingers fondled the glass as though he were touching her body from the nape of her neck all the way down to the narrow rhinestone g-string between her legs. Out of the corner of his eye, he glanced back at me, then drew his lip back against the side of his face and smiled.

I stood up. I would have to find another way to engage Scarface. I couldn't sit there and watch a possible serial killer in the throes of foreplay. I walked back toward the bar. Sam had left. Sheri was still engaged with Mr. Sportscoat, his eyes glued to her God Given Assets and hers on a pink martini she held delicately in her hand like a prop. Rather than interrupt what looked like might be an intimate moment, I went back to my Jeep and sent Sheri a text. *Time to go, Cinderella.*

A few minutes later, Sheri came teetering out of the club and toward my Jeep. It was dark, but not so dark I couldn't see she was tipsy. She stopped when she got as far as the hood of my Jeep and took her shoes off. "You get your interview with your dancing girl?"

"I did." I leaned across the passenger seat and opened the door. Beneath the overhead light, I could see Sheri's lipstick had smeared and her cheeks were flushed.

"What a night." Sheri laughed as she got in and rubbed her feet.

"You had a good time?" I asked.

"You mean watching girls slide down a pole or talking to Max?"

"Max?"

"The man at the bar. We could have talked all night."

"Really?" I put the key in the ignition and started to back out of the parking lot. Sheri was never one to pick up men, but judging from the smeared lipstick on her face, it had been a very intimate conversation. "And just what did the two of you talk about?"

"What does anyone in L.A. talk about? Movies. Books. Theater. Does it matter?"

"No. It's just you seem giddy. That's all."

"And why not? Maybe it's time I got a little excitement in my life. It's been a long time since I felt a man's lips against my ear, whispering how beautiful he thought I was. Besides, I could use a good fling. I gave him my number. He's coming for dinner."

"You gave him your address? He knows where you live?"

"He does now."

"You think that's wise?" I asked.

Sheri poked me in the ribs teasingly. "What, are you jealous? No wonder Cate gets frustrated with you. We go out one night, I get lucky and all of the sudden you become the overprotective mother. I'm a big girl, Carol, I can handle a little romance in my life."

Sheri sat back in the seat and crossed her arms, exactly as Cate had. For the moment I felt like I was driving my daughter home.

CHAPTER 12

Saturday morning the sound of a bell pulled me from my semi-conscious state. In my sleep, Eric had slipped under my radar and we were together again on his boat with me cradled in his arms. Behind the captain's wheel with the cool breeze in our faces as the Sea Mistress skimmed the water's black surface beneath starry skies. I tried to convince myself the sound I heard was the ship's bell, but when the bell rang again, I realized it wasn't the ship's bell at all, but the house phone on my bedside table.

"Sorry to spoil your weekend, Carol. I tried your cell, but you weren't answering. I need you today."

Yesterday's monstrous firestorm had burned through thirty-five thousand acres and caused the evacuation of nearly ten thousand homes, including the home of KTLK's weekend news reporter, and Tyler was suddenly short-handed.

I raised myself up on one elbow and looked at the bedside clock. 8:35.

"When?" I asked.

"Now. But not at the station. In the field. There's a lot of chatter on the police scanner. A fire crew clearing brush uncovered a female body out in Vasquez Canyon. From what I'm hearing, she was strapped in a tree."

Soon as I heard the words "strapped to tree," I stumbled out of bed and hop-scotched toward the bathroom. I tripped over my reporter's bag I'd left on the floor the night before, and nearly dropped my cordless phone. "You think it might be another of the Model Slayer's victims?"

"Hard to say until you check it out, Carol. Could be another model or maybe that missing girl whose boyfriend the police suspected might have helped her disappear six weeks ago. Either way I need you up there."

I slammed the phone down on the bathroom counter, put my hair in a ponytail and five minutes later, I was dressed and out the door.

Six weeks ago, Marilynn Brewer's ex-boyfriend, Brian Evans, had reported his girlfriend missing, and became an immediate suspect. But when the police couldn't find a body, the investigation cooled, and the police suggested Marilynn may have decided to take some time for herself after their breakup and hit the road. According to LAPD's Missing Persons Unit, that's not unusual. Lots of people go missing voluntarily and frequently show up on their own. At no time did the police think Marilynn might have been one of the Model Slayer's victims. She didn't fit the profile. She wasn't at all modelesque. And yet, if it was Marilynn's body the firefighters had found, I was certain it wasn't because she had wandered off into the desert to mend her broken heart and gotten lost, but because she had somehow crossed paths with the Model Slayer.

I checked my map. Vazquez Canyon was a rugged scenic mountainscape of prehistoric rock formations frequently used as a backdrop for movie and photo shoots. Not too dissimilar to the remote locations the Model Slayer had used to pose his previous victims for their last photo shoot. It was also just seventeen miles from the metro station where Marilynn's car had been found.

As I drove toward Vasquez Canyon, the desert road thinned to two narrow lanes, and the air thickened with the dusty smell of smoke. Like a rattlesnake, the road wrapped around the dry desert hills now burnt black as toast. Any signs of life in the area had been singed from the rocky desert floor, leaving nothing but a scorched landscape, like that of some arid, rolling, mountainous terrain, stripped bare for miles. Without warning, an LAPD helicopter swooped from behind a bald mountain and hovered in the air above me. Its rotor blades buffeted over the hood of my Jeep as though its occupants were determining if I was okay. I waved out the window and, like a bird, it swept ahead toward Vasquez's monument of red rocks. I followed its trail. Up ahead, through thick clouds of yellow dust mixed with the smoky residue of the fire, I could see blue and red flashing of lights coming through the haze. An LAPD police cruiser, an unmarked blue sedan, no doubt a detective's car, and a fire truck were parked next to a black coroner's van. Beyond them, yellow tape cordoned off an area of the park usually reserved for hikers.

I knew the area well. Legend had it Tiburcio Vasquez, one of California's more celebrated banditos, had used the area as his hideout. When the kids were little we had hiked the rough, jagged rocks that rose from the barren desert floor like an island of layered sandstone. We pretended it was an alien fortress or partially sunken ship with its red prehistoric rocks tilted at foreboding angles that jutted 150 feet into the air and made for an excellent lookout. Within the mountain itself, deep crevices and narrow caverns created a maze of trails marked with the shallow graves of those foolish enough to have tried to penetrate the fortress and paid the ultimate price.

I parked my Jeep a short distance behind the police cruiser. There were no other news vans in sight. Not a surprise considering every news organization in town was spread thin with their smaller weekend news crews and coverage of the fire and its aftermath.

I grabbed my reporter's bag off the seat next to me and my KTLK baseball cap and threaded my hair into a ponytail through the small adjustable opening in the back, and headed toward a blue canopy tent.

"Hey, Lady. Stop! Whatta you think you're doin'?" A young LAPD officer trailed after me. "You can't go back there. This is a crime scene."

I took my ID from my bag and held it for him to see. "I'm a reporter. Heard some firefighters uncovered a body. You got anyone I can talk to?"

The officer looked over his shoulder, beyond the yellow tape to where the coroner's van was parked next to the tent. "Wait here. I'll see what I can do."

"Fine, but if it's all the same to you, how about I wait over there with the firefighters? I nodded to a group of cottonwoods where three firefighters dressed in yellow jumpsuits squatted with a watercooler between them.

"Suit yourself."

With the young rookie off asking for permission, I approached the firefighters.

"You the men who found the body?" I asked.

One of firefighters looked up. His face was streaked with soot and he had stripped the top half of his yellow coveralls to his waist, exposing his sweat-soaked undershirt. He looked exhausted.

"You a reporter?" With the back of his hand, he mopped his brow and squinted at me.

"I am. Anything you can you tell me about the body you found?"

"Not much. We were clearing the brush. It was our job to clean away any fuel before the fire advanced. I was about to take an ax to that dead tree over there when I saw a body," The firefighter pointed to the area where the body had been found. "Or what I thought was a body anyway."

I took out my notepad. "So the body, it looked like it had been there for a while?" I scribbled the word "date" with a question mark next to it on my pad. If the body had been here for a while, Pete certainly hadn't been. Not if he was with Cate in San Diego.

"Hard to tell. 'Tween what the buzzards and the sun done to her, wasn't much left. Other than hair and bones."

"You're sure it was a woman?"

"Yeah. I'm sure. She was tied to the tree with some kind of rhinestone dog collar 'round her neck."

"A dog collar? You sure it was a dog collar?" If it was a dog's collar, it was the first time the Model Slayer had varied from a rope choker.

"It looked like one of them real fancy kinds. 'Bout two inches wide with lots of jewels on it. I saw one once on some rich lady's poodle in Beverly Hills."

"You notice any tags?"

"Don't know. I didn't get that close, but I did notice she had bracelets on her wrists and high heels. In my book, that's a woman."

I had expected to hear that the body had been tied to the tree. That much matched with the Model Slayer's MO for displaying his bodies. But the idea that this latest victim had been found wearing a rhinestone dog collar made me wonder if this might have been more of a copycat. I wrote the word "copycat" on my notepad and put another question mark next to it.

"Anything else you can you tell me? Color? Length of hair?"

"Dark brown, maybe. Or could be it was just dirty. But it was short. A couple inches at the most."

"And if you had to guess, how tall do you think she was?"

"Five feet. Five two maybe. Hey, I'm sorry, I know it's your job to ask these questions, but soon as we realized what we had, we covered her with a tarp and called the captain. He told us to stay put and wait for the police. 'Tween you and me, if it's all the same, I'd just as soon get back to my unit. Not much anyone can do for that poor girl, and there's no point in our hanging 'round here when there are folks who still need us."

I thanked the firefighters then looked back toward the tent. A harried-looking plainclothes detective ducked beneath the yellow crime scene tape. He had taken off his jacket and his gold LAPD shield attached to his belt caught the midmorning sun. I hurried in his direction.

"Detective?" His white shirt was spotted with dirt and sweat from the heat. "You got a minute?"

"What is it with you people? You don't have enough to report on with the fire?" The detective looked annoyed and turned back toward his car.

"I just need a minute, Detective." I pulled my mic from my bag and chased after him. "Can you tell me what happened here? Do you think this is another of the Model Slayer's victims?"

The detective stopped and glared at me. "What's your name?"

"Carol Childs. KTLK news. And you're?"

"Detective Springer." He reached into the car where his sports coat lay on the seat and pulled out a business card from the inside pocket. "And if it's a quote you're after I'll tell you this, we've got a body. Whoever she is, or was, she's been there for a while. As for whether she was a victim of the Model Slayer, I can't tell you that. So if you'll excuse me, you've got your quote, and I've got an investigation to get back to." He slammed the car door and started to walk back to the tent.

I followed as far as the yellow tape and yelled after him. "How about Marilynn Brewer? The girl that's been missing for–"

"Six weeks." Springer stopped and looked back at me. "I know who Marilynn Brewer is. You satisfied?" Spring's eyes challenged mine. I held his stare, and seeing I wasn't about to back down, he continued. "And no. We don't know if it's Ms. Brewer's body who some psycho killer lynched to a tree and left to die in the desert. And don't quote me on that. I don't need my lead detective coming down on me because I lost it with some reporter who's looking to make a name for herself from the murders of a bunch of young women who thought they were going to a photo shoot and ended up fodder for some newscast."

I let the comment go. A lot of cops were on edge with a nervous public accusing them of not doing enough to protect them.

"The public has a right to know," I said.

"Look, Ms. KTLK or whatever you want to call yourself, I can't tell you who that girl was any more than I can tell you what caused her death. All I can I tell you is what you already know. A couple of firefighters uncovered the body of a dead woman while clearing brush away from the fire."

"How about the position of the body? Did it look like she was posed?" I wasn't about to be cut off. I'd come too far and needed to know how similar the scene might have been to those of the model murders. "Were her hands tied above her head? Was she strangled? Were there any Polaroids found near the body?"

"Polaroids? Are you kidding? You saw the condition of things out here. You're asking for evidence that's long since gone. And you should be too. When we've got something to report, we'll call you."

I knew better than to think a weathered detective like Springer would call me back anytime soon, but I reached back into my bag and handed him my business card anyway.

"Please do," I said. "You never know when we might be able to help each other."

I went back to my Jeep and called Tyler. It was ten minutes to noon, and I knew he would be waiting for my call.

"What you got, Carol?

"Could be another of the Model Slayer's victims. The firefighter who found her said she was tied to a tree. Only not like the others. This one had a rhinestone-studded dog collar around her neck."

In the background, I could hear Tyler's fingers hitting the keyboard as fast as I spoke. "Cops think she was posed?"

"Didn't say. The body was too decomposed, and the detective in charge was tight-lipped. But between you and me, I'd say it's a slam-dunk this is the work of the Model Slayer, and I'm pretty sure it was Marilynn Brewer."

"What makes you think so?" Tyler stopped typing. "She doesn't exactly fit the Model Slayer's profile."

"The story about Marilynn's disappearance in the paper. There was a photo, and you're right she didn't fit the profile. But the article said she was a freelance accountant for some gentlemen's clubs and an aspiring stand-up comic."

"So?"

"When I was at Sky High Club there was a standup working the room between acts. A fill-in so the dancers could get a break and guests could visit the bar. If the Sky High Club was one of Marilynn's clients, maybe she talked them into giving her a break and ran into someone who didn't like her act."

"Like Ely Wade?"

"If I could get hold of Xstacy, she'd know. But she's not returned any of my calls. Give me some time to do a little digging around. If I'm right, and this is the Model Slayer's work, there's no way Pete's involved."

"Pete I'm not concerned about right now, Carol. That body in the desert, that's the story I want, and I want it right away."

"I'll have an audio file to you in five."

I picked up my iPhone and, with a view of the red mountains and the blue tent in front of me, I began my report. iPhones these days are remarkably effective for reporters in the field. A simple app allowed me to record and edit a segment Tyler could insert into the broadcast in a matter of minutes.

"LAPD homicide detectives aren't saying if a body found tied to a tree in the Vasquez Mountains this morning might be the Model Slayer's fourth victim. But firefighters who were clearing brush for the Oh Susana Fire and found the body aren't so sure. The woman's body appeared to have been tied to a tree with a rhinestone dog collar around her neck. Cause of death has yet to be determined. Meanwhile, the recent disappearance of Marilynn Brewer, who vanished six weeks ago from the same area, is still under investigation and police have refused to say if they believe the two cases may be linked together."

On my way home I kept thinking about the grisly scene the firefighters had described. How Pete had been charged with the murders of three young models and was sitting in a jail cell awaiting trial. Would the police find some way to add today's discovery to that list? My head ached as I thought of the possibilities. If the body found today was tied to the Model Slayer, and the date of death was some time in the last six weeks, there was no way the police could charge Pete with her murder. If what Cate told me about her relationship with Pete was true, then the two of them would have still been down in San Diego while Cate finished up the semester at the University. And, if the body was Marilynn Brewer's and I could find evidence she had been doing standup at the Sky High Club, then I might be able to prove a connection to Ely Wade. I picked up my cell and tried to call Xstacy again. When she didn't answer, I left a message and told her to call me. Soon as possible.

Halfway home my phone rang.

"Hi, it's me." Sheri's voice sounded upbeat. A welcome relief from the sight I'd just come from. "You'll never guess what I did."

I mopped my brow with the back of my hand and stared out at the dry desert hills. "Don't make me. It's been one of those days. What's happening?"

"I bought a pole."

"A what?" My hands tightened on the steering wheel.

"A dance pole." Sheri giggled.

"You mean like those we saw at the Sky High Club the other night?"

"Yes. And I'm planning on taking lessons."

"Why?"

"Do you have any idea how many calories you can burn with a pole?"

Sheri was obsessive about her weight and, being a full-figured Italian and a connoisseur of fine food, she made it a point of being up-to-date on all the latest fad diets and workouts. No doubt she knew exactly how many calories she could burn with a half hour on the pole and had already worked out a routine.

"No. But I'm sure you do."

"Trust me, it's a lot. And, I was hoping you could do me a favor?"

"I'm afraid to ask."

"Can you give me the number of the college girl you're interviewing about pole dancing? I thought maybe she might be available for lessons."

I didn't see the problem with giving Sam's number to Sheri. Like any college student, extra work meant extra income. I told Sheri I'd text her Sam's number to her on one condition.

"What do you want?"

"Keep her name between you and me, and don't mention anything to her about the story I'm working on."

"That's two conditions," Sheri teased.

"Actually three," I said. "Promise me you didn't put the pole in the living room where the boys could see it."

Sheri laughed. "Are you kidding? I put it in the bedroom."

"The bedroom?"

"Oh come on, Carol. Think about it. It'll be much more fun there. Particularly for entertaining. Which I plan on doing."

I winced. Sheri's love life hadn't been all that wild or successful. Other than her son's father and a few brief, failed romances along the way, Sheri hadn't had a lot of men in her life and didn't care to. She had no problem telling me she preferred living vicariously through my mishaps, which she believed were more entertaining than those she might have had first hand.

"I take it then you're busy tonight?"

"You're not?" Sheri asked.

"Cate's in Catalina with her dad."

"And Chase?"

"Chase is Chase. I haven't heard from him, and I'm not about to call."

"Well, you should. Because I'm entertaining Max tonight. He's coming by for Paella. I've been shopping all morning. Got chorizo, clams, shrimp. Everything. Things work out well with Max, maybe we can do dinner one night next week. Ciao."

I was layered with red dust and dirt from the canyon when I got home and couldn't wait to shower and scrub the smell of smoke from my hair. My cell rang as I was drying off. Holding the towel around me, I reached into my bag for my phone.

"Mom!" Cate didn't wait for me to answer. "You're not going to believe this."

"What's up? You okay?"

"I'm fine. Dad and I and Steph and the baby sailed over to Catalina yesterday after court. And guess what?" Cate sounded breathless.

"Tell me." I hated playing guessing games, particularly when it concerned my ex, his wife, and the new baby. *What, was she pregnant again?* "What's up?" I asked.

"We were at dinner last night and you'll never believe who walked in."

"Who?" I expected her to tell me some big star. Catalina's famous for star sightings.

"Billy Tyson. Pete's roommate."

"You sure?"

"Positive. I recognized him from the pictures Pete had of the two of them at the house. Billy has this tattoo on his shoulder of a heart with a knife through it. Pete said Billy got it because he wanted to look sexy when he was playing volleyball at the beach. Then last night, when we were at dinner, this guy comes in wearing a sleeveless white T-shirt, and I recognized the tattoo. Sure enough, it was Billy."

"Did you call the cops?"

"Better than that. I snapped a picture of him with my cell phone and sent to it Chase. Then I called and told him where we were. Chase must have notified the local sheriff's department, because the sheriff arrived maybe fifteen minutes later—guns drawn—and arrested him before we finished eating. He looked surprised. I don't think he even knew the cops were looking for him."

"Where are you now?"

"We're still in Catalina. Chase is here with a couple of detectives from LAPD. We met for breakfast this morning. He said Billy told them he'd been sailing for the past week and didn't know anything about Pete's arrest. He had no idea anyone was looking for him. Chase said they went through his boat. He didn't tell me if they found anything. But he said the cops were taking him back to L.A. for questioning."

"That's great news," I said. If finding Billy took the heat off of Pete, it meant the cops would be looking in another direction.

"Isn't it! Mom, I'm so excited. I know this means they're going find Pete had nothing to do with all this and they'll let him go. I'm sure of it."

"I don't know, Catie. But I'm sure if–" I was about to say if Pete was innocent and caught myself. I didn't want to dowse her hopes and have her blame me for suggesting otherwise. Instead, I said, "I mean, when they get a chance to question him, I'm sure it'll help."

"Dad thinks so too. Anyway, I just wanted you to know. Oh, and Mom, don't be mad. I'm going to spend Sunday night at Dad's. I'll see you Monday after work."

Cate didn't have to tell me how conflicted she felt. I could hear it in her voice and felt it in the pit of my stomach. In her mind, her attorney Dad was the sound voice of reasoning. Whereas I was the reporter. The person who brought Pete's name to the forefront of a hideous crime and was keeping it in the news. In theory, I knew Cate understood my job. She appreciated it was my responsibility to inform the public. But when news hits close to home and the court of public opinion is breathing down your neck, it's not so easy to remain impartial. I felt as though Cate viewed me as part of the problem. Part of the machine that perpetuated the non-stop chatter of truths and half-truths. The sooner I could prove Ely Wade was the Model Slayer and that Pete had nothing to do with it, the sooner my relationship with my daughter would get better. Until then, things were going to get a whole lot rockier.

I called Chase as soon as I got off the phone and told him I'd heard from Cate. "She said you're in Catalina."

"For the moment, yeah. We're waiting for a chopper home now."

Chase explained that after he had verified Cate's photo of Tyson with LAPD, he and a couple of robbery-homicide detectives had hopped a police chopper to Catalina. By the time they had arrived late last night, the local sheriffs had picked Tyson up for violating his parole. As a sexual offender, he had failed to notify the authorities that he was living aboard his boat in the harbor next to a beach area where children played.

"You bringing Tyson with you?"

"You bet," Chase yelled into the phone. In the background, I could hear the heavy buffeting of a helicopter's blades. "Got to go, Carol. I'll call when we're back."

I hung up with Chase and called the newsroom. First is always best in the race for news and so far, with respect to the Model Slayer, KTLK had a lot of firsts. Seven months ago, I had been first to report finding the body of Shana Walters in Big Bear. I'd gone there on an assignment for the station. A new ski lift had opened, and Tyler wanted me to report on it firsthand. I did a series of interviews with skiers and restauranteurs and was on the way home when my GPS failed. I took a wrong turn and ended up on a remote canyon road and spotted a body off the side of the mountain. Had it not been for that wrong turn, I never would have seen Shana, or been the first reporter to report on her murder. Then three months later, I was first on the scene again when a commuter was driving up Benedict Canyon and called the station to report what looked like a body off Mulholland Drive. I had no idea the two were related. Again, I was on my way home and Tyler called and told me to check it out. Her name was Kara Stiffers, and when I saw her body, I knew the police were dealing with a serial killer. A month later, I was in the newsroom when I heard a report on the police scanner. A hiker had found a woman's nude body in Griffith Park tied to a tree near the old zoo. I could feel it in my bones. The Model Slayer had struck again. I didn't wait for Tyler to tell me to go. Not every reporter would know the park so well, but I had hiked the trails there as a kid and knew the area around the old zoo well. When I arrived, I was the first reporter on the scene. The police had already strung yellow crime scene tape up, but I could still see the victim. She had been posed exactly like two women I had seen before. It took a while to identify the body and notify her family. Her name was Eileen Kim. And now, I had been first to announce the arrest of Pete Pompidou as a probable suspect. Plus, I had just broken the news about a possible fourth victim in the desert. And KTLK was about to broadcast news that Billy Tyson, a known sexual offender, had been transported from Catalina back to L.A. for questioning with the model slayings. Anyone following the story might think KTLK had an inside track. In fact, it wasn't long before I realized the cops were beginning to think so too.

CHAPTER 13

Sunday morning I went for a run. Overnight it had rained and the direction of the Santa Ana Winds had changed. For the first time in forty-eight hours, the valley was clear of smoke, and the air had been cleansed by the rain and the cooler temperatures. I did a two-and-a-half-mile loop along the L.A. River bed, running from Whitsett to Laurel Canyon, and was starting to feel like myself again, when a van made an illegal left turn onto Ventura Boulevard, and nearly hit me. *Damn California drivers, they never look where they're going.*

I stopped short. With my hand on my chest, I let the van pass. "Hey! Slow down!"

I couldn't see the driver through the blackout windows. But the white van was unmistakable. Two doors. Oversized tires, a dented front fender, and a headlight held in place with gray masking tape.

"Xstacy!" I screamed again and watched as the van traveled west on the boulevard. It had to be Xstacy's, I doubted there could be two exactly like it in the city. Plus, Xstacy had my home number. I'd written it down on the back of my business card when we met and looking me up wouldn't be a problem. I was listed. But I never expected she would try to find me at home. Not unless she was in trouble.

Misty was sitting at the kitchen table when I got home. She looked troubled. In front of her was her glass teapot. The one she brought out for her readings.

"You okay?" I went to the kitchen and got myself a glass of

water.

"There was a young woman here a few minutes ago." Misty cradled her cup in her hands and stared down at her tea. "I sensed she was frightened and that she was running from something. She said her name was Xstacy."

"What did she want?"

"She didn't say, but she wanted you to have this." Misty reached into her robe, took out a small white rabbit's foot and dropped it on the center of the table.

"A rabbit's foot? Why would she—"

"It's a lucky charm, Carol, and I got a reading from it."

While I respected the fact that Misty had worked with the FBI in the past and helped to find missing persons, when it came to personal readings and belief in clairvoyant powers, I had my doubts.

"Misty, I—"

"It's called psychometry, Carol. The art of reading an object to learn about the person associated with it. And before you tell me you don't believe in any of this, let me warn you, you may not now, but you will. Very soon."

There was no point in arguing with Misty. I needed to know what she had learned from Xstacy, and if that required sitting through a reading, then I was willing to do so.

I sat down.

"Alright," I said. "Suppose you tell me what it is you think you're getting from this lucky charm."

"For one, this rabbit's foot didn't belong to Xstacy, Carol. It belonged to someone else." Misty picked the rabbit's foot up and held it in her hand. "It was given to her by a friend. Someone she was trying to help. I feel as though they may have shared a troubled past or present." Misty closed her eyes and shook her head. "The timing of these things isn't always easy to read, but their relationship, there's a darkness about it." Misty put the rabbit's foot back down on the table. "I'm sorry, perhaps if I'd spoken to Xstacy longer, I might know more."

I picked up the rabbit's foot and held it in my hand. Small. Soft. Brown and white with an unusual clasp with three colored beads. One blue and two red. "Not that I believe you, Misty, but if I did, do you have a name of the person who gave it to her?"

Misty put her hand on top of mine and folded my fingers over the rabbit's foot. "No. But whoever Xstacy's friend was, she's dead. She died very suddenly. And recently."

I felt my chest tighten. "Was her name S-s-sam?" I could barely get the name out. Could something have happened to Sam since Friday night?

"I don't have a name, Carol. All I know is Xstacy's frightened. Her friend's passing was violent. Unexpected. I believe she was murdered." Misty's crooked fingers squeezed my own, and our eyes met. "I don't know any more than that, but I sense you do. That's why Xstacy wanted you to have this."

Misty let go of my hand, and I put the rabbit's foot down on the table.

"I need to call Xstacy," I said.

I got up from the table and went to the kitchen counter where I had left my bag the night before. As I searched around for my cell, it started to ring.

"That'll be Chase." Misty got up from the table and shuffled towards the French doors.

"Is that another psychic prediction?" I rubbed my hand down the side of my leg. Just in case the rabbit's foot contained any psychic voodoo.

"Not at all. He called on the house phone while you were out for your run. He tried your cell first. I heard your bag ringing while I was making tea and when the house phone rang, I picked up. I knew it had to be him." Misty pointed to my bag. "Answer it. He sounded anxious. I'll take my tea out on the patio so you two can talk."

CHAPTER 14

"Bad news." Those were Chase's first words. Not hello. Not how are you? Just bad news. Then, "Cate back yet?"

"No. She's staying with her dad tonight. Why? What's wrong?"

"Tyson's lawyer. That's what's wrong. He was waiting for us when we returned from Catalina last night. He's threatened a lawsuit. Says the Catalina police had no right to arrest him. That LAPD's harassing him."

Chase explained that according to Tyson's attorney, Tyson hadn't violated his parole, and he wasn't living on the boat as the police had claimed. Instead, he had gone sailing and had no intention of dropping anchor in Catalina's harbor. He had no idea there was a children's playground close by. His excuse for being there at all was because the weather had changed, and he didn't feel it was safe to sail. In short, Tyson hadn't violated his parole, and neither LAPD nor the Catalina Sheriff's Department has any right to hold him.

"So they kicked him loose?" I asked.

"They don't have anything linking him to the model murders. Not yet anyway, and his lawyer advised him not to say anything."

I squeezed my eyes shut and exhaled. This wasn't the news Cate was hoping for. "Cate thought he might be able to clear Pete."

"That's not the only reason I called. You sitting down?"

"Why? What's wrong?"

"The DA's dropping the charges against Pete. At least for right now. They've scheduled a hearing for ten a.m. with a press conference following. After that, he'll be free to go."

"What happened?"

"Pete's attorney got a judge to rule the evidence the cops took from Pete's van is inadmissible. The search warrant the cops had didn't cover Pete's van, and nothing inside of it—the ropes, the ice chest, the knife—can be used in the case against him. Add to that whatever Cate told the DA about Pete, and the District Attorney started to doubt he had enough evidence to sway a jury. In a case like this, with all the publicity it's getting, the DA wants to make certain he can win before he goes to court."

"This is good news then. They'll have to start over. Build a new case."

"Maybe."

"What do you mean maybe?"

"I ran into someone who knows you last night. He was at the police station when we came in with Tyson. He said you two were old friends. If I'm not wrong, he's the same handsome dude you were talking to at the police station Friday." Chase paused as though he was waiting for some kind of verification.

"Eric?" I said.

"Tall. Good looking FBI agent. Had a lot of nice things to say about you."

"How did he know you knew me?"

"He's FBI, Carol. How do those guys know anything? The thing is, he wanted me to relay a message to you."

Chase paused.

"Go on."

"He thought it might be better coming from me since he's working with the DA and didn't want things to look inappropriate."

Of course Eric would be working on the case. Why hadn't it occurred to me? The FBI always got involved in serial murders.

"What did he say?"

"He wanted you to know investigators think you're a little too close to the case to be impartial."

"They're not the only ones who think that."

"And he's concerned about Cate hanging around a suspected

serial killer. He suggested you might want to have her spend more time with her dad, at least until things settle down."

Was it me or did the world seem like it was getting smaller and making my job more difficult without running into my exes and their opinions?

"Her dad, huh?" I felt like I was about to snap. The stress of the case, the uncomfortable growing distance between my daughter and me and the inexplicable feelings I had for Eric were all coming to a head, and not in a good way.

"Well, if you run into Eric again, be sure to thank him. And tell him he's right. It is inappropriate for him to comment on a case he's investigating or one I'm reporting on for that matter. And as far as my daughter goes, tell him, thank you very much, that Cate's just fine with me, and I don't need him to stick his nose in it."

"Hey, don't shoot the messenger. You ask me, I think you're doing just fine."

I thanked Chase for the vote of confidence, hung up the phone, and called Xstacy. There was no answer, and instead of the call going to voicemail, I got an automatic response.

The person you are trying reach has a voicemail box that is full and is not accepting calls at this time.

Next, I tried Sam. She didn't answer either.

CHAPTER 15

Monday morning, I was back in the very same courtroom where Pete had been formally charged. Just like before, I was sitting shoulder to shoulder with reporters, who like myself had received an early morning communique from the court announcing Pete Pompidou was to be called back before Judge Petrossian at ten a.m. While those on either side of me may have expected the reasoning behind this was to announce additional charges were about to be added to those already against Pete, I knew better.

I sat silently while the prosecutors, the city's best—or the A-Team as I planned to call them in my report—Alverez, Adorno, and Adamson—filed into the courtroom. All identically dressed in dark suits with bold ties, carrying thick briefcases, while the sounds of their wing-tipped shoes echoed on the marble floor. Across from them, Pete's attorney Melinda Croft, stood alone, facing the front of the courtroom. She was dressed in a tight-fitting black skirt and a jacket a size too small for her round frame. She looked nervously around the courtroom, never making eye contact with the prosecution, and held her hands in front of her, rubbing them together while she waited for her client to appear from lockup.

I glanced back at Chase who stood next to the door. Our eyes met. He nodded to me and then to another door near the front of the courtroom where two U.S. Marshals appeared with Pete, who today was dressed in jeans and a chambray shirt. His hands no longer bound by cuffs. The two marshals escorted him to Miss Croft's table, where she greeted him with a hug and told him to sit down.

Moments later, the bailiff came in and asked us all to stand and announced the court was now in session. "The honorable Judge Petrossian presiding."

The judge approached the bench and asked us all to sit. He greeted both the defense and prosecution team warmly, then paused, and looked directly at Pete.

"Mr. Pompidou would you stand, please." I leaned forward in my seat, my pen and pad poised at the ready. "I assume your attorney has told you why I've called you back into court this morning?"

Pete answered. "Yes, Your Honor. She has."

"For the purpose of those here today, let me say this. Mr. Pompidou, it has come to my attention that the District Attorney does not feel there is enough evidence to proceed to trial. In light of this, I am obligated to dismiss the charges filed against you without prejudice. This does not mean, however, these charges and others cannot be brought up again at a later date." The Judge banged his gavel. "Mr. Pompidou, you are free to go."

There was an audible gasp throughout the courtroom. The Judge banged his gavel again and demanded we all remain seated. Croft took Pete by the hand and crossed in front of the A-team who sat stoically behind the prosecution table, the look on their faces like they smelled rotten meat.

I jammed my notepad back into my bag and pushed my way through the crowd toward the elevator. I wanted to be upfront for the press conference. Somewhere I could record sound, ask questions and get answers without being drowned out by the crowd.

Outside on the courthouse steps, the media was ready. News reporters from every news outlet in town huddled together and waited in front of a makeshift podium of microphones that resembled a small forest of trees. While some smoked and others checked their cell phones for messages, I jockeyed for the best position close-up to the mic field and called Tyler and told him to standby.

Finally, the first of the A-Team appeared from behind the courthouse's big double brass doors. Cameramen, with their equipment on their shoulders, began shooting, and I pulled my mic from my bag and plugged it into my cell phone. I could have used the mic on my cell phone, but any chance to get the station's logoed mic flag on camera would earn me extra points with Tyler when the video aired on the evening news. What I needed was a sound bite, something I could edit and include in my report when the press conference ended. I turned on my mic and what I got was gold.

The A-Team approached the mic field. Alvarez, the shortest of the three and their spokesman, began with a statement about how disappointed they were with the judge's action.

"However," Alvarez said, "while we are unable to proceed to trial at this time, I would like to take this opportunity to remind the public that Mr. Pompidou remains a person of interest. The District Attorney's office will continue to investigate the circumstances surrounding the murders of these three young women until justice has been served. Thank you."

Without any further statement, the A-Team turned and walked back toward the courthouse and paused as Croft and Pete appeared from behind the same double brass doors the prosecution had passed through earlier. Making no attempt to acknowledge them, Croft pushed past the three men and led the way to the mic field with Pete behind her.

Standing next to Croft, Pete looked refreshed. He pushed his surfer-blond hair from his eyes and smiled that same slightly crooked grin he had given my daughter the day he had taken our picture at the beach. I followed his gaze.

Standing to my right, at the far end of a line of reporters, was a young woman wearing a baseball hat and large dark glasses. The type celebrities wear when they don't want the public to know who they are. But this wasn't a famous star, hiding from the paparazzi. This was my own flesh and blood.

Cate?

I clicked off my mic and pushed through the line of reporters until I was standing next to my daughter. It was obvious to me Cate had camouflaged her appearance. Her strawberry-blonde hair was tucked under her hat, and she was wearing a long cotton skirt and T-shirt to hide her trim figure.

"Cate, what are you doing here? You can't be here. Not now. Not like this."

"Well, I am." Cate crossed her arms and looked straight ahead. "I need to be. Pete's got no one, Mom."

I grabbed her by the arm and pulled her farther away from the crowd. "How did you know he was going to be released? Did Chase tell you?"

"No. Pete called me this morning. His attorney told him late last night. She said this morning's proceeding was just a formality, and that he'd be released. He asked if I could bring him some clothes, and I promised I'd drive him home."

"Drive him home?" I could feel my blood pressure start to rise. "Where? His place? You're certainly not planning to take him back to our house."

Before Cate could answer, Croft started to speak, and with one warning finger, I pointed in Cate's direction. *We're not done here.*

I stepped back in line with the reporters and held my mic out so that I might get a recording of what Croft was about to say.

"I wish to make a brief statement on behalf of my client. Last Thursday, Mr. Pompidou was arrested for the murders of three young women. His arrest was based largely upon circumstantial evidence that both the judge and the District Attorney don't believe provides sufficient proof of a connection between my client and the deaths of those three young women. Today, I'm happy to say, Mr. Pompidou has been released and all charges against him have been dismissed. I'd like to add that Mr. Pompidou has cooperated completely with investigators and has every hope that the police will continue with their investigation until the real murderer of these young women is caught and properly charged. Until then, I hope that we can all agree that justice was done here today and that the police will not harass Mr. Pompidou with these bogus charges. Thank you."

Reporters began immediately shouting questions.

"I'm sorry," Croft said. "We're not taking questions. My client's spent enough time locked up and has a life to get back to. So now if you'll excuse us."

Croft led Pete down the steps of the courthouse and Cate left my side. I wanted to grab her by the arm and forbid her to go, but I couldn't. She had made up her mind.

In my ear, I could hear Tyler. "Carol, you ready?"

"Yes," I said.

"We're live with Carol Childs from the LA Courthouse. Carol—"

"Thank you, Tyler. In an unexpected move today, Judge Petrossian dismissed without prejudice the murder charges against the suspected Model Slayer, Pete Pompidou. The judge cited lack of evidence for a trial but cautioned Mr. Pompidou that charges could be reinstated at a later date should new information come to light. Meanwhile, Juan Alvarez, head of the city's new A-Team of prosecutors assigned to the case, issued a strong warning to Mr. Pompidou."

I keyed up Alvarez' recorded statement regarding the DA's intention to continue their investigation, then added a brief explanation concerning the meaning of the judge's dismissal of charges without prejudice.

"Without prejudice," I said, "is a temporary dismissal, and will allow the DA more time to investigate further." In an attempt to give equal time to both sides, I followed up with Croft's statement requesting the police not harass her client, then closed. "This is Carol Childs, live from the County Courthouse."

As I reported all this, another more personal drama unfolded in front of me, and I was helpless to do anything about it.

The cameras had followed Pete and his attorney away from the courthouse and caught Cate running up to them. Pete stopped and embraced her. They kissed, and the scene exploded. Cameras clicked, and reporters shouted questions.

"Hey, who's that girl? Is that the girlfriend?" Cate and Pete rushed off, and reporters chased after them. "Miss, what's your name?" "How do you know Pete Pompidou?" "Miss can you give us a statement?"

CHAPTER 16

News that charges against the suspected Model Slayer had been dropped and that Pete had been released was the top story of the hour. Every news outlet in town was leading with it, and KTLK was no different. By the time I got back to the station, the court of public opinion was in session, and show hosts Kit and Carson were in the midst of fielding calls from listeners. Most of them not in favor of showing any mercy to a man they had already prejudged as guilty.

As I passed the large smoked-glass studio window on my way to my office, Kit waved and gestured for me to join them. Careful not to make any sound, I entered the studio, and took the empty stool between the two of them and put on a headset.

Carson had a spirited listener on the line.

"Well, if you ask me, letting that butcher go was a mistake. The cops found pictures of all those models in his apartment. Who knows what else they found they're not talking about."

"Pictures that a lot of other people, photographers for sure, might have had," Carson said.

"Maybe so, but what about that roommate of his? Billy Tyson. He has a record as a sex offender. Go online and check it out. Just type in your zip code, and there they are. Name and address. Everything you need to know. You ask me, the guy was on the run. And what about that other girl, the one they found in the desert tied up to a tree with a dog collar 'round her neck? It's got to be related. Who knows how many more bodies are out there?"

Kit answered. "What are cops going to do? They can't keep a

man in jail, not without proof. That's not the way our justice system works. And the DA didn't think there was enough evidence to proceed to trial."

"Well, they shouldn't have let him go. Far as I'm concerned, they should tie him up to a tree like he did that girl and leave him in the desert to rot. Let the buzzards eat him."

Carson was about to reply when their screener interrupted from the control booth. "Guys, we've got a caller from Sherman Oaks who thinks differently. Shall I patch her through?"

Carson nodded. "Welcome to the show. May I ask—"

"Pete Pompidou's not some serial killer." I recognized the voice. *Damnit, Cate, why are you doing this?*

I reached for the microphone and Kit stopped me. He wanted the next question.

"You sound pretty sure of yourself, Miss—"

"I am. And you should be ashamed as well as everyone listening to your show. Talking about Pete like they know he did it. It's like he's already been tried. They think he's guilty just because he had photos of those girls. But that doesn't make him some serial murderer. He's a photographer. It's what he does. He takes their pictures, and sometimes he doesn't even charge. He's a good guy, not some murderer."

"You sound like you know him pretty well," Kit said.

"He's a friend. I was there this morning when his attorney addressed the press and asked the police to stop harassing him. And I'm asking you to do the same."

Kit's eyes met Carson's. "So, you're the girl on the TV. The one the news caught holding hands with him as you left the courthouse."

"I am." I could hear the conviction in Cate's voice.

I leaned forward, my fingers inches from a control board exactly like the one in the adjoining studio. One slip of the finger and I could override the board in the control booth and disconnect the call.

"You mind telling us your name?" Kit asked.

That was it. I hit the end call button and dumped the call. I didn't trust Cate's self-righteousness to identify herself, and I wasn't about to let my daughter's name be broadcast over the airwaves. A sudden low hollow tone droned through my headphone and into the studio. Kit and Carson stared at me. A look of *why* on both their faces. Inside the control booth, their screener stood up and gestured, his hands in the air. "What the−"

I had no right to do what I did. My maternal instincts overrode my professional side, and I had nothing to say for it. Other than, "I'm sorry. I don't know what happened. My hand must have slipped. I didn't mean to. I−" I took my headset off and stood up. "I think I'm going to be sick. Excuse me."

I ran out of the studio and into the ladies' room. I'd never done anything so unprofessional. I felt clammy and sick to my stomach. I turned on the faucet and threw cold water onto my face, then blotted it and looked in the mirror. I didn't recognize myself. I didn't feel like much of a mother, and with what I'd just done, I was hardly a good reporter. And yet, I couldn't let go of either. I had to find a way to stop Cate from exposing herself, and I had to find a way to prove Pete wasn't the Model Slayer.

I reached into my bag and found my phone and dialed Cate's number. The phone went directly to voicemail. Next, I tried the lab where Cate was interning. Not that I thought I'd find her there. I had no doubt she had left the courthouse and taken Pete back to his place at the beach. But I had to try. An administrator answered and said Cate was off for the day. Frustrated my daughter was avoiding me, I called her cell back and left a strongly worded message.

"Cate, I'll be home around seven. We need to talk. Be there. No excuses."

When I got home, Cate met me at the front door. She gave me a big hug and handed me a glass of red wine. "I'm sorry, Mom. I just can't let Pete go through this alone."

From behind her, I saw Misty seated at the kitchen table with her flowering pot of tea, and two teacups that looked half-full.

"You've been talking to Misty."

"She thought I was I being too hard on you." Cate walked over to the table and stood behind Misty.

"You think?" I didn't need the wine. I followed Cate into the kitchen and put the glass on the counter.

"It's just, I understand reporting's your job and all. And I get what the cops are doing. But sometimes it seems like you're part of the problem, Mom. I guess what I'm saying is, I wish you weren't working on this case."

That was the third time in as many days someone had told me they thought it would be better if I weren't working the Model Slayer's case. Trouble was I couldn't just quit. If I wanted to help my daughter and clear Pete's name, I had to keep investigating. I was the only one who knew about Ely Wade, and I'd promised Xstacy and Sam I'd help. But I couldn't share any of this with Cate.

"Catie, look, I know you think Pete's innocent, but getting involved in a murder case, with a suspect the police believe to be a serial killer...it's just not a wise move. You can't put–"

"What? Myself in the middle of it?" Cate sat down next to Misty. "Why not? The cops don't have a case. Why do you think they let him go? Mom, trust me. I know what I'm doing."

"And what is that, Cate?"

"Standing by him. Mom, the police have nothing. The blood evidence from the crime scenes wasn't just from the models, it was killer's,too. And it doesn't even match."

"How do you know that?"

"Pete's attorney told me so. It's one of the reasons the police had to drop the charges. Whoever killed those girls cut themselves too. The cops had nothing. No match. No motive. Nothing. Besides, I told the cops I was with Pete when Shana Walters was killed."

"When?" I asked.

"When they questioned me at the station. So he has an alibi, and I'm not going to desert him."

I looked at Misty. *Help me.*

"Carol, I think what Cate's saying is, she wants you to respect her judgment."

I sat down at the table. "Cate, please. I know you think Pete doesn't have anything to do with the murders, and I have trouble thinking he's guilty too, but think about it. What do you really know about this guy? Pete Pompidou's not even his real name. And you said yourself you don't know anything about his roommate."

"I know they're innocent. I know Pete wouldn't do anything to hurt anybody. He's an artist, not some crazed serial killer. And I'm not going to stand by and watch him go to prison because the cops haven't looked at anyone else. The police have been following him since we left the courthouse this morning. They're not letting up."

I grabbed Cate's hands and held them in my own. "Cate, you've got to understand. You can't get into the middle of an investigation, no matter how much you think you're helping. When you do things like you did this morning, show up at the courthouse and then call the radio station, you've gone too far. People are going to talk. They'll assume you know things. They'll think you're involved, and I won't be able to protect you."

Cate pulled her hands away from mine. "I don't need your protection. Misty says if I believe in what I'm doing, the truth will protect me."

I glanced at Misty. Much as I appreciated her help, I couldn't have Misty filling Cate's head with nothing more than wishful thinking. "I'm sorry, Misty, but Cate, you can't trust your future to some tea-leaf reading."

"Misty doesn't read tea leaves, Mom. You know that."

"What I told her, Carol, was that she's a lot like you." Misty picked up her tea and swirled what was left of the leafy liquid in her cup. "You work hard enough at something, and things happen. You create an energy about you. There's nothing psychic or hocus-pocus about that. People attracted to that energy come into your life. Some of them with answers and others with questions. But each of them propels you forward. Isn't that what you've found to be true?"

I got up from the table and retrieved my glass of wine from the bar. If Misty was trying to signal me she sensed in some paranormal way that I had drawn Xstacy into my life because I had been investigating the Model Slayer, now was not the time to bring it up. I had no idea how she could possibly know how Xstacy was connected. I certainly hadn't told her about Xstacy's accident or her confession to me, and I wasn't about to tell Cate. I couldn't risk my daughter getting nervous about Pete and leaking what I was working on to the cops.

"Misty's right," I said. "You work hard, and things happen. And I am proud of you, Cate. Standing up for Pete isn't easy, but sometimes you have to realize you can't fix everything. You need to trust the cops will find whoever did these murders and leave it alone. Promise me you won't see Pete again until this over. For your own sake."

"I can't do that, Mom, and I won't. And you wouldn't either."

"Cate, be reasonable."

"No!" Cate stood up and moved away from the table. "You've got to understand. I love Pete, and I won't desert him."

Cate's cell phone rang. She glanced down at the screen and smiled. "I need to take this." I didn't need to ask to know it was Pete. After he had been released, she had driven him back to the beach and came home, exactly as I had asked. She answered with a soft nervous giggle, buried her face in her hand, and turned and went upstairs to her room.

Misty waited until Cate left the room. "You shouldn't be too hard on her, Carol. She's in love. You must remember what that was like?"

"There are times I'd like to forget. Love can make a young girl do crazy things."

"You've done alright for yourself. Two nice kids. An ex who's not altogether a bad guy."

"The kids are great," I said. "The ex, I could have done without." I took a sip of wine and winked.

"I wouldn't worry about Cate. She's going to be just fine."

"Another psychic prediction?" I teased. "Because you must

know, telling Cate everything's going to be okay is only going to fill her with false hope. The police could re-arrest Pete tomorrow. This whole thing would start all over again, and I don't want her anywhere near him when it does."

Misty reached into the pocket of her long skirt and took out the rabbit's foot and placed it on the table in front of me.

"We need to talk about this. It's like I told Cate, you put energy into something, and things happen. Like Xstacy showing up at our doorstep Saturday morning. It wasn't an accident. I don't know how she's connected to Pete or the Model Slayer, but I do know she wanted you to have this rabbit's foot. And I think if you keep it with you, you'll start to understand why." Misty pushed the rabbit's foot closer to me.

"You know I don't believe in stuff like that."

"Do me a favor, hold it in your hand. Close your eyes and tell me what comes to mind."

I picked up the rabbit's foot. Light and soft in my hand with the feel of small twig-like bones beneath the hair.

"What are you thinking about?" Misty asked.

"Right now? Cate. The scene at the courthouse this morning. How upset I was with her for calling the station."

"No. Not that. Anger blocks your vision. Go back to the thoughts running through your mind this morning."

"Chase. The court case. That girl the firefighters found in the desert." My hand closed over the rabbit's foot like a fist, and I started to massage it with my fingers.

"That," Misty said. "Look at your hand. You closed it around the rabbit's foot when you mentioned the girl in the desert. Go with that."

"What do mean, go with that?" I shook my head and looked at Misty. I had no idea what she was talking about.

"It's connected, Carol. I've had this rabbit's foot in my pocket ever since Xstacy gave it to me. And before, when I would hold it in my hand, I could feel her all around me. It's was as though she was right here in the room with me. I've had that feeling before. Last time was when I helped the FBI find that young college girl who had gone missing. It wouldn't leave me alone until I found her. And now when I hold the rabbit's foot in my hand, it's not Xstacy's energy I feel, but that poor girl you reported on in the desert. It was the same dark energy I saw surrounding Xstacy the day she came to the door. In fact, my sense of it is so strong, I feel as though Xstacy and this girl the firefighters found knew each other. That the girl you reported on not only knew Xstacy but gave her the rabbit's foot. It's a definite connection, Carol, and sometime soon, you'll see it yourself."

I put the rabbit's foot back down on the table. "I would agree with you, Misty, except for the fact we didn't have any physical proof how the girl in the desert died or even who she was."

"But I might." Misty picked up the rabbit's foot and held it next to her chest. "I've been thinking about her, and I may have an idea about her name." Misty closed her eyes. "Her name begins with an M. It's Marcy or Mary, something like that."

"Marilynn?" I asked.

Misty's eyes opened. "Yes. Marilynn. And for whatever reason, I sense Marilynn and Xstacy knew one another and Marilynn gave this lucky charm to Xstacy for a reason. And now, Xstacy's given it to you. But I fear she shouldn't have. I sense she's in trouble, Carol, and you need to find her. Before it's too late."

I had no idea if Xstacy and Marilynn knew each other. Xstacy had never mentioned her, and if Marilynn had worked in the Sky High Club, she would have been gone and reported missing by the time Xstacy had killed Ely. Had Xstacy heard my report about the girl in the desert, and suspected she might be Marilynn? Was that why she had stopped by my house? As for how Misty knew what she did, I hadn't a clue. But I had to find out.

CHAPTER 17

Tuesday morning as I drove into work, I kept thinking about Misty's reading of the rabbit's foot. It had left me with an uncomfortable feeling, but not nearly as disquieting as the feeling I had in the pit of my stomach when I tried to call Xstacy again. The call went immediately to voicemail, and I heard the same prerecorded message I had received before. *The person you are trying reach has a voicemail box that is full and is not accepting calls at this time.*

Next, I tried Sam, and when she didn't answer, I left a message. I apologized for the early hour. Told her I'd been trying to reach both her and Xstacy and hadn't received a word back. "Call me," I said. "I'm concerned."

After that, I called Sheri. Ordinarily, I wouldn't dare ring my best friend before ten a.m. But twice a week, Sheri liked to rise early for an online yoga class, part of her new fitness routine, with a master yogi from India. I crossed my fingers this was one of those days, and if she weren't sitting cross-legged in some lotus position and meditating, she'd pick up.

I was in luck. Being careful not to send off any alarms, I told Sheri I was on deadline to wrap the story about college girls working strip clubs. I had tried Sam's number, but she wasn't answering.

"I thought since you were taking pole dancing lessons with Sam you might have another number or know how I could get hold of her."

"You could try Pamela's." Sheri sounded out of breath. I

pictured her in some pretzel curl on the floor with the phone in front of her. "We talked last night. She said she was working out at a new dance studio down on the boulevard and wanted me to come. It's not far from your place. In fact, you should come with me. I'm anxious to get in a couple more workouts before Max gets back."

"He still a thing?"

Sheri giggled. "Of course he's still a thing. Or at least he is for now. He's been out of town for a couple days, so who knows? But I'm having fun, and between my yoga and the pole dancing, it's a great way to keep toned. Why don't you come with me tonight? Might be fun."

I couldn't imagine a worse way to spend the evening. I was familiar with a number of local businesses on the boulevard, restaurants, nail salons, and gyms. Dance studios, yoga, Pilates and now pole dancing salons were the new *it places* to go after work and meet people. To me, they all looked like giant fish tanks. Over illuminated white box-like studios, with big glass windows and high ceilings that allowed passersby to leer-in at their spandex-clad clientele. The idea of caressing a pole and hanging upside down in front of a group of strangers like some monkey in the zoo didn't strike me as appealing.

"Sorry, I have to work late tonight. Rain check?"

"I've got a better idea. How about, you, me, Chase, and Max get together for dinner some time? Give me a chance to introduce him to my friends."

"As long as it doesn't include spandex or pole dancing, I'm good. But, it's got to be next week. This weekend is crazy."

"Monday, then."

"Monday, it is."

I hung up the phone. At least Sheri had talked to Sam. As for Xstacy I still had no idea where she was or how much trouble she might be in.

Tyler called as I was about to pull into the station's lot. "Carol, where are you?"

"Outside.Why?"

"Turn around. We got a call from a listener. There's police activity at Venice beach. Somebody found a body tied to a post on one of the volleyball courts. Sounds like it could be another victim of the Model Slayer. I need you to check it out."

"Please, tell me this body's nowhere near Pete's place." I gripped the steering wheel tighter, my knuckles white. At least Cate was home this morning.

"Don't jump to any conclusions, Carol. Just get us the story."

I pulled a U-turn in front of the station's gate, waited for the light to change, and sped down La Cienega to Venice Blvd. If this was the Model Slayer's work, he had chosen a convenient location, so close to Pete's house. Too close, I thought.

CHAPTER 18

I parked my red Jeep off Washington Boulevard, near the Venice Pier. The same spot where I'd parked when Cate had called me about Pete's arrest. From the backseat, I grabbed my to-go bag. Inside was a pair of tennis shoes and things I might need in the field like a baseball hat, sunscreen, and a candy bar. I slipped off my heels, put on my tennis shoes and pulled my hair up into a ponytail and pulled it through the hole in the back of the baseball cap. Then hiked my pencil skirt above my knees and jogged down the bike path towards the volleyball courts.

Ahead of me, the police had already cordoned off the area, refusing access to anyone, including reporters. Yellow crime scene tape circled the volleyball court but did little to block curiosity seekers who were gathered two and three deep behind the tape.

The police had done what they could to hide the victim's body from the public's view without disturbing the scene. A privacy shield about four feet high provided circular coverage of the area. What lay beyond was anybody's guess. With no access to the police, I queried the crowd, looking for possible witnesses. I spotted a runner, standing off by himself.

"Excuse me. My name's Carol Childs. I'm a reporter." I handed him my business card. "You know what happened?"

"Not really. I came along right after the cops got here. A couple of joggers said they found a body on the beach and called it in. They're talking to the police now." The runner pointed to the yellow crime scene tape where three men in matching T-shirts and shorts, who looked like they might all be members of a local running club, were talking to investigators. "The tall one told me they were jogging on the beach when they saw a woman's body strung up on one of the volleyball poles. Said she was tied to it, with her hands above her head. Like those models who got killed."

Overhead the sky was filling with news choppers, all vying for a shot of the beach. While around me, TV reporters had started to arrive and were doing their best to set up live shots with the volleyball court and the ocean in the background. If I were going to get the story on the air, I needed to act now.

"You mind sticking around?"

"Not if you're gonna put me on the air I don't. I'm a big fan of Kit and Carson. You work with them, right?"

"Yeah," I said.

"Cool. Name's Jason Holder. I'm a personal trainer. I work out on Muscle Beach. Think you could mention it when you introduce me?"

"Sorry," I said. It never ceased to amaze me how, even in the midst of tragedy, some people would seize on the moment for self-promotion.

I punched star five, speed dial on my phone for the station, and told Tyler I was in Venice. "I'm standing on the bike path with a witness who's pretty sure the body on the beach is the work of the Model Slayer.

"Hold on, Carol. I'll patch you into the morning show. And good work. You break this before anyone else in town and we're four for four." I assumed that meant because I had been first to report on the murders of the three models. If today's body on the beach was the Model Slayer's fourth victim, I had set some record. Not quite the record I was going for, but I knew Tyler was anxious to claim credit for KTLK being first to break the news of the Model Slayer's latest kill.

With Jason standing next to me, I took my earpiece out of my bag and plugged it into my iPhone. The earplugs allowed me to hear the station and use the phone in place of my mic, a simpler solution when I wasn't in a large public setting. Tyler came back seconds later, interrupting Kit and Carson's morning show with breaking news.

"We've got news of another possible Model Slaying in Venice Beach. Carol Childs is there now. Carol, can you tell us about what's happening?"

"Thanks, Tyler. The police discovered a female body this morning. I'm standing here with Jason Holder, an early morning jogger who said he was here when two other joggers found the body and called the police. Jason, can you tell us what you saw?"

"It's like I told you. She was tied to the pole. With her hands above her head."

"There's a lot of speculation among the crowd here this morning, this might have been the work of the Model Slayer. Do you think so?"

"I can tell you this, that girl, whoever she was, didn't get there by herself. And from what I've read about the Model Slayer, sure looks like it. She was nude and the way those other joggers described her, she had been posed."

"Anything else?"

"I heard one of 'em say she had dark hair and tattoos."

My throat tightened. *Tattoos?* Was this how I was going to find out the body on the beach was Xstacy?

I forced the words from my mouth. "You see anything else unusual this morning?"

"No, but seems strange doesn't it?"

"What's that?"

"That suspect the cops let go Monday? That photographer. He lives just up the beach. 'Course it probably wouldn't be too smart if it was him to go kill some girl in his own backyard, but then some people aren't too smart, right?"

I wished I could have cut Jason's last remark from the broadcast, but I was live, and there was no stopping his words as they slipped out over the airwaves. I wrapped my report and thanked Jason for his help.

Tyler whispered into my earpiece. "Good job. Carol. Now I

need one more thing."

I knew before Tyler asked what he wanted me to do. And there would be no negotiation about it. I either wanted my job, or I didn't.

I asked anyway. And stared down the bike path towards the small salmon-colored bungalow Pete called home. "What do you need?"

"Check out Pete's place. You can probably see it from where you are. Find out if he's home. If he is, interview him."

Down the beach, a small crowd had already begun to gather on the bike path outside of Pete's small bungalow. Some pointed back in the direction of the yellow crime scene tape where a coroner's van had arrived. If I had any chance at all of talking to Pete, I couldn't approach the house from the ocean side.

Instead of the bike path, I chose Speedway, the narrow alley-street that ran directly behind the homes facing the ocean. From behind the houses, I could approach the back of Pete's bungalow without drawing attention to myself.

I picked my way down the alley-street, pockmarked with potholes and dumpsters. The narrow blacktop thoroughfare was a community of its own. Shared by the residents—who lived in multi-million-dollar homes and drove expensive imports—with dozens of homeless with their makeshift camps and shopping carts.

When I reached the back of Pete's house, I stopped. His van, a VW Bus, like Misty's only much newer and without all the peace symbols painted on it, was parked in the carport. Next to it was a late model BMW coupe with personalized plates. BILLYBOY. I took that as a sign both Pete and Billy might be home.

I checked to make sure I hadn't been followed, then dashed across the street. Quietly, I slipped between the two cars, then approached the back door, and knocked.

The door opened, as though the wind had pushed it. With my hand still on the doorknob, I entered.

"Pete. Are you here?" I looked around the kitchen.

No answer.

"Billy? Pete, it's Carol Childs. Hello?"

Still no answer. In front of me, a kitchen sink was filled with dirty dishes. An empty pizza box had been left on the kitchen table. I poked my head into the front room. The curtains were drawn, and the room was small and dark with minimal furnishings. A leather couch. Chair and big screen TV. I peeked through the front window, careful not to be seen. The crowd was beginning to disperse. I went to the foot of the stairs and yelled again. No answer. The house was empty. I checked upstairs anyway. Two bedrooms. Both beds appeared to have been slept in, the sheets tossed and clothes scattered on the floor. The small bath, between the rooms, looked as though it had been ransacked. Drawers open. Men's cosmetics scattered on the counter. The shower stall showed no evidence anyone had taken a shower recently. At least not today.

I went back downstairs and checked the kitchen once more for any evidence that might tell me when they had left. Coffee or breakfast cereal. There was nothing. Wherever Pete and Billy had gone, it looked as though they'd left in a hurry.

It wasn't until I left the house and was in the driveway facing Speedway that I noticed it. Parked directly across the street was a two-door white, utility van.

"Xstacy?"

I ran towards the van and knocked on the driver's window. "Xstacy!" I cupped my hands and tried to see inside, but it was useless. The only thing I could see was my own frantic reflection in the blackened window. "Xstacy!" I screamed again. I hoped she was asleep in the back. That the body on the beach, the tattooed girl, hadn't been Xstacy.

I pounded harder on the window, and when there was no answer, I tried the door. It was locked, and one of my fingernails broke off as I tried to open it. I stood back and prayed I was wrong. Maybe this wasn't Xstacy's van. Maybe someone else with a white van had parked it here. Then I noticed the dented front fender and that telltale damaged headlight secured with gray duct-tape.

I put my hand on the window of the van and made a vow. *If it's*

you, Xstacy, I'll find who did this. No matter where the trail leads.
I ran back toward the volleyball court. I needed to talk to the officer in charge of the investigation. A small four-post tent had been set up, and more police along with several blue-jacketed FBI agents were working the beach, scouring the sand for any signs of clues.
I approached the cordoned off area and held out my business card. "I need to talk to the detective in charge. It's about the body. I think I know who it is. If I'm right, her van's parked down the street off Speedway."

My meeting with Detective Soto, the lead investigator on the case, had a bad beginning and an even worse ending. He started with questions I couldn't answer. Like, why I was so sure I knew who the victim was? And what exactly was my relationship with her? None of which I could explain. Even if I wanted to share what Xstacy had told me, I couldn't. Dead or alive, Xstacy was a confidential source and so was Sam. And Sam's safety depended upon my silence. All I could tell Detective Soto was that while covering the story this morning, I got a description of the woman's body from a jogger on the beach, who had talked with another jogger, who had called the police to report the body. And from that description, I thought I might know who she was.
"Third hand, huh?" Soto looked down at my business card and scribbled something beneath it on his clipboard. "So that's how you reporters work. With third-hand sources? No wonder they call it fake news."
I didn't appreciate the put-down. I reminded him the cops weren't exactly talking to the press when I showed up. They had cordoned themselves off and restricted access. Finally, feeling like I was being treated more like a suspect than a reporter willing to share inside information, I came back with, "Hey, you want this lead or not?" I didn't care if I sounded flippant. The sooner I confirmed it was Xstacy's body on the beach the sooner I could get

to work on finding the murderer.

"Alright, Miss Childs, if you can't tell me how it is you know this victim, why don't you start with telling me what it is you think you know about her."

"I know she's tattooed and drives a white van, and that it's parked over on Speedway behind those houses." I pointed down the beach to Pete's house, where several LAPD's finest were combing the sand with metal detectors. "If you check the registration on the van, you'll find it's registered to a Stacy Minor, aka Xstacy." I remembered the name from the pedestrian accident reports I'd pulled for the station's Town Hall Meeting. "At least, that's the name I know her by."

"And just exactly what is it you and this Stacy Minor have in common?"

"I'm afraid I can't share that with you. It's confidential. But I'm sure if you check the van out, you'll find it belongs to the girl on the beach."

Soto signaled for two officers who had been standing guard over the crime scene to go look for the van, then glanced back down at my business card.

"You're Carol Childs. *The* Carol Childs, the reporter who's been breaking all these news stories about the Model Slayer." I nodded. I had an uncomfortable feeling I wasn't going to like his next question. "Seems to me, Ms. Childs, when the Model Slayer hits, you have an uncanny way of being first on the scene. You have any way of explaining that?"

"It's a big story," I said. "Reporters are competitive when it comes to something like this."

Soto unclipped my card from the clipboard, glanced at it again, then put it in his pocket. "Wouldn't have anything to do with the fact your daughter's friends with our principal suspect, would it?"

There it was. Soto had linked Cate and me together.

I rallied back, "Pete Pompidou? Not at all. In fact, curious as it is to find a body so close to his residence on the beach, I don't think it was him at all."

"You sound pretty confident."

"I know my daughter wouldn't be involved with a serial killer."

"Let's hope not." Then Soto looked back at the blue tent and asked if I planned on hanging around.

"No. I've got what I need. But, I'd appreciate it if you confirmed the van is Xstacy's you call and let me know. You've got my number."

"Don't worry, Ms. Childs. If you're right about this, we'll be doing a whole lot more than just talking."

CHAPTER 19

I tried to call Sam from my car as I left Venice Beach. If Scarface from the club had been the Model Slayer's partner and had been following Xstacy and killed her, Sam needed to know, and fast. I didn't want Sam hearing about it on the news. While the police weren't about to release Xstacy's name until they had a positive ID, I knew once Detective Soto checked out the van, it wouldn't be long before they would put two and two together and the name Stacy Minor would be everywhere. My call went immediately to voicemail. Rather than leave another message, I decided to drive over to UCLA and wait at the Tri-Delt house for Sam to return from class. Bad news was best delivered in person.

I was met at the door of the Tri-Delt house by two sorority sisters. Both blonde and smiley, and similarly matched in size and shape. It made me wonder if sorority sisters had all been cast and dyed from the same mold, they all looked so much alike. Both had gold delta lavaliers around their necks, books in their hands, and appeared to be on the way to class.

The taller of the two asked if she could help me.

"I'm here to see Sam," I said.

"Sam?" The girl frowned and shook her head. "Sorry, we don't have any Sams here. You sure you have the right house?"

"Samantha maybe? She's a dancer," I said.

"Oh, you must mean Sam Miller. You do know she doesn't live here?"

"And she's not a sister." The shorter girl scrunched her nose like I should know better.

"But I was just here a week ago. She was teaching a yoga class. We spoke in the parlor."

"That may be," the shorter girl said. "She teaches a yoga class here. But she's not a Tri Delt."

I bit my lip to keep my mouth from falling open. If she wasn't a Tri Delt, who was she? Was she even a college student?

"Do you know where I can find her?"

Both girls looked at each other, then back at me and shook their heads in unison.

"You might check over at the Wooden Center." The tall girl pointed across the street to campus. "They do dance classes there. Maybe someone knows there. Sorry."

"Thanks," I said.

I watched as the two passed by me in their short mini-skirts and laced up sandals. Then picked up my phone and called Sam again and left another message.

"Sam, it's Carol Childs. I need to see you. It's important. I'm on campus, and it's almost noon. Call me when you get this."

My next call went to Cate's cell phone. If I were going to be hanging around the university, I might as well grab lunch with my daughter. When she didn't answer, I tried the UCLA pathology department directly. An administrative assistant answered, and I asked to speak to Cate.

"I'm sorry, Cate called in sick today. Is there someone else who might be able to help you?"

Sick? Cate wasn't sick. If anything she was still stewing about last night and my request she not see Pete again. "No," I said. "I'll call back later."

My number one priority quickly went from Sam to my daughter. At least I'd seen Cate's car parked next to mine in the garage when I left this morning. But if she hadn't come into work, where was she? And why?

I called the house, Misty answered as though she had been

waiting for my call. The first words out of her mouth were, "It's Xstacy, isn't it?"

"The cops don't know yet. But I think so. Is Cate home?"

"Not now. But she was. She got a call right after you left this morning and bolted out of here. Didn't even finish her breakfast. Then about an hour ago, she came back." I felt my breakfast roll in my stomach. "She wanted to borrow my van, and she wasn't alone."

"She had Pete with her?" I asked.

"Not only Pete, but his roommate too."

I closed my eyes and bit my bottom lip. *Cate, what are you doing? We talked about this, you know this isn't a good idea.*

"What was I going to do, Carol? She had the keys in her hand and said she needed to get Pete and Billy out of town. They couldn't be seen in Pete's van, and her car is too small."

"Did she say where she was going?"

"It looked to me like they were going camping. She took extra blankets and water with her."

"Dammit, Misty. She can't be doing this. The cops will arrest her for being an accessory."

"Carol, you need to trust her. Cate's a smart girl. She'll be fine."

"I wish I could be as confident of that as you are, Misty."

I called Chase when I got back to my office. I was relieved when he picked up and I could hear his voice. It was good to know somebody had my back. In a world that was beginning to spin out of control with dead bodies and my daughter missing, he felt like a solid rock.

"I need you," I said.

"About time."

"I'm serious, Chase. Cate took off with Misty's van this morning. Both Pete and Billy are with her."

"I know."

"You know? How?" I felt like I had been hit with a cold dishrag. Any warm fuzzy feelings I had about Chase burst into flames of frustration. How could Chase know something about my daughter I didn't?

"Cate called this morning. She told me she was on her way to Venice Beach to get Pete. He called her after he heard the police helicopters hovering above his place and saw a mob gathering out front. You ask me, Cate did the only thing she could do. Got those boys out of there before the neighbors pulled them out of the house and LAPD had an incident on their hands."

"What are you talking about? My daughter just became an accessory to a—"

"Hang on there, Mom. It's not all bad news. After Cate called me, I phoned my buddies over at robbery-homicide and told them what Cate was up to. Turns out they appreciated me sharing with them what she planned to do. And—" Chase paused.

"And, what?" I screamed.

"You sitting down?"

"I am now." I threw my bag on my desk and collapsed into my chair.

"They actually thought it was a good idea."

"Good idea? What are you talking about? How is any of this a good idea?"

"Hear me out, Carol. LAPD's had a couple of undercover guys following Pete around since his release. Billy too. So far they haven't seen a thing, and to their knowledge, once Pete got home, neither he nor Billy left the place. But the public doesn't know that, and the cops were worried if Pete got curious about what was going on at the beach and came outside, with as much publicity as he's been getting for the model slayings, his neighbors might grab him and tear him apart. The last thing LAPD needs right now is a bunch of vigilantes going after Pete like they did with Richard Ramirez."

I was in grade school when Richard Ramirez, the Night Stalker, was apprehended by an angry neighborhood mob. There wasn't a girl in my class who hadn't heard about him and worried he would sneak into her bedroom in the dead of night and strangle her. Over a two-year period, Ramirez had terrorized, raped and tortured more than twenty-five women. He had killed thirteen more before he was caught one night trying to steal a car. Neighbors recognized him from a photo the press had circulated and took matters into their own hands. By the time the police arrived, Ramirez had been clubbed on the head with a tire iron and surrendered to police without an incident. Much as I wasn't wild about Pete, I hated to think of something similar happening to him.

"So then neither Pete nor Billy could have had anything to do with the body on the beach this morning?" I asked.

"Unless those boys are some Houdinis, they didn't leave the house last night."

"Then they're no longer suspects?

"They're not home free yet. But it does mean the cops are widening their search."

"Meanwhile, they just let Cate take them?"

"Cate did what they couldn't, got Pete and Billy out of there without blowing their cover. Pretty cool, huh?"

"Unless you're her mom."

"Relax, Carol, she couldn't be safer than if she were the president's daughter. She's got two of LAPD's finest trailing her. Besides, she's driving Misty's van, which isn't exactly hard to spot. That old rig of hers can't go faster than fifty-five. It's not like she'll outrun them."

"You're not making me feel any better, Chase."

"I could try," he teased.

I hung up the phone and checked my office line, then my computer, and cell phone again for messages. I was hoping for something, anything from Sam. There was nothing. No voicemail. No emails. No texts. Not even so much as a Post-it note from Tyler stuck to my computer screen telling me Sam had called. There was, however, a voicemail on my office line from Detective Soto.

"Ms. Childs, this is Detective Soto, LAPD." His voice sounded less like a drill sergeant and more engaging than he had this morning. "I wanted to thank you for alerting me to the van parked over off Speedway. Turns out, after my investigators went through it, you were right. The van's registered to a Stacy Minor. Off the record, I'd say Miss Minor was a match for the body on the beach. 'Course we'll have to wait for the coroner to make the final call on that. But we did find a Post-it note stuck to the dashboard with Pete Pompidou's address scribbled on it. I think it'd be helpful if we talked. Give me a call."

Soto left his number, and I saved the message. I fully intended to call him back, but not until I had talked to Sheri. After our last conversation about Sam, I had called Pamela's to see if Sam was working, but she hadn't come in. If Sheri had any other ideas as to where Sam might be, I wanted to know.

"Hi, it's me," I said.

Sheri yawned a sleepy hello.

"Did I wake you?"

In the background, I could hear the whisper of a male voice.

"You're not alone," I said.

"Not quite." Sheri giggled. "Max came by last night."

I winced. "Sounds like it's not a good time to talk."

"It's fine. We were just about to get up anyway. Max went to make coffee. We're doing massages later this afternoon. I need it after last night. I treated him to a martini spin."

"Please tell me that's a drink and not something Sam taught you to do on the pole." I had visions of Sheri hanging upside down on the dance pole in a death spiral.

"Don't make me laugh. It hurts too much. I don't know how those girls do it. I feel like a pretzel this morning, and I can't straighten up. That girl makes everything look easy."

"Speaking of Sam," I said. "I checked Pamela's. She wasn't there. I was hoping maybe you'd heard from her again."

"No. I'm not scheduled to see her again 'til next Monday. But I do know she mentioned she'd be working a new club on Thursdays. Stilettos downtown. You want to go?"

"As long as it doesn't involve me and a pole, I'm in. Meanwhile, if you hear back from Sam before then, ask her to call me. Tell her it's urgent."

* * *

By the end of the day, I still hadn't heard from Sam. I could only assume, with all the different news stations reporting the cops finding a body on the beach and the rumors circulating about another possible model slaying, that Sam was spooked and lying low. If she had tried to call Xstacy like I had, she would have heard the same *mailbox full* announcement, and by late afternoon with no message from her, it would have been even worse. TV stations had all begun to air video of the volleyball court where the joggers had found the body along with footage of Xstacy's van being towed from behind Pete's bungalow. One TV reporter, doing a live stand-up from the beach in front of the volleyball court where Stacy's body had been found, was quick to point out the body was just a block up from LAPD's prime suspect in the case. It wouldn't take much for Sam to think the body on the beach was that of her girlfriend.

Meanwhile, Detective Soto had called twice more, once on my office line and again on my cell. The sound of his voice had grown ever more serious with each call. At one point he implied he hoped I wasn't dodging his calls. It was important we talked. I saved the messages, and as I headed home, called him from the car. My call went directly to Soto's voicemail. I left a brief message explaining I was sorry to have missed his call, I'd been in and out of the studio, and would try again later.

My key was barely in the lock to my condo when the door swung open. Misty stood in front of me. From inside the house, the air was perfumed with the smoky scent of cedar, an incense I knew Misty used to help rekindle her psychic powers.

"It's Xstacy, Carol." Misty stared at me, her eyes covered with milky white cataracts. "I can feel it."

"We still don't have confirmation. But I think so." I walked past her to the kitchen, put my bag on the counter and reached for a wine glass above the bar. After today I needed something. Misty followed.

"It's my fault, Carol. I should have done something. I should have known. I should never have let Xstacy leave the house that morning."

"Misty–" I stopped myself, the empty wine glass still in my hand. I wanted to say her feelings were unfounded, but who argues with a psychic? Misty believed what she believed. Who was I to tell her differently?

"Listen to me, Carol." Misty put her hand into the pocket of her skirt and pulled out the rabbit's foot Xstacy had given her. Then took my wine glass from me and thrust the rabbit's foot into my hand. "You need to keep this with you. Xstacy wanted you to have it. I sense it's connected to the case and whatever its purpose, it will reveal itself. And very soon."

I ran my fingers across the rabbit foot's soft fur. "You sound a lot like a psychic again, Misty."

"The incense helps. It clears my senses."

I closed my hand over the foot. "If it'll make you happy, Misty, fine, I'll keep it with me. But if there's anything at all to this *lucky charm*, I'd be happier if Cate had it with her. Have you heard anything from her?"

"She called. She wanted me to tell you she's okay. And not to worry."

"Not worry?" I picked up my empty glass and filled it with wine from the open bottle of red on the bar. "How can I do that? My daughter's off with a man and his roommate the police consider to be possible suspects in a serial murder case, and I'm not supposed to worry? Why doesn't she call *me*?"

"She doesn't want to upset you."

"I'm already upset."

"Don't be. You don't really think Pete's capable of murder. What you're really worried about is Cate forsaking her future for a man you don't think is worthy of her."

I took a sip of my wine. "What are you playing psychologist now, Misty? Because if I had a choice, I think I'd prefer you stick to your psychic predictions and tell me that's not going to happen."

"Cate's a smart girl, Carol. It's you I'm worried about. I've had this feeling lately it's you who's in danger. That somebody's watching you. Listening to you. Do me a favor. Keep the rabbit's foot with you."

CHAPTER 20

Wednesday morning as I pulled out of the garage from beneath my condo, I noticed a small black Toyota parked across the street. I didn't think much of it until I drove away from the curb and headed down Dickens Street. The car followed and took a left turn directly behind me as I turned onto Coldwater Canyon and again as I turned onto Ventura Boulevard. Misty's warning that somebody was watching me had me looking over my shoulder. It was probably nothing. Just another early morning commuter headed out of the valley. But when I pulled into a gas station a block later with the Toyota on my tail, my stomach dropped.

The Toyota pulled directly behind and tapped my rear fender. Trapping me behind a larger SUV. Fast as I could I locked the doors and watched in my rearview mirror as a short, stocky man wearing a baseball cap got out of the car. He approached the driver's side of my Jeep glanced at a KTLK decal on my windshield, then rapped on the side window with the back of his knuckles.

"Your name Carol Childs?" He asked.

I nodded. My head shaking involuntarily. I didn't dare open the window.

He grabbed the left wiper blade. Slapped a blue envelope against the windshield, then replaced the blade and tapped the glass with the palm of his hand. "You've been served, ma'am. Have a good day."

I watched as he got back in his car, slammed the door, then put the Toyota in reverse and peeled out from behind me and down Ventura Boulevard. With my heart pounding and hands shaking, I unlocked my door and snatched the warrant off the windshield.

Order to appear before LA County Court...in the matter of Stacy Minor, at the request of LAPD Detective Miguel Soto, you are ordered to appear before the court Monday, July 3rd at 10:00 a.m.

I crumpled the subpoena in my hand. I should have known this was coming. When Soto called and said he wanted to talk, I suspected it wasn't just a friendly chat he had in mind. But what could I say? He wasn't going to be satisfied if I told him Xstacy was a just fan of the station. That she had contacted me to say she didn't believe Pete was the Model Slayer. Not after I had identified her van, parked so close to Pete's bungalow. Not when the police knew Cate was dating their number one suspect. Anything I said would lead to further questions. Questions I couldn't answer without violating my promise to her.

Tyler was in his office when I arrived. Per usual he was hunched over his keyboard, eyes glued to his computer screen. "What's up, Childs?"

I laid the subpoena on his desk. "We need to talk."

Tyler's eyes glanced sideways from the screen and froze on the blue envelope on the desk marked Subpeonea, then looked up at me. "I was afraid this would happen, Carol."

"Tyler, I'm scared. I can't go to jail. I've got two kids. My son's at camp and coming home next week and Cate's off with her boyfriend who the police think might be the Model Slayer. My plate's full."

"You could tell the police what they want to know about Xstacy. How she and her girlfriend killed a man they think was the model slayer. 'Course if you do, you'd be violating your promise to her, and you wouldn't be working here anymore. And good luck trying to find another job as a reporter." Tyler didn't have to tell me reporters who squealed to the police about their confidential sources and what they told them would be out of luck when it came to finding another job. Sources wouldn't trust them, and potential employers had a pool of fresh young talent to choose from as opposed to a reporter who had burned her sources.

"I can't do that, Tyler, and I won't. Xstacy may be dead, but Sam's not. If I tell the police and they put out a warrant for her arrest or her name leaks out somehow, whoever killed Xstacy will have Sam's real name and come after her."

"I'm sorry, Carol. But if you're going to work investigations, these things can happen. You had to know that." Tyler handed the subpoena back to me. "Seems to me you've got until Monday morning to do some soul-searching. I'll call Mr. King. Whatever you decide, you're going to need the station's attorney to go with you Monday."

"Unless I find whoever killed Xstacy first."

Tyler raised his brow. "Yeah, that would be helpful. Meanwhile, you've got a guest waiting in the Green Room for you."

"Who?" I wasn't expecting anyone.

"Brian Evans. Name ring a bell?" I shook my head. "Marilynn Brewer's ex-boyfriend. The man the police suspect may have caused her to disappear."

"I thought they cleared him of that?"

"That was before the cops found the body in the desert. Now they're talking to him again, and he wants to talk to you."

"Me? Why?"

"Don't know. All he'd say was he wants to talk to you. Said he'd wait all day if that's what it took. I told him I'd tell you he was here soon as you came in."

The Green Room is where we usually park VIPs before they go on-air. Not that it's a great place to hang out. The room is small and stuffy, with no windows and a coffee maker that spits burnt coffee into paper cups. But if some Hollywood bigwig or political heavy didn't want to be seen waiting in the lobby, what it lacked in creature comforts, it made up for in privacy. The only reason I could imagine why Tyler would want to stuff Brian Evans in the Green Room instead of leaving him in the lobby was that the man didn't want anyone to know we were talking, and Tyler had agreed. Brian stood up when I walked in. He looked every inch the bookish accountant earlier news stories surrounding Marilynn Brewer's disappearance had reported him to be. He was dressed in blue chinos, a white collared shirt with a pocket protector with a half-dozen ballpoint pens, and he was holding a Dodger baseball hat in his hands. He was roughly five foot eight, early thirties, slim with black framed glasses and thinning blond hair and a slight goatee, barely visible against his pale white skin.

"Brian?" I introduced myself. "I'm Carol Childs. Tyler said you wanted to see me."

"I do." Evans leaned forward and anxiously offered me his hand, then sat back down on the sofa. A gray mid-century utilitarian affair, about as comfortable as a park bench. "I wanted to talk with you because you were there that day."

"That day?" I wasn't sure I understood. The day police had found Marilynn's car, or the day firefighters had found the body in the desert? I had reported on both. I clutched my notepad to my chest and waited for his response.

"The day the firefighters found that girl's body in the desert. I assume your boss told you I was Marilynn's ex."

"He did. What I don't understand though is why you're here?"

"The police are questioning me about Marilynn again. I have to talk to someone. I thought maybe you might know something." Brian rubbed his hands together and looked around the room. "We alone? I mean, nobody's able to hear us in here, right? You're not recording any of this?"

I assured him we were alone and under California law, I couldn't tape a conversation without his knowledge. "You don't need to worry," I said.

Brian crossed his legs and clenched fists in his lap. His eyes focused downward. "Marilynn didn't have a family. She grew up in foster care, so I guess I'm the closest thing she had to kin, and now that the cops have a body, they've come back with all kinds of questions. They wanted the name of her doctor and her dentist. So they can make a positive ID."

"That's all pretty standard stuff, Brian. I'm sure you understand."

"Maybe, but they've also been asking me about those murdered models as well." Brian looked in my direction then jerked his head away.

I was glad Brian was looking at the wall and didn't see the surprise on my face. If this is what Chase meant when he told me the cops had expanded their search and the police were now talking to Brian, I wanted to know why.

"I'm sorry. This has got to be a very difficult time for you."

"I never would have hurt Marilynn. But you were there. You saw the body. I was hoping if I came by and talked to you today, you might be able to help me."

I stood up and took a paper cup from the water dispenser. "Brian, I didn't see the body. I talked to the firefighters who found her. But I don't see how I can help."

"I heard your report, Carol. I need to know if you saw something. Anything. Something that might make you think it was the Model Slayer that killed her."

I took a sip of water. If the police thought Brian was a possible suspect, I needed to couch my next words carefully.

"It could be anyone, Brian. One of Marilynn's clients maybe? I know she was an accountant–"

"Bookkeeper," Brian said. "The newspaper got it wrong. It's how we met."

I scribbled a note to myself. "I had also read Marilynn did stand-up for some of the clubs where she kept the books."

Brian scoffed. "Yeah, right. Gentlemen's clubs. Not exactly the type of place a nice girl should be working."

"I'm not judging."

"We fought about it all the time. I didn't like her hanging out at a place like that with all those Jezebels. Teasing men for money. Marilynn wasn't a stripper. The only reason she worked there was that she wanted to be a comedian. You believe that? She thought working between the acts at the clubs might be a way for her to break in."

Jezebels? The word reminded me of something Xstacy had said about Ely. That it was his job to take pictures of the models so that other young women wouldn't follow them into temptation. An odd word and even odder choice of phrasing. It made me wonder if perhaps Brian knew Ely, and the two of them had some crazy pact to rid the world of what they saw as wanton women and evil temptresses.

"Did Marilynn ever work the Sky High Club near the airport?" I asked.

"It was one of her accounts. As for doing stand-up there, I wouldn't know. She didn't like to talk to me about it."

"How about a man named Ely Wade? She ever mention him?" I kept my eyes focused on Brian, looking for some sign—some facial tick—the name meant something to him. I got nothing. No flinch, no masked reaction.

"Name's not familiar," he said.

"What about Xstacy?"

"You mean the drug?"

"No. Xstacy was a young woman about Marilynn's age," I said.

"She the one the cops found at the beach yesterday?" Brian looked up at the ceiling.

"Could be."

"Then I supposed you're going to want to know where I was Monday night?"

"Excuse me?" Brian's response wasn't what I expected.

"The police didn't call her Xstacy. They said her name was Stacy Minor. Nobody I knew, but they asked me about her alright. Wanted to know where I was Monday night. Whoever she was, I think the cops think I killed her." Brian got up off the couch and pulled a paper cup from the water dispenser and took a sip.

"Did you?" I braced myself against the wall.

Brian tossed the cup in the trash and sat back down on the couch. "I'm not a killer, Ms. Childs and I don't know anything about the people Marilyn worked with. Maybe I should have. Probably would have made me a better boyfriend if I did, right? I'm pretty sure that's what people think."

"People think all kinds of things when there's a murder, Brian. And the police ask questions. Uncomfortable questions. It's their job."

"Well, I didn't do it. I didn't kill Marilynn, and I didn't kill any of those models or that other girl, Xstacy or Stacy or whatever her name was." Brian stood up and reached into his pocket and handed me a business card. "Look, I came here looking for help. Hoping maybe you saw something or heard something that made you think Marilynn was one the Model Slayer's victims and could help get the cops off my back."

"I'm sorry. The body was badly decomposed. The coroner said it had been there for a while. For all we know the body the firefighters found might not even be Marilynn. We don't have a positive ID yet. There's still a chance it's not your girlfriend."

"Yeah, but judging from the way the cops have been talking, they don't think so."

"Like I said, Brian, cops ask a lot of questions. They have a job to do."

"Well, if you think of anything, you have my card."

Brian was halfway out the door when he realized he had left his hat with car keys on the side table. When he picked his hat up, the car keys tumbled out onto the floor.

I leaned down to get them up and noticed the keychain, a rabbit's foot similar to the one Misty had insisted I keep with me. "This yours?"

"Yeah, Marilynn gave it to me. She had one too. Exactly the opposite, with two ruby red stones with a blue sapphire in the middle."

I palmed the rabbit's foot, convinced I had its match inside my reporter's bag back in my office. "Did Marilynn have hers with her the day she disappeared?"

"It wasn't with her things when the cops found her car. I went with them to identify it. Her keys were still in the ignition, but the rabbit's foot was missing."

"You don't suppose she gave it to someone else?"

"Maybe. She was pretty upset after the breakup. Why, you think it's important?"

"I don't know." I handed the keys back to Brian. "But if you think of anything else, call me."

I showed Brian out and hurried back to my office anxious to sort through what he had just told me. If Brian had killed his girlfriend, the manner of death was too similar to the models' deaths not to cause suspicion. If Brian wanted to know what the cops knew and was trying to stay a step ahead of the investigation, talking to a reporter who had covered the murder scene might be a pretty good start. And then, there was the rabbit's foot. Clearly, it was a match for the one Xstacy had left for me. Misty was right. As to what it meant, I didn't know. But clearly it was a clue, and proof Marilynn and Xstacy knew each other.

CHAPTER 21

For dinner Wednesday night, I made myself a bowl of microwave popcorn and grabbed a diet soda from the vending machine in the employees' kitchen. The idea that in five days I would be facing a judge who would likely sentence me to jail for refusing to answer questions concerning my relationship with Xstacy weighed heavily on my mind. I wanted the time alone to do a little research and squared myself away in my office in front of my computer.

Unlike some gossip magazines or tabloid news shows like *TMZ*, most news stations don't have budgets for private online investigative sources. It's up to the reporter to get creative, and I planned to dig up as much information as I could from free social media sites available to me. It's amazing what people will post about themselves. Given a little time and effort, it's not too difficult to compile enough information about someone to get a pretty good idea of who they are.

I started with a list of names: Brian Evans, Ely Wade, and Samantha Miller. If I had a name for the scar-faced man at the bar, I would have included him too. But with no name and nothing to go on, I stuck with the names I could research and added Pete Pompidou, aka Peter Phillips, to my list. If Pete really was some freelance photographer from Canada who had stolen my daughter's heart, I wanted to know as much about him as possible.

What I learned about Brian Evans blew me away. Evans maintained a professional LinkedIn profile along with a list of his clients, and a Facebook page with a cache of posts and photos going back five years. Most recent were pictures of Marilynn. The two of them together. Smiling. Dancing. Typical couple shots. Going back further Brian had posted pictures of his dog, his car, then several of what appeared to be a previous girlfriend, Melissa Morgan. I scrolled over the photo of the girlfriend, highlighted her name, then clicked over to her Facebook page.

Melissa Morgan was active on Facebook, and from the looks of the photos on the page, she had moved on from Brian. She was single, pregnant and happy to display photos of her bulging belly. I dug deeper into the photos and found an old picture of Melissa with Brian. Including a rather unflattering one of Brian along with a long passage about their break up and news that she'd taken out a restraining order against him. She had even posted a copy of it. I zoomed in on the paperwork. The order was dated November 13, 2016. No wonder the police had continued to question Evans. If they knew about the restraining order, they certainly had reason to think Brian might be a person of interest when it came to Marilynn's disappearance. I clicked on Melissa's contact information and bingo. She'd listed her phone number. I jotted it down and moved on to Ely Wade.

Wade didn't maintain a Facebook page, but, like Brian, he did have a listing on LinkedIn which read like an online resume. Along with his picture, Wade had listed his residence as Pasadena and his occupation as gaffer, an electrician hired to oversee the lighting of a TV show or Hollywood set. Included for references were a dozen or more small production companies and photo studios where Wade had worked. Most of them I hadn't heard of, but one stuck out and stopped me cold. Lenny Marx Photography. The name of the photographer Chase said had hired Pete when he first came to California. Feeling like I'd just stuck my finger in a light socket, I skipped over to the online white pages, typed in Lenny Marx Photography, and called the number. Voicemail came back with a British accent.

"You've reached Lenny Marx Photography. Unfortunately, Darling, I can't take your call right now. I'm away on assignment. Leave your name and number. I'll call you back."

I hung up the phone. If Pete and Ely knew one another there wasn't much I could do at this hour. I clicked back to LinkedIn and continued scouring the listings of Wade's former employers and stopped at another name. Evelyn Wade Photography. I skipped back to the white pages and could find nothing for Evelyn Wade Photography. Hoping Evelyn might have a Facebook account, I typed in her name.

Several listings for the name Evelyn Wade came up, but the Evelyn Wade I was looking for was easy to identify. She looked exactly like the photo I'd seen of her younger brother on his LinkedIn page. Her profile picture showed a shy looking woman with a low brow, short dark hair, square jaw, and small eyes. And like most people, naive to the problems of posting personal information on the web, she had completed her online profile. Evelyn was single, forty-nine-years-old, listed her occupation as seamstress and her interests as photography and gardening. Better yet, she had included a large number of pictures on her page, several of herself with Ely, along with lots of nature shots, photos of flowers and trees. Her latest post caught my eye. Headlined, *Pasadena Property for Rent*, showed a photo of herself standing in front a small cottage-like duplex. Two bedroom, single bath. Shown by appointment only.

I punched the number listed beneath the photo into my cell and hoped I wasn't calling too late.

A woman's voice answered. "Hello?"

"Hi, I'm calling about the Pasadena rental? Is it still available?" I crossed my fingers. If this was Ely Wade's last residence and I could get inside, I might find a photo or some souvenir he had taken from one of the models. And if I were lucky, maybe even something leading me to Scarface's identity.

"It is if you've got references. Ain't letting no riff-raff in. Place belonged to my brother, and I need to rent it. I'm not used to strangers livin' next door."

Bingo! I gripped the phone tighter and leaned into the desk. "I can't blame you. In fact, I've been looking for a small place close to the college. I'm a student, or was..." Suddenly I remembered Sam's comment about my looking like somebody's mom. I guess I couldn't pass as a student anymore. "Actually, I'm a returning student. I've been trying to finish up my theology degree at Fuller Seminary, and I need a quiet place where I can study." I thought throwing in the seminary angle was a good approach. Everybody in Pasadena knew the Fuller students weren't big partiers. "Any chance I could come see the place, and we could meet?"

"Not 'til next week. I'm still moving some of my brother's things, and–"

"If it's all the same. I don't need to see it all cleaned up. And the sooner I can find a place the better. I promise it's not a problem."

"Saturday morning then. But don't expect the place to be all spic and span. My brother wasn't much of a housekeeper." Evelyn gave me directions to the house and made me promise not to be late. "One o'clock, I've things to do in the morning, and I don't plan to wait around all afternoon."

I assured her I would be on time, hung up, and dialed Melissa Morgan. With a little bit of luck, I might be able to meet with two sources before the weekend was out.

The call went immediately to voicemail. But the message was unlike any I'd ever heard.

"Sorry to miss your call. Baby's on the way, and so are we! Valley Pres here we come!" Then came, three quick breaths, a scream, laughter and what sounded like another stifled scream. "Leave a message."

Tyler returned as I was packing up and stopped in the doorway to my office.

"You're still here. I thought by now you would have called it a day. You should get home. It's late."

"We need to talk." I followed Tyler back into his office and sat down in front of his desk.

"What's up? You look beat."

"Last time I met with Sam, she told me Xstacy was afraid of a man at the bar. She described him as scar-faced and said he sat up by the stage with Ely when she performed. I tried to meet with him, but I couldn't get a name. But I've been doing some research, and I was able to get something more on Ely Wade and Brian Evans tonight. You won't believe what I found."

"Start with Brian. I want to know why he was here today."

"It's like you said, he wanted to know more about the girl the firefighters found. I think he suspects it might be Marilynn. At first, I thought he was just grieving the loss of his ex-girlfriend and needed closure. Maybe he felt talking to a reporter might help. But then he said the police had been talking to him again, and he needed my help."

"Your help?"

"In addition to Marilynn, the cops were also talking to him about Xstacy. They wanted to know if he knew her."

"Did he?"

"He said he didn't know any of Marilynn's friends. But I think he's lying. He referred to the dancers in the club as Jezebels. Odd term isn't it? I mean, who uses a word like that anymore?"

"A little Old Testament, maybe."

"That's what I thought too. Like temptress. That's the word Xstacy told me Ely Wade used to describe the dancers. Said he was taking their pictures so that other girls wouldn't be drawn into temptation. But it's more than that."

I explained how Xstacy had left a brown and white rabbit's foot with Misty for me, and that Brian had a similar rabbit's foot on his keychain with three very distinctive, but similar looking beads attached to it.

"When I asked him about it, he said Marilynn had made it for him, and that she had one exactly like it. The only difference between his rabbit's foot and hers were the beads. They represented their individual birthstones and were in reverse in order. Other than that, the rabbit's foot Brian had was an exact copy of the one

Xstacy had left with Misty for me, with red, blue and red beads."

"You're going to need more than a nervous ex-boyfriend with an old-world vocabulary and a lucky charm to pin Brian to the model slayings, Carol."

"Hold on. That keychain got me thinking Brian might be hiding something, and when I checked him out on the internet, I found Brian had a previous ex-girlfriend. It appears our milk-toast accountant's a bit of player. Seven months ago, Brian was involved with a girl named Melissa Morgan. Looks like he might have had both Marilynn and Melissa going at the same time. Anyway, he and Melissa broke up, and Melissa served him with a restraining order. Even posted a copy of the order on Facebook. I doubt he'd give me the full scoop on their relationship, so I did a search for Melissa and got her phone number. And guess what?"

"I can't wait."

"She's pregnant."

"Pregnant?" Tyler laughed and shook his head.

"And not just pregnant. But nine months pregnant and ready to pop. When I called, I got her voicemail. She was on her way to the hospital. I plan to make a visit to the hospital sometime tomorrow to check her out."

"And Ely Wade?"

"I really hit pay dirt with that one. Wade was an electrician, a gaffer. Looks like he worked mostly non-union jobs for a bunch of small production studios I never heard of. Except for one. Lenny Marx photography. Where..." I paused and looked up at the ceiling. I couldn't believe what I was about to say. "Pete Pompidou had worked. I can't prove if they knew each other or not, but it's an uncomfortable coincidence and, unfortunately, not one I'm going to be able to get answers for right away. I called Marx's studio, and got a recorded message. They're away on assignment. However, I did learn Ely had a sister. She's living in Pasadena in a duplex. Right next door to where her brother lived. And, wait for it," I held my hand up. "The plex is for rent."

"I assume you contacted her."

REASON TO DOUBT   135

"I have an appointment to see her Saturday afternoon. She wouldn't see me earlier, or I'd be there now if I could."

"So you got a couple of suspects." Tyler reached for a bag of M&Ms on his desk and popped them, one at a time, into his mouth. "Some nameless scar-faced man at the bar you haven't been able to talk to. Brian Evans, who the police suspect killed his girlfriend. And whether you want to accept it or not, your daughter's boyfriend, Pete, and his roommate. Or maybe just his roommate Billy Tyson." Tyler put the candy down. "You should work late more often, Childs. Anything more on Sam?"

"Unfortunately, I couldn't find anything more about her than I already knew. For a millennial, Sam's covered her tracks pretty well. The only online reference to her was on the UCLA website promoting their dance program. Her picture was there twice, once in a group shot, the other as the recipient of a Bob Fosse Scholarship. What I did find, however, was her mother."

"You think she might have gone to see her mom? Girls in trouble sometimes seek out their mothers."

I rolled my eyes. "Not always. In fact, sometimes when they're in trouble, they don't even talk to them." I took a couple of the M&M's from the bag. "Sam's mother lives in Las Vegas. She's active on Facebook. She's got lots of photos of herself and a few of Sam. I would have thought Sam might have gone there too. But, Sam's mom posted she eloped and is honeymooning in Italy."

"So maybe Sam's there?"

"Not likely. In addition to her mother posting a photo of herself with her new husband leaving the church on Sunday, there was also another photo posted just today. It seems her mother arranged to have the house fumigated while they were away. Bed Bug Exterminators had slapped a photo on her Facebook page of her house all tented-up. Only a fool would go inside now. The only other contact I had for Sam was the sorority, and guess what? She doesn't live there. She's not even a Tri-Delt. So right now I'm coming up blank. Xstacy's dead and I don't have a clue where Sam is."

Tyler stood up and turned off the low hum of the intercom, silencing the pre-recorded overnight programming.

"Go home, Carol. You need to get some rest."

I ran my fingers through my hair. I was exhausted. "It's funny, up until tonight, I had hoped when the cops found Xstacy's van and realized she'd been involved in an accident," I used air quotes around the word, "resulting in Ely Wade's death, that they'd start to put two and two together and think Wade was the Model Slayer."

"And then the cops would get suspicious and wonder if Ely had a partner. Maybe somebody who knew Xstacy had killed Ely and come after her."

"That was the plan. And I was hoping the cops would find that somebody was Scarface. Only now I'm worried once the cops start looking into Ely Wade, they're going to discover both Pete and Ely worked for Lenny Marx Photography. It won't matter if they worked there the same time or not, Pete'll be right back in their crosshairs, and Scarface will be just another drunk at the bar leering at the dancers."

CHAPTER 22

Thursday morning I woke early and dressed casually, black slacks, white cotton T-shirt with a tan blazer and a pair of campy white tennis shoes. I figured since I had little more than three days left of freedom, I might as well be comfortable. Quietly, I snuck downstairs, fixed myself a cup of coffee so as not to wake Misty, and poured it into a travel mug. I got as far as the front door when I heard my name.

"Carol? Where are you going?" Misty was sitting in a small, gray swivel chair by the front window and stood up. She was dressed in a white, long-sleeved men's shirt, something she frequently wore when out-and-about to protect herself from the sun, with her burlap bag slung over her shoulder.

"Work," I said. "Where else?"

"Not without me, you're not." Misty shuffled to the door and placed her hand in front of it. "I heard you come in last night. You hardly slept. And don't tell me differently, I could hear you thrashing around. Something's up. I'm worried about you."

"Misty," I laughed out loud, the idea she could help me ward off any danger was as dear as it was preposterous. "There's no rea–"

"No?" She cut me off. "You're investigating a serial killer, Carol. One of his victims was at our front door on Sunday morning and wanted to see you. Why wouldn't I be worried? I'm coming with you."

"To work? Misty, that's ridiculous. If someone were after me, the safest place I could be would be inside the station."

Years ago when the station was built, broadcast studios were thought to be a potential target for groups looking to commandeer the station's signal. Great care was taken in their design to prevent that from happening. Outside KTLK's six-acre campus, the antenna field was secured by twelve-foot-high fences topped with barbed wire. Nobody got in or out without passing through a security gate, and once inside, the station itself was like a small fortress, built with thick block walls in the shape of a pentagon. The broadcast studios and the newsroom, or what Tyler liked to call the station's cerebral cortex, were located in the windowless center of the building. Surrounding the studios like a castle moat was an eight-foot-wide circular hallway that served as a barrier between the studios on one side and a bevy of small business offices on the other. The conference room, sales bay, kitchen, bathrooms and employees' lounge all faced the outside wall of the building. I couldn't have been safer if I were inside the Pentagon itself.

"Maybe so, but you're not going alone, Carol. I've had a vision. Someone's holding you against your will. And until the police find who's behind these murders, I'm sticking with you."

I didn't want to tell Misty I'd had the same concern, that the person or persons holding me against my will wasn't the Model Slayer at all, but LAPD. All night long, all I could think about was how I was going to explain to the kids, particularly Cate, why some judge had plans to lock me up while a madman was still on the loose killing young girls. Cate would say I chose my job over my family. She couldn't know what I was doing was trying to clear Pete's name before the police arrested him again. Like a small tank, Misty stood in front the door and refused to allow me to pass.

"Alright, Misty. You can come with me. However, you have to agree to remain in the lobby or the employees' café. You cannot, absolutely must not, under any circumstances, disturb me in the studio or step foot inside the newsroom."

Misty smiled, a broad, closed-lip grin across her round, age-spotted face, then turned around and opened the door. "Shall we go?"

I knew I'd regret my decision to take Misty to work, but it

wasn't until I had finished the eight-a.m. news update and was coming out of the studio that I realized the mistake I'd made.

Tyler approached me in the hallway and pointed over his shoulder in the direction of the employees' lounge. "Did I just see Misty Dawn in the café?"

I nodded and rolled my eyes beneath my lids. "She's had a vision. She's afraid someone's following me and insisted on coming to work."

"She's your bodyguard?" Tyler raised a brow.

"She's concerned I may be in trouble."

"Well, she's right about that. Your *friend* Detective Soto was over at Channel Nine this morning. I recorded the interview. You're going to want to see it. Come with me."

I followed Tyler down the hall to the newsroom, a mid-sized bay area with four desks, file cabinets, water cooler and a big screen TV mounted on the wall. Tyler's office, a small eight-by-ten room, was directly off the newsroom. As I entered, his eyes swept from me to an empty chair in front of the TV. I sat down and focused on the big screen.

Tyler picked up the big screen's remote control and hit the play button. I watched while Channel Nine's cheerful morning duo finished their report about a pair of bear cubs swimming in a backyard pool, followed by a weather report warning of more severe temperatures. Today's high was expected to set a record of 114 in the valley.

The station went to commercial break, and Tyler fast-forwarded to a shot of Detective Soto. He was seated on a couch in the studio's mock living room with Cynthia Madden, one of Channel Nine's perky morning hosts. In front of them, for the sake of station ID, were a couple of KCAL 9 Coffee Mugs.

Cynthia introduced Detective Soto and set up the interview. She recapped the latest news about the young woman whose body had been found at the beach and how frightened people were that a serial killer was on the loose.

"I'm hoping, Detective, you're here to tell us you're close to making an arrest."

Soto shifted his heavy frame on the couch as the camera moved in for a close up on the detective's face. The bags under his eyes made it clear the man hadn't slept much in the last forty-eight hours.

"Before we begin, Cynthia, I want to thank you for allowing me to join you here today."

I glanced over at Tyler. "Is he kidding?" Every station in town wanted Soto for an interview. He'd hardly have to ask permission.

Tyler raised his hand, a flat palm in my direction, his attention still on the screen.

Soto explained he had chosen Channel Nine to share with the public LAPD's latest findings because he appreciated their professionalism and fine reporting of the Model Slayings.

"Really? Fine reporting?" I talked back to the screen. "They took their sister station's feed of the first model's murder and ran it as their own. Heaven forbid little Cynthia leave the studio and get her hair all messed up."

Tyler looked over at me and snarled, his fingers scratched cat-like in my direction.

I deserved that. The morning Shana Walters' body was found I had slipped on the muddy hillside while filing my report. I still held it against Cynthia, whose camera crew had arrived by helicopter right after I broadcast news of the murder. Channel 2, KCAL's affiliate in the market, had filmed the area up near Big Bear as a body bag was loaded into the coroner's van. Cynthia delivered the news of Shana's murder along with the film, all from the comfort of KCAL's mock living room studio while I was stuck driving back to the radio station in a pair of soggy sneakers.

I turned my attention back to the big screen. Soto said he wanted to bring the public up to date on what the police now knew about the Model Slayer.

"We've identified the woman whose body we found on the beach Tuesday morning. Her name was Stacy Minor. I'll get to the details of Ms. Minor's death in a moment. But first, I'd like to begin by letting the public know we're no longer looking for just one serial killer. We believe the Model Slayer has a partner.

"You mean like the Hillside Strangler?" Cynthia asked.

"The Strangler didn't work alone. Kenneth Bianchi worked with his cousin Angelo Buono. The two raped and murdered fifteen women and terrorized the city back in the late seventies. Which is why I'm here today." Soto took a sip from the KCAL mug in front of him. "As you know, the models we found each had a blood-smile painted on their face. It troubled our investigators for obvious reasons. It appeared as though whoever killed the women had cut them and painted the smiles as part of some blood ritual. As a result, our forensics team paid a lot of attention to the blood on the girls' faces and found something unusual. The blood used was not only that from the model but looks to have been deliberately mixed with blood from her assailants."

"Agh," Cynthia gasped and put her hand to heart. "Like some Indian blood ritual?"

"We're not sure," Soto said.

"And from the blood, have you been able to determine anything more about the killer or killers?"

"I can tell you, from the test results we know one of the men is a very rare blood type. AB Negative. The other is more common. Type O."

"Anything else?" Melissa asked.

"We believe the women all knew their killers or at least one of the killers."

"The newspaper said it seems likely the women all thought they were meeting with a photographer."

"We're not ruling anything out. But we did find black and white Polaroids like those professional photographers sometimes use at each of the murder sites. They were laid at the feet of the girls. Whoever killed them posed the girls and took their pictures post-mortem."

"I didn't read about the Polaroids, Detective."

"You wouldn't have." Soto picked up his coffee cup and took

another drink.

"Of course not!" I yelled back at the scene. "I was there, Detective, remember? You asked me not to include anything about the photos in my reports. And I didn't."

A lot of good that did me now. Soto was spilling information to my competitor, and all I could do was sit back and take notes. The message was clear. *You don't want to talk to LAPD, we don't want to talk to you.*

"We didn't publicize it, Cynthia, and for obvious reasons. In high profile cases like this, we sometimes withhold information that may be useful when questioning suspects later on."

"And what about Stacy Minor? She was a cocktail waitress, not a model. You think she knew her attacker as well?"

"We have reason to believe she did. In fact, Ms. Minor's murder and her employment at a strip club has caused us to rethink not only the killers' motives but their possible connections to their victims as well."

I leaned into the set, my elbows on my thighs. This was good. Of course, Soto had reason to believe Xstacy knew her killer. He had her ID. He knew her work history. Her van. If Soto was rethinking the killers' connection to their victims, then he had to have been curious about Xstacy's accident and Ely Wade's death. No investigator worth his salt would have passed up on that. And with the cops' latest discovery, there had been a second killer, it wouldn't have been much of a stretch to think if Wade was the Model Slayer, that his partner might have been at the Sky High Club the night of the accident and had targeted Xstacy as a result. I felt myself rooting for Soto to put the facts together and crossed my fingers Scarface was on his radar as Ely's partner. Unfortunately, Cynthia's next question and Soto's answer crushed my hopes.

"I have to ask, Detective, the young man our sky team filmed last week as LAPD pulled him from his home in Venice Beach, he's a photographer. He lives just down the beach from where Stacy's body was found, and—"

"Mr. Pompidou," Soto added.

"Is he still a person of interest? For a brief moment, we all believed LAPD had a suspect in custody. Then Monday morning, the charges against him were dropped, and we all watched as he walked away from the courthouse with his attorney and his girlfriend."

I stood up. "Don't you dare use Cate's name." I balled my fist.

Tyler glanced over at me again and shook his head.

Soto continued. "The wheels of justice move slowly, Miss Madden, but they do move. Frustrating as it can be for officers investigating crime scenes as grisly as these, we do have to abide by the law. The District Attorney didn't believe we had substantial evidence to try Mr. Pompidou, and as a result, we had to release him."

"Is there anyone else you're talking to?"

Now was the time for Soto to say, yes, of course. That the police had uncovered evidence of Ely Wade and Brian Evans or maybe even the scar-faced man at the club. But Soto remained straight-faced and said while he wasn't at liberty to discuss the details of the investigation with the public, both Mr. Pompidou and his roommate Mr. Tyson remain persons of interest, and he hoped both men would make themselves available for questioning again soon.

"And what about the body of the young woman the firefighters found in Vasquez Canyon this weekend, Detective? People are wondering, is there a connection there as well?"

"I'm afraid, Cynthia, we just don't know. I'd like nothing more than to tell you we've been able to make a positive ID, but unfortunately, we can't. Not yet. But there were similarities."

"Like?" Cynthia asked.

"Whoever she was, she appeared to have been tied to a tree and she may have been strangled. Although we don't have an official cause of death. We're still waiting for the coroner's report."

Misty pushed into the room and pointed at the TV screen. "They can wait all they like. Pete didn't do it."

I had no idea how long Misty had been there, but long enough to know she didn't like what she heard. "That man has no evidence at all Pete killed those models. And that reporter, Carol, why weren't you interviewing him?"

Tyler looked at me. "Good question, Misty. I take it, Carol, you haven't told her?"

"Told me what?" Misty shuffled closer to me.

"Carol's been subpoenaed," Tyler said. "The detective thinks she's withholding evidence pertinent to his investigation."

"And unless I can find the Model Slayer by Monday morning, I'm due to appear before a judge who's planning to send me to jail."

Misty looked to Tyler for verification, then back to me. "So now what? You have to do something. You can't go to jail."

I stood up. "To start with, Tyler, I'm going to need some time off. I'll be back Sunday for the Townhall Meeting, but until then–"

"Go." Tyler waved a hand at me. I was free to leave, and we both knew why. Soto's obvious snub of both the station and me rendered me useless as a news reporter until I either coughed up the information about Xstacy the cops wanted or found the killer myself.

I grabbed Misty by the hand. "And you and I, Misty, we're going to go check out a baby."

CHAPTER 23

Once inside my Jeep, I explained to Misty that while Detective Soto claimed the coroner didn't know the identity of the girl whose body the firefighters had found in the desert, that I did. And so did she.

"You and I both know it's Marilynn Brewer, Misty. You picked up on it from the rabbit's foot, and in a way, so did I." I took the rabbit's foot from inside my bag and attached it to a lanyard holding my press pass that hung from my rearview mirror. "Her boyfriend confirmed it yesterday. He's carrying one exactly like it on his keychain."

"You believe me now?" Misty crossed her hands on her lap and leaned back into the seat as we drove out of the parking lot. She looked contented.

I turned left onto LaCienega and stopped at a light and glanced in the rearview mirror. I wanted to make sure we weren't being followed.

"To be honest, I wasn't sure when you first told me. But yesterday, Marilynn's ex-boyfriend came to visit me at the station. His name's Brian Evans. Detective Soto had been questioning him, and Brian wanted to know what I had seen in the desert that morning, and what I thought the cops knew about her murder. I told him I didn't think I could help him, and when he started to leave, he dropped his keys. That's when I noticed the rabbit's foot."

"You think the ex-boyfriend did it?"

"I'm not sure. But I got a creepy feeling about him. The guy's odd. Something's off about him. Maybe he's just a square accountant-type and hard to read. I don't know, but if he killed

Marilynn, I suspect he either wanted to make it look like she was one of the model slayer's victims, or he is the Model Slayer."

The light turned green, and I glanced over at Misty. I could see she knew I wasn't telling her everything.

"Carol, Detective Soto said the police were looking for two men. He believed the Model Slayer has a partner. If Brian killed his girlfriend and the other girls too, I just don't sense a connection with Pete. But I do feel there's another connection with Pete you're worried about."

I focused on the road ahead. "It's not a connection between Pete and Brian I'm worried about, Misty. It's between Brian and a man Xstacy knew named Ely Wade, a man she was afraid of. Soto hinted about him this morning when he was on the air. He said the police were looking into all of Xstacy's connections and her employment at the club. If I'm right, Ely Wade's going to pop up big time, and the cops are going to think maybe that connection wasn't so healthy." I couldn't share with Misty that I knew this because Xstacy had gone into great detail about Wade and her suspicions about him. "But what worries me is that Ely and Pete share a work history, and that doesn't look good for Pete. If I know that, I'm afraid Soto does too."

"Which would explain why Detective Soto talked about Pete this morning, and never mentioned Brian."

"I think Soto suspects there's a good possibility Ely Wade is the Model Slayer. And I'm convinced based upon the fact he's been talking to Brian that he believes Brian killed his girlfriend. But I don't think Soto believes Brian had anything to do with the model slayings. What Soto's waiting for is the coroner to make a positive ID on the body. When the report comes in, Soto will arrest Brian and say he killed his girlfriend because he was angry over their breakup. That Brian tried to make Marilynn's murder look like the Model Slayer killed her so he could get away with it."

"Which would explain Brian asking you about the murders."

"Soto'll call it a copycat killing. But my hunch is Brian was Ely Wade's partner and that he killed Xstacy too."

"But you can't prove it?"

"No. And Soto will use Pete's connection to Ely to say they were partners and move on with his investigation against Pete and possibly Billy."

Misty sighed. "This doesn't sound good, Carol."

"The only thing I know for certain right now is that the cops think Xstacy was killed by the Model Slayer, or his partner, anyway. And if I can prove it was Brian who killed her, then there's a pretty good chance I can prove Brian's the second man the cops are looking for in the model slayings as well."

"And if you can't?"

"I'm still holding out hope for Scarface."

"Scarface?" Misty looked at me quizzically.

"A man at the club. A scary looking dude who used to sit at one of Xstacy's tables."

Misty closed her eyes and sat silently, then asked the question I knew had been brewing in the back of her mind. "If Xstacy was scared, why did she come to you? You're a reporter, not a cop. Why didn't she go to the police and ask for help?"

"It's complicated. Xstacy had a troubled background. There were things she did she didn't want the cops to know about, and she didn't trust the police. She didn't think they would believe her." I paused. I had to be careful how much I told Misty. "And she made me promise not to share it with anyone. She was afraid if things came out, she and her girlfriend might get hurt."

"You mean murdered," Misty said.

"Yeah. And I'm afraid she was right. I'm sorry, Misty, I can't tell you more than that. You're going to have to trust me."

The traffic ahead of us slowed, and we were stuck waiting at the corner of Sunset and Laurel Canyon, while a woman pushing a baby stroller with a toddler in tow trotted past us. "Oh, and the bit I told Tyler about our going to seeing a woman with a bab–"

"I was wondering about that," Misty said.

"She's Brian's previous girlfriend. She's pregnant, or was anyway. She had a baby last night, and I think the baby might be his." I explained how I'd found Melissa Morgan's profile online while researching Brian and learned not only was she his previous girlfriend, but that she had also filed a restraining order against him. "She's at Valley Presbyterian."

"Pull over." Misty pointed in the direction of a small shopping center.

"Why?" I asked.

"Because you can't go charging into a hospital looking like you're going to an execution. You're going to need flowers. There's a store on the corner."

Misty was right. While most hospitals welcomed family and friends during the day, coming in empty handed would signal a red flag to the attendants. The flowers would provide an obvious cover and help get us past the nurse's station. If security suspected I was a reporter, I'd be out on my Keds before I reached the elevator. I parked in front of the flower shop and went in and purchased a large bouquet of pink and blue carnations.

Valley Pres was familiar territory for me. A year ago, my ex and his wife had given birth to a baby girl at the hospital. Rob had insisted the kids come by and welcome their new sibling. The hospital had an open-door policy for friends and family during visiting hours, and I had tagged along, staying well out of sight while the kids stared through a large glass window at a pink bundle who reminded me a lot of Cate at the same age. I crossed my fingers the hospital's policy would be the same today, and our unannounced visit wouldn't present a problem.

The maternity ward was on the fifth floor. I stopped at the same viewing window I had stood at a year earlier and searched the names above the bassinets. If Melissa had chosen to include her last name instead of the father's, as many single mothers were doing these days, it would be easy for me to get her room number from the card above the baby's head. I was in luck.

Baby Morgan—no father's name listed—seven pounds, eight ounces, a healthy-looking boy, was in the second row. He had on a blue knit cap and snoozed contentedly behind the glass. According to the card attached to his bassinet, his mother was in a private room marked E-405.

Misty took the flowers from my hand and led the way from the viewing window and past the nurse's station. With a friendly, five-finger-wave to the nurse on duty and an air of confidence only Misty could have pulled off, she announced how glorious it was to be a grandmother again and tapped lightly on the door to Melissa's room.

"Fresh flowers for the new mommy." Misty entered the room and busied herself arranging the flowers on the bedside table like a hospital volunteer.

Melissa struggled to sit up. In her semi-conscious state, I could see she was confused.

"Flowers?" She asked. "From whom?"

"KTLK." I stood at the end of the bed with my hands on the railing.

"Did I win something?"

I could understand Melissa's confusion. Like a lot of radio stations, KTLK was always running contests and giveaways. Surprising our listeners in unsuspecting places was part of what we did.

"No, I'm sorry. My name's Carol Childs, I'm a—"

"Reporter. Yes, I know, I've followed your reports about the Model Slayers." Melissa sat up and tucked the blanket in around her legs. "You're here about Brian, aren't you?"

I nodded. "I'm really sorry to bother you, now of all times. But I think you may be able to help."

"You're a little late," Melissa said. "The police already asked me about him."

"Then you know homicide detectives questioned him about Marilynn Brewer's disappearance."

"And likely murder. They wanted to know if I thought Brian had anger management issues."

"Did he?" I asked.

"Brian had a lot of issues. Mainly commitment. But if you're curious about the restraining order I filed, and why...it was because we had a fight about the baby. He said it couldn't be his and we argued. I pushed him, and he pushed back."

"You had a witness?" To file a restraining order in California, Melissa would have had to have someone verify the abuse charges before a court would have accepted the filing.

"My sister's an attorney, what do you think?" Melissa took a blue flower from the vase and smelled it. "And wasn't like it was the first time. Brian and I had what you'd call a hot and cold relationship. We'd get hot. I'd want more, and he'd get cold feet and then try to come crawling back to me. Then it'd start all over again. Finally, when I was done arguing, and he'd pushed me for the last time, I filed a restraining order to keep him away from me and the baby. End of story. I don't need Brian Evans in my life, and I don't want him anywhere near my baby. Ever."

"Well, you did the right thing." Misty took the flower from Melissa's hand and broke off the stem and placed it behind her ear. "You're going to be just fine, Dear."

A nurse's sing-song voice interrupted us and announced it was time for someone's feeding and wheeled Baby Morgan's bassinet into the room. I stepped back from the bed, the nurse smiled and handed the bundled baby to Melissa. "Someone's hungry."

Melissa accepted the baby, cupped the back of his head gently with her hand and nestled him to her breast like a natural.

"I don't know how Brian would have been with Marilynn. I know he didn't like surprises. He thought I'd deliberately gone and gotten myself knocked up so he'd have to marry me. Can you imagine? We'd been together for four years. It's not like I'd been with anyone else. Not like him anyway. As to whether he killed that girl, I don't know."

The baby started to cry. Melissa placed her hand on her breast and compressed it against the baby's mouth.

"I'm sorry. My milk's not coming in, and the baby's fussing. You're going to have to leave. I need time alone with my son."

I apologized for the interruption. "Handsome boy," I said. On the way out the door, I paused at the bassinet and stared down at the nameplate. "You got a name, yet?"

"Galen." Melissa looked up at me and smiled. The baby had started to suckle. "It means peace. I could use that in my life after Brian."

I glanced back at the name card on the bassinet. Baby Morgan. Blood Type: AB positive.

"Thanks," I said.

On my way out, I double-checked the name card on the door to Melissa's room. It indicated Melissa's name, age, doctor's name, and blood type. Melissa's blood was type B. The baby an AB. The question was, what blood type was the father?

I put my arm through Misty's, and we strolled past the newborns' window. "Cute, aren't they?"

"They are, but that's not really what you're thinking, is it?" Misty looked up at me out of the corner of her eye.

"You're right. I'm thinking if the baby's blood type is AB and Brian's the father, there's a good chance he might be the rare blood type the police are looking for."

"And if he's not?"

"There's still one other possibility."

"Who?" Misty asked.

"Scarface, the man at the club."

"And you're going to go check him out."

"Yes, but you're not. I need you to do me a favor, Misty. Call Cate. She's not taking my calls, and she's ignored my texts. But if you use the house phone, she'll think it's you and answer. Tell her I need to talk to her. That it's important. I need to know something about blood types. It might help with the case against Pete."

CHAPTER 24

Sheri called just before five o'clock full of news about Max, their couple's massage, and catered dinner. Not nearly as good as the Coq Au Vin she planned to make for him once he returned from his trip this weekend. Then switching the subject, she asked if I had heard back from Sam and if we were still on for tonight.

"No. And yes," I said. No. I hadn't heard back from Sam. And yes, I still planned on going to Stilettos.

"Good, because I'm ready to play your wing-girl if that's what you need. Long as I'm driving."

I didn't fight Sheri on her choice of transportation. It wasn't much of a contest between my aging red Jeep and Sheri's new convertible sports coupe. Experience had taught me if we arrived in her Mercedes, the valets would not only help us out of the car, but past the bouncers and all to the way to front door. One look at my Jeep with its dented fenders and balding tires and they would wave us on to self-parking. No wonder Southern California is the luxury import capital of the world. The cache of driving a car that cost nearly as much as my daughter's college education ensured respect in L.A.'s car-obsessed culture.

Sheri and I arrived at Stilettos just after nine p.m. as a crowd of upscale urbanites was beginning to gather outside the door. Stilettos, like any number of trending nightclubs, was housed on the ground floor of a mixed-use building in a popular area east of Little Tokyo that had recently undergone a renaissance of modernization. Now known for an artistic community who bought into newly reconverted lofts and nine-to-fivers, who worked downtown to avoid the freeway commute, it offered affordable housing in glass towers with views of the city's ever-changing skyline.

Inside, Stilettos was another world. Once through the door, it was like being transported back in time to a nineteenth-century cabaret with neon crimson lighting and champagne that flowed freely from a fountain beneath a crystal chandelier. The servers, all scantily clad young women with heavy eye makeup and rhinestone lashes, were dressed in bustiers with fishnet hose and garters. They all looked as though they might at any moment drop their silver serving trays and join the bevy of beautiful girls on stage in G-strings and six-inch heels.

A hostess showed Sheri and me to a high-top table in front of the bar where we had a good view of the stage. Sheri ordered a martini while I stuck with the complimentary champagne and scanned the crowd and the tables up close to the stage. If Sam was here, I wanted to make sure Scarface hadn't followed her from the Sky High Club to her new digs. Judging from the crowd, Stilettos attracted a much more cosmopolitan group than those who frequented the Sky High Club. I doubted someone like Scarface would have made it past the bouncers.

On stage, a racy Cancan number entertained the crowd with a line of exotic dancers. All Vegas-like showgirls, their bodies bare-breasted and dusted with glitter, glistened beneath the lights. Dressed in nothing but short little tutus, they did a line of high kicks and bare-bottomed dips, followed by hand blown kisses to the audience. Near as I could tell, Sam wasn't one of the dancers. Next up was a striptease. A number that could have been choreographed by Bob Fosse and left nothing to the imagination. Finally, when the stage lights went dark for intermission, I asked a hostess if she knew of a dancer named Jewels. She said the name meant nothing to her, but that the girls frequently danced under different names. It was almost midnight, I suggested to Sheri we leave. I stood up and felt a hand on my shoulder.

"Buy you ladies a drink?"

I glanced down at a hand on my shoulder and recognized Chase's Army Ranger ring.

"Are you following me?" I asked.

"Should I be?" Chase let go of my shoulder and squeezed between Sheri and me. "How about you, Sheri? You like another?"

Sheri took an olive from her martini, popped it in her mouth, and holding a near-empty glass by the stem, wiggled it under Chase's nose. "Shaken not stirred, please."

Chase raised a finger, caught the attention of one of the servers, pointed to Sheri's drink and ordered another, shaken not stirred, and then asked, "So, what are you ladies doing here tonight?"

Sheri answered before I had a chance. "She's working on a story."

Chase winked at me and looked at Sheri. "Isn't she always."

"It's about college girls working in strip clubs to help pay their college loans," Sheri said. "Who knew, right?"

A server with glittered nails as long as toothpicks and heavy eyelashes to match leaned in between us and put another drink down on the table for Sheri. "And what about you, handsome?" The server batted her lashes at Chase. "Something special you might like?"

"Club soda," Chase answered.

"Straight up?" She smiled.

"With a twist of lemon, if you can."

The fact Chase didn't drink and was hanging out at Stilettos should have been my first clue this wasn't an accidental meeting. My second was the smell of cologne and the Ranger Ring on his right hand. Chase seldom wore jewelry, particularly when he was working. And cologne was a big no-no. It left a trace and was easily identifiable.

"So why don't tell me, if you're not following me, why are you here?" I asked.

"I could tell you I was spying on you. Checking out my competition. That I thought maybe you might be out with your ex, but–"

"Eric?" I snapped. "That'd be none of your business."

"Hey," Chase scoffed. "I wouldn't blame you. Guy's pretty enough I'd go for him too."

"Very funny." I knew better than to think Chase was the jealous type. If he wanted to spy on me, I'd never know it. "What is it? You here for the dancers or because you just can't resist the urge to follow me?"

"Misty was worried about you. She called and suggested I keep an eye on you. Make sure you weren't getting into any trouble." Chase put his hand back on my shoulder and squeezed it lightly.

I looked at Sheri and shrugged. What was I going to do?

Sheri stood up and whispered in my ear. "I think the two of you might like a little time together." Then handing me her keys, she said, "It's getting late, and I can see this might be a private conversation. I'll Uber home. You two have fun. Ciao."

I palmed Sheri's keys, hugged her goodbye then turned back to Chase.

"So how did you know I was here?"

"I'm a detective, Carol. Trade secrets." Chase put his elbows on the table and bumped my shoulder with his and smiled. "Can't tell you everything. But I will tell you Misty wasn't alone in her concern."

"Oh yeah? Who else?"

"Mr. King."

"The station's attorney?" I asked.

"After the police questioned your daughter, King suggested I keep an eye on you."

"Me?"

"He seemed to think you might be in a lot more trouble than Cate. I thought he was worried you were overprotective of her. Then King called me back yesterday. He said Soto had gone to the DA with a request for a subpoena and that you'd been served."

I picked up the glass of champagne I'd been nursing and took a drink. "Soto wants to talk to me about Stacy Minor. He wants to know how I knew the van parked behind Pete's place at the beach was hers and what I knew about her. And I can't tell him. Not without revealing what she told me off the record."

"And you're willing to go to jail for that?" Chase leaned closer to me. Our shoulders touching.

"If it means protecting my source and what she told me, yes. I'm a reporter, Chase. This isn't about me. Reporters depend upon their sources for information. Sometimes, the only way to get that information is off the record. And if it means not revealing who gave it to me, then so be it. Without reliable sources, and the anonymity the press provides for them, we don't have a story or a free press." I picked my glass up and tossed back the last of my drink.

"Don't give me some institutional line, Carol. I'm talking about you. Spending time alone in a six-by-eight cell until some judge decides to let you out. You prepared for that?" Chase put his hand on top of my wrist.

I pulled my arm away from Chase. "Don't even think about trying to change my mind. I know what I'm doing and why. And if you don't like it, you can get out of my way.

Chase sat up straight, both hands on his drink. "I didn't say I didn't like it, Carol. And if you'll let me, I'm willing to help. You don't have to tell me everything, just let me know what I can do."

I took a breath. Despite the fact I wanted to keep Chase at a distance, I could use his help.

"Alright, but you have to understand I can't and won't tell you everything. What I can tell you, is that Xstacy called the station after Pete was arrested. Among the things she told me was that she didn't believe Pete was guilty because she knew the Model Slayer was dead. The man's name was Ely Wade, and Xstacy believed she had accidentally run him down when she was leaving the Sky High Club one night." I left out the part about Xstacy confessing to me how she had planned to run Ely down and that the accident, while she had reported it to the cops as such, was definitely premeditated. "The thing is, Xstacy thought Ely had a partner, and I think Xstacy was afraid he'd come after her."

"You think Ely's partner killed her?"

"I don't know. But Xstacy had a friend, a dancer at the club she was protecting named Jewels. If I were to tell the police Xstacy believed the man she ran over was the Model Slayer I doubt they'd believe me. Not with Cate dating their leading suspect. Soto would think I was throwing a wild card in their direction to get them to look at someone other than Pete Pompidou for the murders. And, if I told them everything I know about Xstacy and her girlfriend, I could very well end up jeopardizing the safety of someone Xstacy was trying to protect, and who might well end up the Model Slayer's next victim."

Chase paused and took a sip of his drink. "So this girl you're protecting, is she the college girl you told Sheri you're doing a story on?"

"Her real name's Samantha Miller. She goes by Sam for short, and that's about all Sheri knows. Other than she's a student at UCLA and teaches dance on the side. Sheri hired her for a few pole dancing lessons."

"Pole dancing lessons?" Chase furrowed his brow

"It's Sheri's latest new exercise routine," I explained how Sheri had gone with me to check out Sam at the Sky High Club and afterward Sheri wanted her number so she could take private lessons. "Beyond that, Sheri hasn't a clue what I'm really investigating, and I want to keep it that way. The problem is Sheri hasn't been able to make contact with Sam since Xstacy was murdered and neither have I."

"So you're here then to find Sam?" Chase said.

"If I don't talk to Sam before Monday and learn who she thinks killed Xstacy, I go to jail. And I won't be much good to anyone if I'm sitting in a jail cell."

Chase leaned closer to me. I could smell the faint scent of his cologne as his shoulder touched my own. For a moment it felt like we were the only two people in the room.

"What can I do?" Chase put his hand on my forearm and

squeezed it.

"For one, don't ask me anything more about what Xstacy told me. And no matter what happens, don't try to convince me to give up what I know to the cops."

"You want me to trust you then?" Chase asked.

I looked down at my drink. Chase was right to question whether or not he could trust me. In the past, I hadn't been a hundred percent forthcoming with him concerning a case we were working on. Ultimately, it had been for his own good, and when I explained it to him, he had forgiven me. Although my confession had led to our falling into bed together. It was a delicate situation we had been dancing around ever since.

"I'm afraid trust is all I've got."

"Actually, I could think of a few other things, but if that's what you want, I'm in." Chase picked up his drink and swirled the club soda around like it was a vodka tonic. "Besides, Misty would kill me if I didn't say yes."

"Okay, then," I clicked my champagne glass to his. "If I can't find Sam before Monday, I've got one other option, and maybe you can help me with that."

"Fire away. What do you need?" Chase asked.

"I need to prove that the girl the firefighters found in the desert this weekend was Marilynn Brewer and that her murder is related to Xstacy's and the models."

"You think there's a connection?"

"I'm sure of it," I said.

I explained Brian Evans and his surprise visit to the radio station and how he said the cops had been talking to him about Marilynn's disappearance. "He wanted to know what I had seen in the desert and if I thought there were any similarities to the model murders. Strange, don't you think? I got the idea he was trying to find out what the cops knew."

"What did you tell him?"

"Not much. In fact, after I listened to him, all I could think about was how you told me the cops had expanded their search after they released Pete. I thought for sure it was because they suspected Brian. Then this morning, I saw Detective Soto on Channel Nine, and everything went up in smoke."

"Why?" Chase said."

"Soto said the cops believe the Model Slayer hasn't been acting alone. That he has a partner. And when Soto was asked about Marilynn Brewer's murder, he never brought up anything about Brian. Add in the fact that the cops found Xstacy's body at the beach along with her van just down from Pete's bungalow, and I'm certain Soto's thinking Pete's good for it." I explained how I had found Xstacy's van behind Pete's house and gone to Soto and identified it. "By now I'm certain Soto must have learned about Xstacy's accident and Ely Wade and checked into his background."

"Probably so," Chase said. "Soto's a very thorough investigator."

"The problem is after I started digging around into Ely's background, I found a connection between Ely and Pete. They both worked for Lenny Marx photography. I don't know if they worked there at the same time or not. But if I found it, I know Soto's found it too, and he's going to want to talk to Pete again."

"Let me get this straight. You think Brian Evans is the Model Slayer or his partner anyway, and the cops have been talking to him, or were up until they may have learned that Pete and Ely Wade knew each other. And now you're hoping that Sam may know something to help you convince Soto that Pete's not his guy and Brian is."

"I've one other possibility," I said.

"What's that?"

"Xstacy thought Ely's partner was a regular at the Sky High Club. She said there was a man who always sat up front by the stage. She didn't know his name, only that he was a big tipper and always paid cash. When Sheri and I went to the club last week to meet Sam, she pointed him out to me. I tried to talk to him, but I couldn't."

"You think you could identify him if you saw him again?"

Chase asked.

"I can't get his face out of my head. He had a scar the size of Texas running down the side of his cheek from the inside of his eye to his jaw."

"Tomorrow night then. You and me, the Sky High Club." Chase swigged down the last of his club soda. "Unless, of course," Chase gently traced my chin with his finger. "I can convince you to come home with me tonight?"

From behind us, the lights on the stage dimmed, and a huge spotlight swung wildly around the room and came to focus on a dancer, standing alone in the center of the stage. With her siren-red hair piled high upon her head and wearing nothing but a pair of rhinestone heels, she covered herself with large white feathered fans reminiscent of the famed burlesque dancer Sally Rand.

I nodded to the stage, grabbed Chase's finger and held it in my hand. "I think it might be better if I left you here with the fan dancer. Less complicated, and Sheri's expecting me home with her car."

CHAPTER 25

Friday morning, I woke to the soft, soulful sounds of Amy Winehouse singing "Love is a Losing Game." For the moment I forgot where I was and wondered if I had given in to Chase's tempting offer and gone home with him. I curled the sheets up around me like a cocoon and allowed the thought to play out in my fantasy. Then stopped myself. This was ridiculous. I didn't need to be going down that path. Not again, and certainly not now. I sat up in bed. The low hum of the air conditioner filled the room. It had been cranked down to a cool, sleepable temperate, and blackout drapes cloaked the room in darkness. Definitely not Chase's house. I squinted at a bedside clock. Next to it a photo of Sheri with her son, Clint, stared back at me. The time read 8:35. I had slept late for a workday.

Which wasn't a surprise. After leaving Chase at the club, I returned Sheri's car, fully intent on taking my Jeep and returning home. But when I arrived, Sheri was still awake, and we ended up splitting a bottle of red wine and chatting. Or more correctly, I listened as Sheri talked about Max, who she described as a tall, smooth-talking Brit with an appreciation for the finer things in life. "Of which," she giggled, "I think I'm quickly becoming one."

Finally, about two o'clock, concerned I shouldn't drive home, Sheri fixed the guestroom. Not that it took much fixing, the room was always ready and like a five-star hotel, complete with luxury linens and complimentary toiletries. Sheri even placed a plush terry robe on the foot of the bed and told me to make myself at home.

I put the robe on and followed the music barefoot down the

hallway to Sheri's big master suite. Her bed, a kingly-looking Victorian with a hand-carved headboard that had once been part of a movie set like everything else in the house, was unmade. Across the room, in front of a large bay window, overlooking the canyons with a view of the city and the ocean beyond, was Sheri, hanging upside down from a dance pole.

"You're here." Sheri dismounted from the pole, legs over her head somersault-style, like a gymnast. She was dressed in a pair of short black exercise shorts and a sports bra. "I thought you would have gotten up early and left for work already."

"Tyler gave me the day off," I said. It wasn't a lie, but I wasn't ready to explain the subpoena or get into what I intended to do with my time off. "I had it coming with the overtime from the fire."

"You sleep okay?" Sheri asked.

"Better than you," I teased. "At least I didn't wake up feeling like I had to hang upside down like a bat."

"Don't knock it, Carol. I've lost an inch around my waist and two pounds already. Can't tell you the last time that happened." Sheri grabbed a hand towel and wiped her hands. "By the way, did you find Sam last night?"

"No," I answered.

"You try the Tri-Delt house? If she's not answering her cell, maybe you could leave a message."

I wasn't about to tell Sheri I knew Sam wasn't a Tri-Delt, but she did have a point. If Sam was hiding, what better place to hide than inside a sorority house where she could mix in with a lot of young girls?

"When's the next time you're meeting with her?"

"Not 'til Monday, unfortunately. Max is back Sunday, and I'd really like to get one more session in with her. Spice things up for his return."

I glanced back at the pole. "Based on whatever it was you were doing on that pole, I'd think things between the two of you were spicy enough."

Sheri walked over to a large antique armoire and stared at

herself in the mirror. "I know, right? Like who could turn this down?" With her hands on her hips, Sheri looked at me and rolled her lower lip outward, like a pouty child. "But, things aren't always what they seem. Nice guy and all, but more of a looker than a toucher, if you know what I mean."

I raised my hands above my head. "TMI, girlfriend. And a little too early in the morning." I backed towards the bedroom door and pointed in the direction of the kitchen. "How about I go downstairs and make us breakfast?"

"And eat toast that tastes like cardboard?" Sheri asked. "You can forget that."

While I showered and dressed, Sheri went downstairs and fixed breakfast. By the time I got to the kitchen, the corner bistro table where Sheri liked to serve light meals was set with colorful linen napkins, a basket full of fresh, homemade cranberry scones and a copy of today's *LA Times*.

I was about to sit down when I read, "Police to Exhume Body in Model Slaying Case."

"Did you see this?" I held the paper up as I skimmed the article.

"No, why?" Sheri looked over her shoulder at me while she removed a tray of sliced tomatoes with melted parmesan cheese from the broiler. "What is it?

"It says the police are planning to exhume the body of a man believed to have ties to the model slayings." I read aloud from the paper. "In a bizarre turn of events, detectives have uncovered an accident report connecting Stacy Minor, a cocktail waitress, whose body was found on Venice Beach Tuesday morning, to the death of a man she accidentally hit with her car behind The Sky High Club, three weeks ago."

"The Sky High Club?" Sheri grabbed a napkin and sat down at the table. "I wonder if Sam knew her?"

I shook my head and kept reading. The less Sheri knew about Xstacy's connection to Sam the better. "Detectives believe Ely Wade, 41, an unemployed photographer, may have visited the club with a friend the night Wade was struck by Ms. Minor's vehicle."

"Wow! Now that is bizarre," Sheri said.

I jumped ahead in the story. "Police suspect Ms. Minor's murder to be the work of the Model Slayer and are asking anyone who may have information about the accident behind the Sky High Club, Ely Wade, or the man police believe may have been with him the night Ms. Minor's van struck and killed Wade to call LAPD."

"So why aren't you jumping up and down, Carol? Sounds to me like the detectives have reason to believe Wade had connections to the Model Slayer, and that his friend killed this cocktail waitress as retribution for her running his friend over. Certainly somebody will remember seeing the two of them together, and Pete will be off the hook."

I reached back into the basket for another scone. "I hope you're right."

Sheri's cell rang. She glanced at the screen and smiled. "That's Max. I've gotta take this. He's back Sunday. Any chance you and Chase could come for dinner Monday night?"

"Monday?" I paused. It'd be a miracle if I weren't in jail.

Sheri held a finger up, signaling me to wait, and answered the phone. "Hi, handsome. Can you hold a minute?"

Then turning back to me she held her hand over the phone's small speaker. "Please, Carol. I'd love for you to meet Max, and the boys are coming home Monday. We could make it a big family dinner."

Coming home? How could I have forgotten? Charlie and Sheri's son Clint were due back from sports camp Monday. We always celebrated their return together.

"Can I let you know? Tyler's got me scheduled for something. If I can't make it to the school, I was hoping you could pick Charlie up."

"As long as you're home in time for dinner. And ask Chase. It'll be more fun that way."

CHAPTER 26

Cate called as I left Sheri's, and she wasn't happy. The detectives who had been trailing them since they had left the city had approached their campsite and suggested Pete and his roommate might like to accompany them back to Los Angeles where they could chat.

"Might like to accompany them?" Cate screamed into the phone. The tension in her voice pulsated against my ear. "Are you kidding me? Everyone knows that's code for they're going to arrest them again."

"You don't know that, Catie. They're just doing their job."

"Mom, I'm scared. The detectives told me the girl whose body was found in Venice—"

"Stacy Minor," I said.

"That her van was parked behind Pete's house the night she was murdered, and they found Pete's address scribbled on a sticky pad on the dashboard."

"Slow down, Catie. Catch your breath."

I didn't know if I was talking to my daughter or advising myself. The cops were closing in on Pete, and there was little I could do other than tell Cate to stand down.

"It's going to be fine. But you have to do what the cops tell you to do. No funny business, Cate. Promise me."

Cate sniffed. "Okay, but Mom?"

"Yes?"

"Call Dad for me, will you? I didn't tell him what I was doing. I don't think he knows."

I was pretty sure Rob didn't know, or he would have been on the phone with me wanting to know how it was his daughter had escaped with a possible murder suspect without my knowing. I didn't relish that conversation.

"I will. But before you hang up, Catie, there's something else. I need your expertise."

"Does this have anything to do with the message Misty left about the blood types?"

"It does. And there's an outside chance it may help Pete too."

"How?" Cate's voice sounded hopeful.

"The DA dropped the charges against Pete because he didn't believe there was enough evidence to proceed to trial. Mainly because he wasn't a match for DNA found at the crime scene."

"That's what Pete's attorney told us."

"But, since releasing Pete, detectives have come out and said they believe the Model Slayer had a partner. That's one of the reasons why they're asking Pete to come in again and talk."

"Yeah, right. Talk," Cate said bitterly.

"But the good news is, I think I may have a lead on someone else who might be a match."

"You think you know who the Model Slayer is?" Cate asked.

"I don't know that for sure. But I might know someone who may be a match for the rare blood type the cops are looking for. If I'm right, I might be able to at least point detectives in another direction and take the focus off of Pete."

"So what are you asking?"

"If a woman gave birth to a baby and you knew both their blood types, would it be possible to know the father's?"

"Sure. It'd be easy. Why?" Cate said.

"There's this woman, who's possibly related in some way to a man who I believe might be a suspect. She gave birth yesterday to a baby boy, and I think the baby is his."

"What's her blood type?"

"B positive," I said.

"And the baby?" Cate asked.

"AB positive."

"Then the father has to be either an A or AB."

"And what if the father is AB negative?"

"Wouldn't make any difference. But it'd be rare. Only one percent of the population is AB negative. Just because the father is negative, doesn't mean the baby would be."

Cate's answer wasn't a hundred percent proof that Brian Evans was the Model Slayer. But if he were the baby's father, and an AB blood type, I felt like I was one step closer to finding evidence to connect Brian to the murders.

"One more thing. I need you to come home. Something's come up. It's personal, and I'm going to need you here."

"What's wrong?" Cate sounded concerned. "You okay?"

"I'm fine, honey, but something's come up at work, and we need to talk. It's important." I wasn't about to tell Cate on the phone about the subpoena, but I needed to tell her before she found out about it after I was in jail.

I met Chase outside the Sky High Club just before ten p.m. The street, little more than a narrow, poorly lit, rutted alleyway, ran parallel to the 405 Freeway. It was littered with trash and shopping carts that made parking and two-way traffic difficult. I found a place to leave my Jeep behind a liquor store a block away, locked it and picked my way around the potholes while I dodged oncoming cars in a pair of ankle boots and a tight leather skirt.

Chase smiled as I approached. He was standing with one of the bouncers, a beefy looking man with arms like watermelons in a black T-shirt. The word SECURITY printed boldly in white letters on the back. Night and day from the silk suits the guards outside of Stilettos had worn.

"Little different than Stilettos," Chase said.

"Different clientele," I responded. "You'll see inside. Follow me."

I led the way through the door, toward the bar where I had

met Sam. Chase took the stool next to me and ordered a sparkling water for himself and a glass of white wine for me. On stage, a trio of identical platinum blonde dancers in G-strings and six-inch heels entertained the crowd with a pole dance. I scanned the tables by the stage, then, spotting the man I'd come looking for, bumped Chase lightly on the shoulder and tilted my head in the direction of Scarface.

"That's him," I whispered.

Without a word, Chase picked his drink up off the bar and wandered down toward the front of the stage where Scarface was seated at a table by himself. Chase stood casually by the table, nursing his non-alcoholic beverage, and waited for the trio of blonde dancers to finish their number, then engaged Scarface in a conversation. I had no idea what Chase must have said. Whatever it was, Scarface nodded to the empty seat next to him, and Chase sat down.

A barmaid served up a tray of drinks, pushed the tray in my direction and waited for one of the servers to pick it up. "Hey, Blondie, weren't you here last week?" A heart-shaped name tag attached to her bustier said Red, an apt description of her curly, flame-red hair.

"Yeah, why?"

"You look familiar that's all. That your boyfriend?" She pointed in the direction of where Chase was sitting.

"Make a difference if he were?" I asked.

"Hey, I'm not hitting on you. Just curious. The gal you were talkin' to last week, she's a friend of mine. Thought if I saw her again, I'd tell her you were in. That's all."

"You know how I might get hold of this friend of yours? Because I've been trying to get hold of her and she's not returned any of my calls."

Red picked up a dishrag and started wiping the bar in front of me. "If you can't find her it's 'cause she don't wanna be found. She's probably scared, like a lot of us are. Particularly after what happened this week."

"You talking about that girl's body the cops found on Venice Beach Tuesday?"

"Yeah, Xstacy. And Marilynn Brewer before her too. I knew 'em both. Girls around here are scared, wondering who's gonna be next."

"You tell the police?"

"They came by. I told 'em some. People like me, we don't really like to talk to cops. You open your mouth and next thing you know, they're asking you all kinds of questions about things you'd rather not talk about. And the management here would just as soon boot you out the door than have a lot of cops hanging 'round. Not exactly their clientele."

I slid my business card across the bar. "I'm not a cop, Red. I'm a reporter with KTLK. Will you talk to me?"

Red picked up my card, flashed it under a dim light by the cash register and read my name aloud. "Carol Childs, this you?"

I nodded.

"You work with Kit and Carson?"

"I'm on in the mornings with them. I do the news."

Red looked back down at my card. "I love that show. Sure, I'll talk to you. But you gotta leave my name out of it." Red tucked my card inside of her bustier. "What do you want to know?"

"You mentioned Marilynn Brewer. How do you know her?"

"I know she was the bookkeeper. Usually came by during the day when things were slow. She'd order a Rum and Coke, and we'd chat at the bar."

"What'd you talk about?"

"Nothing special. Work. Hobbies. Her boyfriend."

"She talk to you about Brian?"

"That was his name? I don't remember. Only that she said they were having troubles."

"She say what kind?"

"He didn't like that she wanted to be a standup comic. Too bad. Maybe she should have listened to him. In my opinion, that's what got her killed."

"What do you mean?"

"She convinced management that if they let her work the last call, she'd cut her rate for bookkeeping." Red dunked a couple of beer glasses in a sink behind the bar and continued to talk as she wiped them clean. "One night, she got her big break, and got up on the stage and started making jokes about the Model Slayer. It was right after that third model was found dead and everyone was talking about it. I remember Xstacy was up front and started shaking her head at Marilynn like this wasn't a good idea. Marilynn couldn't see her though, 'cause the lights up on stage are so bright it's impossible to see anything beyond the first row."

"Xstacy and Marilynn were friends?"

"Friendly as you can be in a place like this. More casual than close."

"And you think Marilynn may have pissed somebody off?"

"Maybe. Most of what she did was pretty rank. Big surprise, right? In a place like this, what isn't? The girl had a foul mouth and wasn't afraid to use it. Thing is, for whatever reason, she hits on the subject of the Model Slayer. Talks about how he was prejudiced. Always picking on the pretty girls. Like that was supposed to be funny. Then she points to this guy at Xstacy's table and says, 'So what about us ugly girls? We not good enough for you?' It was as though she was accusing this guy. Anyway, one of the bouncers got up and pulled her off stage. Later, I hear she was fired, and she wasn't going to be doing the books anymore. I didn't think much about it. Not until I started reading in the paper that she'd gone missing. Gave me a real uneasy feeling. Girls like Marilynn just don't vanish. Then those firefighters found that body, and I just knew it had to be her. She used to tell me how much she liked to go hiking out near Vasquez Canyon. I mean who else could it be? Then next thing I know, Xstacy showed up dead and far as I'm concerned, that's too close for comfort. Know what I mean? Now we're all thinking something's going on and we're looking over our shoulder wondering who's next."

"Do you remember the last time you saw Marilynn?"

"It was the night she did her performance. 'Bout six weeks ago. May 4. I got stiffed that same night for a $150 bottle of wine. Some guy at the bar orders it, places a couple of Ben Franklins down, waits for the change, then takes the bottle to a table. Next thing I know, I'm stuck with a couple of bogus bills, and he's nowhere around. My manager wanted to fire me. Only reason he didn't is 'cause it'd be too much trouble to train someone new to deal with the lowlifes who come in this place. He stapled the phony Franklins to the bill and told me next time to run it under a black light. The real thing should glow pink." Red reached behind the register for the receipt, the date circled in red, and handed it to me.

I made a mental note of the date and asked after Marilynn was fired if Xstacy had ever talked about her again.

"Once. Xstacy had come by to pick up her paycheck like usual. Kid was always out of money and wanted to cash her check soon as she could. I offered to fix her a drink while she waited. I remember she looked kinda nervous and was playing with this keychain. Had a rabbit's foot on it. She said it had belonged to Marilynn. That Marilynn had given it to her as kind of thank you for her helping her out."

"Helping her out? I don't understand."

"You know, talking to management. Helping Marilynn get the gig. I don't know what went on between them, but I do know this: that rabbit's foot was no lucky charm. First, it's Marilynn's, and she gets killed. And then it was Xstacy's, and now she's dead."

I thought about Xstacy's timing, how she had shown up at my condo right after the firefighters had found the body in Vasquez Canyon. No doubt she had suspected, like we all did, the body was Marilynn Brewer's. The question was, had Xstacy stopped by my condo because she knew Marilynn had been a victim of the Model Slayer? Or was she worried Marilynn's ex-boyfriend Brian had killed her and Xstacy wanted to tell me she believed he was Ely Wade's partner? And when I wasn't there to talk, did she leave the rabbit's foot as a clue?

A server sidled up to the bar with a tray and ordered six Pretty

Pink Ladies on the Rocks. Red apologized for the interruption and said she had to get back to work.

"If you think of anything else," I said.

"Don't worry." Red patted her right breast where she had hidden my card. "If I do, I'll call. But remember, no names."

I turned back to the stage and with my elbows behind me on the bar, scanned the room until I found Chase. I watched as he stood up from the table where Scarface was seated.

Whatever had transpired between the two men, I didn't need to wait for Chase to tell me it was nothing. As he approached the bar, his eyes met mine, and he shook his head slightly from side to side. His expression told me everything.

"Sorry, Carol, he's not you man."

I looked back at the table where Scarface sat staring up at the stage. A long-legged dancer, dressed in a red sequined leotard, pirouetted on the pole and crouched down with her back to him, then held her head backward and with her long hair swept the floor.

"You sure?"

"The guy's a wounded warrior, Carol. He spotted my ring and asked me to sit down."

"That's it? You guys are brothers-in-arms, and now you don't think it's possible he's involved?" I checked myself. Chase's own record as an injured vet was a sensitive issue I had learned to tread lightly on. "Xstacy was sure he was involved. She told Sam—"

"The man's wearing a prosthesis. His left leg was blown off when his truck hit a landmine in Afghanistan. Took his left eye too. I'm surprised you didn't notice."

"That explains the scar, but—"

"If he were anywhere near the site those models' bodies were found, his footprints would have been everywhere. And it would have been obvious the killer was walking with the aid of a prosthesis. It's not him, Carol. I'm sorry, Xstacy was wrong."

I closed my eyes and considered what Chase had said. If Scarface wasn't Ely's accomplice, then it had to be Marilynn's ex-boyfriend. I opened my eyes and met Chase's. "Fine. Then I think we should go."

I was about to grab my bag and leave when I caught sight of Brian Evans over Chase's shoulder. He was coming through the club's door.

With one swift move, I picked up my bag and wrapped my arm around the back of Chase's neck. Without saying a word, I pulled Chase's face to mine and kissed him hard on the lips. I didn't dare let Brian see me. Not until I knew what he was doing here.

Chase responded willingly. His hands slid around my back as he kissed me, then broke slightly. With our lips still touching, he whispered, "Something I missed?"

"Just kiss me, you idiot."

I'd forgotten how mind-numbing Chase's kisses could be. I forced myself to focus. With one eye open, I watched as Brain passed behind Chase and worked his way through the crowd to a small table by the front of the stage, next to Scarface.

"You plan on doing that again?" Chase smiled. "Because if you are, I may have to order myself a real drink."

"Save that for when you may need it," I said. "You'll never guess who just walked in."

I pointed in the direction of the stage, to the table next to where Scarface was sitting. "That's Brian Evans, Marilynn's ex. He told me he never came to any of the clubs Marilynn worked. Said he didn't know any of her friends. So why's he here?"

Chase and I sat at the bar and watched as Brian ordered a drink and exactly like Xstacy said, paid cash for it. Men frequenting a bar like the Sky High didn't want to leave a trail. Maybe it was Brian all along? Sam said the lights from the stage made it difficult to make out who was in the audience. Could be Sam was mistaken about who she thought had been sitting with Ely. Maybe it wasn't Scarface at all, but Brian.

I nudged Chase with my shoulder. The last act was coming to a close. I suggested we leave. I didn't want Brian spotting me sitting at the bar as he left. Chase and I went back to his SUV parked across the street from the club where we had a good view of the Sky High's front door and waited.

"What are you planning on doing?" Chase asked.

"I'm not sure, but I'm not leaving until I've got a picture of Brian coming out of the Sky High Club." I took my iPhone from my bag and clicked on the camera app. From this angle, I could get a good shot of Brian as he left the club.

"Might be a while." Chase leaned back against the seat and prepared to wait.

"Or not," I said. Across the street, Brian walked out the front door and paused beneath the club's neon sign. I opened my window and clicked off several pictures before I realized I had left on the flash.

Brian's eyes snapped in our direction.

Chase pulled me from the window. "Get down, Carol. He's spotted you."

With his foot on the accelerator, Chase peeled away from the curb.

CHAPTER 27

The next morning, no matter what I did, I couldn't get the image of Brian Evans out of my head. The sight of him walking into the Sky High Club had been a total surprise, and after Chase had dropped me back at my car, I replayed every ounce of my conversation with Brian as I drove home. Everything he had said to me about Marilynn. How he didn't like the clubs where Marilynn worked. How he didn't approve of her clients or the *Jezebels* who danced in the clubs. Or that she wanted to be a standup comic. Yet there he was at the Sky High Club, staring up at a bunch of strippers like it was no big deal. I couldn't stop wondering about him. The thought of Brian showing up at the Sky High Club had kept me awake all night, and by five a.m. the next morning, I had given up on trying to sleep. I rolled out of bed, threw on a pair of shorts, a T-shirt, and my running shoes and before I went for a run, checked on Cate. She was home, safe and sound asleep in her own bed. I brushed a strand of her sandy blonde hair from her face, kissed her on the head, and promised her it was all going to be okay. Then quietly crept out of her room and went for a run.

I did two miles along the river walk, my mind pounding out the facts as I ran. Brian had lied to me. He not only knew the clubs Marilynn worked for, but if last night was any indication, he had visited them as well. Plus, the rabbit's foot Xstacy had left for me that had clearly been Marilynn's was evidence the two women knew each other. And while I didn't have the final word on Brian's blood type, if he was the father of Melissa's baby, it had to be either A or AB. If it was AB Negative, it would be too coincidental for Soto to ignore. I quickened my pace. I had less than forty-eight hours to build my case against Brian and convince Soto that Brian had not only killed Marilynn Brewer but that he, not Pete Pompidou, was the Model Slayer's accomplice.

By nine a.m. I was outside KTLK's security gate waiting for the guard to wave me through. On the other side, I spotted Tyler as he trekked across the parking lot from the station's old Airstream trailer parked out behind the antenna field. A year ago, Tyler gave up his apartment in West Santa Monica and staked his claim on what had once been a small temporary office for visiting tower engineers. Tyler claimed he preferred the efficiency of the trailer's tight quarters to his near-empty apartment. It allowed him access to the station twenty-four seven, something that fit his workaholic nature, and eliminated the need for a commute. He waited for me as I parked my Jeep.

"What's the problem, Childs? Can't stay away?"

"Can't sleep." I fell in with Tyler as we walked towards the station lobby.

"How's the investigation going?"

"Not as well as I'd like. Scarface is no longer a possibility." I explained how Chase had gone with me to the Sky High Club last night and discovered Scarface was an amputee and wounded war vet. "Plus, he's partially blind in one eye. Not exactly a likely suspect."

"And Brian?"

"Still a mystery. I came in this morning because I wanted to call the coroner's office. See if they've made an ID on the body in the desert. It's been a week. There must be something."

"Let me know what you come up with," Tyler said. "I'm just down the hall. If you need anything, just ask."

Tyler and I parted company in the hallway. He went his way back to the newsroom, and I went back to my office and hoped by the time I left today, I would know more than what I came in with.

Not every reporter in town had the L.A. Coroner's inside line. But I did. When I first began reporting, Dr. Gabor, the Chief

Medical Examiner, had insisted I attend an autopsy. Standard "operating procedure" he said for reporters who wanted access to the coroner's office. It wasn't, but I didn't know that at the time and naively agreed. The fact I didn't faint or toss my lunch as Gabor pulled innards, like spaghetti, from a corpse while Vivaldi played in the background, earned me his respect. Ever since we've had a nice working relationship. More than once he's taken my call and explained in layman's terms the doctor-speak written on an autopsy report.

I picked up the phone. If memory served me correctly, despite the fact it was a Saturday, and most people had yet to have breakfast, Gabor would have been at work for hours. The coroner's office was responsible for twenty-five to thirty autopsies a day, and frequently Gabor's hours were anything but orthodox. He worked six days a week, and despite his rigorous schedule, the man was a creature of habit. By now, Gabor would have cleared his desk for lunch, placed a white linen napkin down along with a diet soda, and was about to launch into a thickly-sliced, pastrami on rye, with a pickle on the side. His favorite. A staple he picked up on his way to work every day from Art's Deli in Studio City, where *Every Sandwich is a Work of Art.*

Gabor must have recognized my number from the caller ID on his phone. He started talking before I could say hello.

"Well good morning, Ms. Childs. How's my favorite investigative reporter doing this bright summer day?"

"Hoping you might be able to tell me you've made an ID on the woman's body the firefighters found in the desert last week."

"So, this isn't a social call?"

"Sorry, Doc, I'm on kind of a tight deadline," I said.

"Always working, Carol. Someday you're going to have to slow down. Smell the roses as they say. Before it's nothing but formaldehyde and dead bodies. But, you're in luck if that's all you want this morning. I've got good news. We made a positive ID late yesterday."

I gripped the phone tighter. "Can you give me a name?"

"Don't see why not. The report went out last night. Not my fault it's so late. We were stuck waiting for dental records. Turns out our girl hadn't seen a dentist in several years, and her doctor retired right after her last exam. Top of that, the office hadn't digitized any of their patient's records. We had to wait for someone to get them out of storage."

"But you know who she is?"

"Name's Marilynn Brewer. We sent a complete report to LAPD last night. Or as complete as we could make it."

"What do you mean, complete as you could make it?"

"We've yet to rule on the cause of death. Could be accidental."

"Accidental?" My voice cracked. "Did I hear that correctly? Marilynn's body, or what was left of it anyway, was found hanging from a tree with a dog collar around her neck. How's that accidental?"

"The girl was dead before she was ever strapped to that tree. Gruesome I know, but that's not what killed her."

"Then what?"

"Blow to the back of the head. Could be a fall or someone hit her from behind. I'm waiting on another forensic pathologist for a second opinion. But it was definitely the blow that killed her."

"Any idea how it might have happened?"

"Sorry, I can't tell you that, Carol. I've got twenty-five medical examiners here, some of them working round the clock and a half dozen investigators in the field. I wasn't there when the body was found. I've no idea what led up to her being tied to that tree. And the crime scene, as you know, was pretty much destroyed by the firefighters clearing brush. In fact, the only reason I'm doing the autopsy at all is the police put a rush on it. They want to know if I suspect her death might be related to the model slayings."

"Is it?" I asked.

"I don't think so. The Model Slayer strangled and stabbed all his victims. This girl's death, like I said, was probably a blow to the head. I have trouble thinking Brewer's murder is related. Might have been someone trying to make it look the Model Slayer's work though. A copycat maybe or even a rush job by the Model Slayer. I don't know. I'm a medical examiner, not a detective. I can tell you the cause of death and pretty much how it happened. Beyond that, you have to talk to the cops."

I thanked Gabor for his time and laughed to myself. The cops weren't about to talk to me. Not if Soto had anything to say about it. I picked up my bag and headed to Tyler's office. I needed to get news of the coroner's IDing Marilynn's body on the air.

Kari Rhodes, KTLK's weekend entertainment host, had perched her birdlike frame on the stack of newspapers in Tyler's office and was nibbling trail mix from the palm of her hand when I walked in. From above her round, red-framed eyeglasses, she raised her brow when I began to speak.

"Tyler, I need a favor. It's Marilynn Brewer," I said. "The coroner identified her body last night."

Kari jumped off the stack of papers, obviously irritated at my interruption, and wiped her hands. "Well, that's it. I'm out of here."

"Stop!" Tyler pointed to Kari. "This may concern you too."

"Moi?" Kari put her hand to her chest and batted her eyelashes. The woman never ceased to amaze me. She was a cliché, a gossip columnist personified. Beyond thin, beloved by fans, and dripping in fake jewelry.

Tyler rolled his eyes, shook his head and started to bark orders.

"Carol, I'm going to need you to get me something about Marilynn Brewer for the top of the hour, but first, before you go, we need to talk. Kari, sit down."

Kari plopped herself back down on the newspapers while Tyler explained to me that Kari's morning guest, the acclaimed Hollywood Diet Doctor, Dr. Olivia Johansen, had come down with the flu. More likely a reaction to her awful green glob, Kari said. But whatever the reason, Kari was suddenly rudderless, looking at filling the first half of an hour-long live talk show with no prospects.

"Here's what's going to happen. Carol, you're going to fill in for Kari's missing diet guru, and your topic this morning, ladies, is the Model Slayer. If Detective Soto thinks he can show up on Channel Nine and try to steal our lead on the story, let's show him what we can do. Carol, this is your story. You were the first to report on the Model Slayer murders, and I want you to fill us in, bring us up to date on everything you know, beginning with the coroner identifying Ms. Brewer. Now's your chance. You're no longer sitting in the news booth and restricted from opinions. You're a guest. Free to discuss the case any way you like. Meanwhile, I'll handle the news update. Now go."

Ideally, under KTLK's new management, Tyler had drawn a line between his news department and those on-air persons considered to be talent. Reporters were strictly news people. Limited to the top of the hour news programming, field reports, and the occasional more in-depth news wraps like the upcoming Townhall Meeting where reporters would interview those who make the news. In short, reporters were not paid to editorialize and forbidden to do so. That job was for talent, and they had much more leeway. Talent could interact with listeners and express their opinions. Which were usually outrageous, because that's what drove ratings. Only if an on-air personality was ill would Tyler wrangle a reporter from the newsroom and sub them in as talent.

Tyler included news of the coroner's report IDing Marilynn's body with the station's top of the hour news, and Kari took the story, exactly as Tyler had suggested, and used it to open her show.

After introducing me, referring to me as KTLK's star reporter, an accolade I could have done without, Kari asked what I thought about the coroner's announcement.

"Are you surprised, Carol? I mean you of all people, you must have suspected when firefighters found the body it might be Marilynn Brewer. The girl had been missing for six weeks. I know we all thought maybe...but the way she was found? Tied to a tree like that in the desert with a dog collar around her neck. Who does that kind of thing?"

"I can't answer who, Kari. At least not yet, but I can tell you I'm not surprised the body the coroner IDed this morning was Ms. Brewer, any more than I'd be surprised to learn she was another of the Model Slayer's victims. But, before I share with your listeners why I think so, it might help if I explained what I know about the murders and why I think the police have mistaken Ms. Brewer's murder for a copycat and been reluctant to include it with the others."

"A copycat? You really think so?"

"I believe the police think so."

"Well, you've certainly piqued my interest. So why don't you tell us why you think the police haven't included Ms. Brewer among those of the Model Slayer's victims? After all, you of all people would have some idea. You were the first reporter to uncover the murders."

"Which in all honesty, Kari, was an accident. The result of my Jeep's navigation system sending me in the wrong direction." I explained how Tyler had assigned me to cover the reopening of one of the ski lifts in Big Bear, and how I was on my way back to the station when my GPS went wacky. "I was lost and driving slowly, inching along when I spotted a body off the side of the road. Thinking somebody had slipped from the roadside, I parked my Jeep and hiked down the mountain to a muddy ravine. That's where I found Shana Walters."

"And she was dead?"

"There was no doubt about it. Someone had tied a rope garrote around her neck, and she had been stabbed in the abdomen. I called the police immediately."

"And then three months later, there was another body. And again, you were the first to report it."

"I was on my way home, back to the valley, when Tyler called and said there was chatter on the police scanner and asked me to investigate. A commuter had been cutting through Benedict

Canyon, coming up from the city towards the valley when she spotted something off Mulholland Drive and called the police." I adjusted my headset, the vision of Kara Stieffers body still in my head. "When I saw the body, tied to a tree with a rope garrote around her neck I knew we had a serial killer on our hands. It was too similar to Shana's murder, plus Kara had been a model."

"I remember that day. I think everybody does. And then less than a month later we all woke up to a report that another young woman's body had been found in the hills. By then, I think everyone knew we were dealing with a serial killer."

"I know I did. Particularly when I saw the body. Her name was Eileen Kim, and she was a beautiful young Asian woman. Her body was found by hikers in Griffith Park, and like the other women, Ms. Kim was a model. After her murder, we in the press started calling the killer the Model Slayer."

"Because of the photos," Kari said. "I heard the police found small black and white photos with each body."

"The police thought the killer had left some type of signature behind. Originally detectives asked the press not to include anything about it in their reports, but there were definitely photos. I saw them with Shana's body, and again when the police found Kara and Eileen. They were scattered beneath their bodies. The type of instant Polaroid photos some photographers like to use to check for composition."

"That must be why detectives think they're looking for a photographer or maybe two photographers. I heard Detective Soto on TV the other day. He said police now think the Model Slayer had help. And that each of the girls appeared to have been posed, like centerfolds."

"Or pole dancers," I said.

"Pole dancers? That's an odd term, Carol. Why would you say that?"

"Because I think that's where Detective Soto and his team have missed the point. These girls weren't centerfolds. They were models alright, and like you say, detectives found black and white Polaroids with each girl, but they weren't posed as centerfolds for some erotic photo shoot."

"You don't think so?"

"No. I don't. Not one of the models had a reputation for doing anything the least bit erotic. Shana Walters was a nursery school teacher. Kara Stieffers worked at her church as an administrator, and Eileen Kim was in law school. They were all hoping to make a little extra money on the side doing commercial work. Girl next door type of stuff."

"Then why do you think they were posed like pole dancers?"

"Because the last victim, Stacy Minor, whose body the cops found on the beach—"

"Just down from where the cops arrested that young photographer."

I let Kari's remark slide, the more I could keep Pete's name out of the news the better.

"She worked at the Sky High Club. That's a gentlemen's club, near the airport. Known for their erotic pole dancing. Stacy was a cocktail waitress, and investigators believe she may have known her attacker."

"I'm not following, Carol. What are you saying?"

"The woman whose body the coroner IDed this morning, Ms. Brewer. She had connections to that same gentlemen's club. And the last time Marilynn was seen in public was when she did a stand-up comedy act there."

"You think Stacy and Marilynn knew each other."

"I know they did."

"And because the cops believe Stacy was killed by the Model Slayer, and Marilynn and Stacy both worked at the Sky High Club, you're convinced there's a connection?"

"I don't think its coincidental Marilynn's body was found hanging from a tree six weeks after she was last seen at the Sky High Club. And I suspect, now that the coroner's made a positive ID, there'll be an arrest. Initially, I believe Detective Soto thought Ms. Brewer's murder might be a copycat. Someone close to her wanted to make it look like she had been murdered by the Model Slayer. Before I knew Stacy and Marilynn knew each other, I might have agreed with that. But now I don't think so, and once the police learn these two women knew each other and worked together, I think they'll see Ms. Brewer's murder wasn't a copycat at all. Whoever killed her is the Model Slayer and had reason to want to hush her up."

"Are you saying you think Stacy and Marilynn may have uncovered information about the Model Slayer that got them killed?"

"I wouldn't be at all surprised if whoever killed Stacy and Marilynn had been frequent visitors to the club. That they had a fixation on pole dancers and found models, innocent girls, who they would hire to carry out that fantasy. The murderer may have told the girls he was a photographer and lured them to a shoot. Then murdered them and took their photos for souvenirs."

CHAPTER 28

By eleven o'clock I was home. Chase was sitting at the kitchen table with Cate next to him and Misty at the stove. Misty was sautéing a pan of yellow squash with tomatoes she had brought in from the garden. The things Misty could coax from the ground, particularly from outside my back door that until her arrival had been nothing but weeds, amazed me. This morning she had mixed her fresh sautéed special with scrambled eggs. My stomach growled as I entered.

"Hungry, are we?" Chase stood up and looked at me as though my appetite might be more a result of last night's kiss than food.

I gritted my teeth. Both to control the buzz I had begun to feel in my chest when in his presence, and to hide the involuntary smile I feared would flood my face at finding Chase's in my kitchen. Again.

"You're early," I said.

"I tried your cell. You didn't pick up, so I called the house, and—"

"And Misty answered and asked you to breakfast." I dropped my bag on the kitchen counter. "Why am I not surprised?"

"Guilty as charged." Chase raised his hands in surrender.

Last night, after I explained to Chase what I knew about Ely Wade and my appointment with Ely's sister to see her brother's place in Pasadena, Chase invited himself to go along. After spotting Brian in the club, he thought it best if I didn't go anywhere alone, at least until things settled down. And I agreed.

With a glass of orange juice in one hand, Chase motioned to an empty chair at the table.

I ignored the invitation and went directly to Cate and hugged her. "I'm glad you're home."

"Me too, Mom. But I haven't heard from Pete or Billy since the detectives picked them up. Chase says they're probably still questioning them."

"Since yesterday?" I glanced at the clock on the wall. It was almost eleven thirty, which meant they had been in LAPD's custody for nearly fifteen hours.

I knew the police could hold them up to twenty-four hours before LAPD had to charge them with a crime. With nine hours to go, it was going to be a long day.

Chase cleared his throat. "I'm afraid it doesn't look good, Carol. That's why I called. I wanted to give you a heads-up. It's looking like the cops have something."

I asked Cate. "What about Pete's attorney, have you tried to call?"

"She's not answering her phone. She's a public defender, Mom. What do you expect? It's not like she's got a large staff." Cate's tone was sharp.

"And Tyson's attorney?" I looked from Chase to Cate. "Didn't Billy call him or his dad? Last time the cops picked him up, his attorney raised holy hell."

Cate answered. "His attorney told him he'd meet him at the police station and to shut up and not say anything. Mom, I don't know what's going on, but I think somebody's setting Pete up."

I took Cate by the hand and sat down at the table. "We need to talk."

"What's wrong?" Cate's fingers gripped tight around my own. They felt damp.

"Does the name Ely Wade mean anything to you?"

"No." Cate shook her head nervously. "Why? Should it?"

"How about Stacy Minor?" I asked.

"That's the girl whose body the police found on the beach near Pete's place."

"She also went by the name of Xstacy. She was a cocktail waitress for the Sky High Club, a strip club near the airport." I studied Cate's face, waiting for any sign of recognition. Something about Xstacy's name or the Sky High Club that might jog her memory. She stared back at me blankly.

"So?"

"Xstacy called the radio station after Pete was arrested. She wanted to talk to a reporter about the model slayings. At first, I wasn't sure she was on the level. She claimed she knew Pete. That he had taken pictures of some of the girls at the club and–" I paused. A lot of what Xstacy had shared with me, I couldn't tell Cate.

"And what, Mom? Stop hedging." Cate shook her hand away from mine. "What did she say?"

"She said Pete couldn't possibly be the Model Slayer because she knew who the Model Slayer was."

"What? Why didn't you say anything?" Cate asked.

Carefully as I could, I shared with Cate that some of what Xstacy had told me had been confidential and that I couldn't divulge what she had said without violating that privilege. Instead, I repeated the facts exactly as I had reported them in the news, leaving out Xstacy's confession to me about deliberately running Ely Wade down.

"After Xstacy was found dead, the cops found her van parked behind Pete's place and ran her plates. That's when they learned Xstacy had been involved in a pedestrian accident that had resulted in the death of Ely Wade, a regular at the Sky High Club. And once investigators started looking into the accident, based on the way Xstacy was murdered, they got suspicious and began to wonder if maybe Wade was the Model Slayer and that somebody–his partner maybe–had been with him the night he was hit. From everything I know, I think his partner may have been following Xstacy ever since that night, and for some reason, Xstacy either went to meet with him, or he followed her to Venice Beach."

"Which might explain," Chase said, "why the police found a

sticky note attached to the dashboard of Stacy's van with Pete's address posted on it."

I frowned at Chase. *How did you know that?*

Chase read my mind. "My buddies with LAPD told me."

"Well, you know it wasn't Pete." Cate looked up at Chase, "The cops had been following him since he left the courthouse Monday morning. It couldn't have been him."

Chase cleared his throat again. "Unfortunately, Cate, we don't know that for sure. The undercover guys watching Pete, from what I understand, didn't see him leave the house because they were watching from the street, not from the beach. For all they know, Xstacy could have been in the house all along. Maybe waiting for Pete when he got home from the courthouse. Pete, or Billy for that matter, could have killed her inside the house, then snuck her body out the front door. Stuffed her in a shopping cart and rolled her along the bike path to the volleyball courts. Investigators found a shopping cart parked next to the Volley Ball court, and nobody remembers seeing anything unusual. Not surprising considering all the homeless around there. Anybody in a hoodie pushing a shopping cart wouldn't attract a lot of attention no matter what time of day. Right now, all investigators know is that they didn't see either Pete or Billy leave the house until you showed up, and then they were under orders to let you go."

"Who then?" asked Cate. "Who killed her?"

"That's what I'm trying to find out," I said.

"But you know something, Mom, I know you do. That's why you wanted to know about blood types. You said it might have something to do with the case."

I explained to Cate that in addition to Pete, I knew the cops had talked to Brian Evans. "His ex-girlfriend, Marilynn Brewer, was the body the firefighters found in Vasquez Canyon. After I reported it, Brian showed up at the radio station. The coroner hadn't IDed the body yet, and Brian wanted to know if I thought it might be his ex-girlfriend."

"How would you know?"

"I wouldn't. But I don't think that's why he came by the station. I think he wanted to know what I'd seen and if I thought there were any similarities to the model slayings. And if so, what they were."

"Ugh. That's creepy," Cate said. "What did you do?"

"I told him I didn't know much. That I hadn't seen the body, and then he got all weird. Said the cops had been talking to him about Marilynn and her disappearance and they might be thinking he was the Model Slayer."

"Are they?" Cate's breath caught in her throat.

"I'm not sure. After Brian left, I started to search the internet for anything I could learn about him. I found his previous girlfriend. The woman he was with seven months ago. She was pregnant and about to have a baby."

Cate's eyes widened. "Which is why you wanted to know what blood type a child might be if you knew the parents' blood type."

"It was worth a shot. Misty and I visited the hospital, and it turns out Brian's ex is a type B, and the baby's an AB positive."

"And if you're right, and Brian is the father, that would make him an A or AB, which is rare."

"Even rarer if he's an AB negative. Which just happens to be the blood type the coroner matched to the scene of the models' murders."

"Then why are the cops still talking to Pete?"

"Because I think Detective Soto's ruled Brian out for the Model Slayings. He may believe Brian murdered Marilynn alright. That Marilynn found out about Brian's previous girlfriend, the baby, and it caused a rift between them, and Brian killed her. Maybe even accidentally. The coroner said she had been hit on the head or maybe fell. He couldn't be sure. But however she died, I think Soto believes Brian tried to make it look like the Model Slayer killed her, and up until the coroner made an ID on the body last night, Soto couldn't make an arrest."

"So that's it then? You're not going to do anything?"

"I'm not sure what I can do, Cate. I'm convinced Brian's guilty, but when I was researching his background, I also did a search on Ely Wade and found he worked briefly for a big-time fashion photographer named Lenny Marx. You may remember Chase mentioned Marx's name when the cops first arrested Pete. He said Pete had worked for him for a while."

"So what?" Cate shrugged and shook her head. "Pete worked for a lot of photographers when he first came to L.A. What's that got to do with anything?"

"Well, that connection, in addition to everything else they have on Pete—"

"Which is all circumstantial," Cate said. "And not enough for the DA to hold him for trial."

"But it's what has Soto and his team thinking Pete might be Ely's partner."

"It could be anybody," Cate said.

"It could be anybody with type O blood. Ely's body was exhumed earlier this week. If the medical examiner finds Ely was AB negative, it explains why Soto wants to talk to Pete again."

Cate dropped her head to her chest. "Because Pete's a type O.

I nodded. "Yeah, because Pete's a type O, and so is their second suspect."

"Maybe they should be talking to Lenny Marx," Cate said. "Maybe he's type O."

Chase put his hand on Cate's shoulder. "I'm sorry, Cate. The police don't like Marx for the Model Slayings. They talked to him early on when they were checking out Pete's background. Marx is seldom in the county. He doesn't waste his time shooting neophyte models. His clientele are all artists, political bigwigs, and Hollywood superstars. People who want the Marx name on a life-sized black and white portrait of themselves and hope to see it hanging in a museum."

Misty came over to the table with a large serving platter full of her sautéed scrambled eggs and placed it on the table. "I think you need to tell her what else is going on, Carol."

"What's happening?" Cate asked.

"I've been subpoenaed," I said.

"Why? What do the police think you know that you're not telling them?"

"Think about it, Cate. I was the one who found Shana Walters' body. I was the first reporter on the scene when each of the other models were found. My daughter's involved with a man detectives suspect to be their principal suspect, and the police know I had been talking to Xstacy. They want to know what she told me and why."

"Then tell them what you know. Tell them what Xstacy told you. That she didn't think Pete did it. Tell them that."

I took a deep breath. "That's just it, Cate. I can't just tell them that. There were things Xstacy told me off the record. If I were to reveal what she shared with me in confidence not only would I be violating my promise to her, but it might expose another woman she was trying to protect. Who could well be the Model Slayer's next victim."

"It's Pete or this woman, then? You're honoring some commitment you made to a dead woman when you know something that could help Pete?" Cate stood up.

"Cate, it's not that simple." I reached for her hand, and she pulled away.

"What if it was me, Mom? What if it was the other way around and I was living somewhere else and got accused of something I didn't do? What if Pete's mother knew something that could help me and refused? Pete could be executed or go to prison for the rest of his life. The rest of his life!" Cate's eyes met mine. "You realize what you're doing? You're choosing your job over the man I love."

Cate brushed behind me and rushed up the stairs. I heard the bedroom door slam shut. Suddenly, I didn't feel like eating.

CHAPTER 29

Chase insisted on driving to Pasadena. Probably a good move on his part. If I'd been behind the wheel, I might have missed the turnoff to Ely Wade's house and driven all the way to Palm Springs. As it was, I was having trouble clearing my mind of the argument with Cate and worried she would never forgive me.

"What if I'm wrong, Chase? What if I can't prove Brian was Ely's partner, and Pete goes down for it?"

Chase glanced over at me, then back to the freeway. "You're a long way from there, Carol. You've no idea what you'll find inside Ely's house or what you'll learn from his sister. For all you know, she'll tell you Brian and her brother were best buds. Or maybe you'll find a stack of nude photos of the murdered models with Brian's fingerprints all over them."

With his free hand, Chase opened the console between us and took out a couple of lollipops, popped one in his mouth and offered me the other.

I refused. "And if I don't?" I looked out the window through the haze at the city's skyline. The once familiar scene of L.A.'s skyscrapers appeared to have doubled, with new buildings reaching for the sky like wildflowers, hiding yesterday's city in their shadow. *Damnit, Sam. You're out there somewhere. Where are you?* "Maybe I should tell the cops about Sam? Let them question her about Ely's partner."

"Carol, don't. You're upset about your argument with Cate, and you're second-guessing yourself. Your instincts are good. Everything Soto's discovered is because you've been in the driver's seat the whole way. You found the first body. You called the cops. You pointed Soto in the right direction after finding Xstacy's van. Between you and me, I'm convinced you're going to find something to tie Brian to the other murders, and when you do, Cate's going to understand why you had to play this out to the end."

"I hope you're right."

Chase turned onto a treelined street full of small, adobe duplex units that had been built after the Second World War. Aside from the landscaping, each of them looked identical. Spanish style with red-tiled roofs, small front patios, arched front doors, and a paned picture window. Exactly like I'd seen on Ely's sister's Facebook page. Halfway down the street, I spotted the For Rent sign.

Evelyn Wade was seated on the patio in a small metal rocker, eating a bag of pistachios. She stood up and dropped the shells on the patio and brushed the crumbs from her hands as Chase and I approached. "You the one who called 'bout the unit?"

"I am." I didn't bother to give her my name or offer to shake her hand, and she didn't seem to care. Her eye was drawn to Chase.

"You didn't mention you were looking for a place for the two of ya." Evelyn gave Chase the once over, her eyes scanned him like a TSA Agent. "I'm not renting to no couples."

"We're not a couple," I said.

"'Cause I don't want no women moving in and entertaining gentlemen callers. If that's what you're looking for you best move on."

"It's not a problem. Like I told you on the phone, I'm a student at Fuller Seminary. This is—"

"A friend," Chase said. "I'm just in town for a short time and helping her check places out. If it's okay, we'd like to look around."

"Long as you understand. I like to keep things quiet. This was my brother's place, and he kept to himself mostly, so I'm not used to anyone making a lot of noise."

Chase went in ahead of me. The house was small and stuffy. The living room was sparsely furnished with an overstuffed plaid rocker and bookshelves crammed with books and old black and white photos and memorabilia. I moved toward the shelves.

"You decide to take the place I'll have all this stuff out of here 'fore you move in." Evelyn came in and stood behind me.

"That's okay. Didn't mean to snoop. I was just curious." I picked a photo up off the shelf. "This a picture of you and your brother?"

Evelyn looked over my shoulder. "It is. And the one next to it, that's a picture of my brother and me with my mother back when we were kids. Don't know why he bothered to hang on to it. She wasn't much of a mother. More of a run-around. But back in the day, she was a real looker. Used to be a swimsuit model 'fore she up and left us to fend for ourselves."

Chase called to me from the kitchen. "Hey, you see this?" He pointed to the stove. "Gas. And look at that." Above the stove, in a cubby that had been fashioned in the day to hold cookbooks was a Polaroid camera. "Haven't seen a camera like that in years. Still work?"

"I wouldn't know. It belonged to my brother. Don't know why he had it. He had a dark room in the garage."

A dark room? I looked at Chase. I had to find a way to get into the garage. If there were photos of the models, maybe one with Brian or souvenirs Ely had taken from them, it might be the evidence I needed. I was about to ask if we could see the garage when there was a heavy knock on the front door.

"Your name Evelyn Wade?" I recognized the voice instantly.

"Who wants to know?" Evelyn took a step toward the door.

"LAPD. We got a search warrant."

I glanced from the kitchen to the front door where Detective Soto stood on the other side of the screen with Eric and two plain-clothed detectives behind him. Soto opened the screen door and handed the warrant to Evelyn. Then seeing me with Chase, he smiled. "Well, well, now, just who do we have here? Doing a little house hunting, Detective?"

"Detective?" Evelyn looked at back at Chase and me. "Just who are you?"

"These two?" Soto said, "Let me introduce you. The woman, her name's Carol Childs. Maybe you've heard her on the radio. She's been investigating the Model Slayings, which by the way, is why we're here."

"And who's he?" Evelyn pointed to Chase.

"Private PI. And two people I'm going to ask to wait outside on the patio while we check the place out. Sorry, ma'am, but you're going have to let us in. Unless you'd like us to force our way inside."

"Doesn't look like I have a choice," Evelyn said.

"Afraid not," Soto said.

"Then I'll be next door." Evelyn stomped out of the house and went into the adjoining cottage while Chase and I waited on the patio for Soto and his team to search the place.

"Look at it this way, Carol. Soto saved us a call. If you'd found anything, we would have had to call him anyway, and I don't need to tell you it would have looked suspicious coming from you."

"I don't know if that makes me feel any better, Chase. What if he finds something? What if he finds something I'm not expecting? What if instead of Brian, it turns out it's Pete? Then what do I do?"

"Then we deal with it, Carol."

"We?"

Chase paused and reached into his jacket. "Lollipop?"

"Why not." I took the pop from Chase's hand and put it in my mouth. I had done as much as I could. Whatever Soto found inside Wade's house would determine what happened from here on out. All that I had left to do was face the music with the judge Monday morning.

"You want to explain why you're here, Ms. Childs?" Soto stood on the step to the front door and looked at me.

I stood up. "I think you know why, Detective. In fact, I think we're both here for the same reason. To confirm Ely Wade was involved with the model slayings and to see if we can find evidence as to who he was working with."

"That's where you're wrong, Ms. Childs. We *were* both trying to confirm Wade was the Model Slayer, but with what I just found in the house and in the garage, along with the Polaroid camera in the kitchen, I doubt we'll have to wait long to find out. And, if the prints on the camera are a match to Wade, and your daughter's boyfriend, I think we'll about have it wrapped up. Now if you'll excuse me, I've got work to do." Soto pushed past me. In his hand, he held a brown paper bag marked evidence.

My chest tightened. If Soto had found the Polaroid camera used to take pictures of the models and Pete's prints were on it, there was nothing I could do. Without thinking, I reached for Soto's arm to stop him.

Chase grabbed my wrist and pulled me back to him. "Don't, Carol."

"And what about Brian Evans? What if it's his prints on the camera?" I asked.

Soto stopped in front of his unmarked car and stared at me. "Is that what you're hoping for?"

I took a step closer to Soto. "The coroner IDed his girlfriend's body last night. I'm surprised you haven't made an arrest. I know you've been talking to him."

"About Marilynn? You bet, but there wasn't any evidence."

"What do you mean?"

"Oh, you were thinking Brian Evan's was a match for the rare blood type we've been looking for?" Soto took a step closer to me and shook his head. "Too bad. You must have missed the department's press release this morning."

"What press release?" I asked. "The one you didn't send KTLK, maybe?"

"You think I'm playing favorites, don't you? Come on, Carol, you were on the air this morning, and you probably missed it. Not that I tune in and follow your reports, but Kari Rhodes is my wife's favorite Saturday morning show. She loves all that Hollywood gossip. Listens every week. You can't imagine my surprise when she came running into the kitchen and told me to turn on the radio." Soto opened the trunk of his car and placed the evidence bag inside. "Nice job by the way. But you should know, after the coroner IDed

Marilynn's body Friday afternoon, we had another little talk with Brian, and we concluded you were right. Marilynn was one of the Model Slayer's victims. Thing is, Brian didn't kill her. Not any more than he killed any of the other girls."

"Brian wasn't a match?"

"For the rare blood type? No. That was Wade. The DNA tests we did on the body after we exhumed it confirmed the match. That's why we came to check out the house. As for Brian, the guy had a GPS tracking device on his car. He kept a record of exactly where he went, how many miles he drove, and when. Accountants. You gotta love 'em." Soto shook his head. "Backed up his story entirely, he wasn't even close to the murder sites." Soto opened the door to his car and got in. "But I wouldn't worry about it, Ms. Childs. I'm sure if you have anything else we should know, you can tell us on Monday. Right?"

As Soto pulled away, Chase grabbed me by the arm and pulled me back toward his car. "Come on, Carol. There's nothing more you can do here."

We got as far as the curb when I heard Eric's voice. He was coming out the house. "Carol, you got a minute?"

I left Chase in front of his SUV and met Eric in front of his Town car, tanned and handsome as ever. "What?"

"I just wanted to say, I know tomorrow's a big day for you, and nobody's going to think less of you if you give up what you know."

"Eric, you know me better than that."

"Think about it, Carol. Soto's got this. Ely Wade's dead, and Pete's going to go down for the Model Slayings. He'll either be executed or go to prison for the rest of his life. Maybe you need to take a step back and do what you can right now for your daughter. You don't want her visiting Pete in prison."

"Stop! You don't need to tell me what to do, Eric. I know full-well what I'm doing, and I understand the stakes. And as far as Cate's concerned, that girl's got her head on straight and I couldn't be prouder of her. So thank you very much for your concern, but we're doing just fine."

CHAPTER 30

Sunday morning Cate didn't come down to breakfast. Not a big surprise since she hadn't shown for dinner the night before either. Misty said she preferred to take her meals in her room by herself. Pete had called Saturday afternoon while I was out. He had used his one call the police had given him to tell Cate he had been re-arrested for the murders and was headed to the county jail and would be arraigned Monday morning. About the same time I was expected to be called before Judge Hensley.

"And that's not all, Carol." Misty stood in the doorway of the French doors and stared out at the back patio. "The cops let Billy go."

"His attorney?" I said.

"I think he cut a deal. He got Billy released, but not before Billy told the cops Pete snuck out Monday night to get a pizza. He took the bike path so nobody would notice him."

I pinched my eyes shut and exhaled. Of course Billy would say that. After twelve hours of questioning, I wasn't surprised. Whether any of it was true or not, it didn't matter. Soto would use whatever Billy gave him to see Pete convicted and there was nothing I could do about it.

"There's a story in the *Times*." Misty pointed to the paper on the kitchen table. "I saved it for you to read."

I picked up the paper. "Suspect Arrested in Model Slayings. Public Breathes Sigh of Relief."

LAPD has re-arrested their prime suspect in the Model Slayings. Pete Pompidou, a photographer, who investigators believe had ties to the girls, was arrested late Sunday afternoon in connection with the murders of five young women whose deaths have terrorized the city for the last seven months.

Detective Soto, the lead investigator on the case, said interest in Pompidou resurfaced when the body of Stacy Minor, believed to be the Model Slayer's fifth victim, was found on Venice Beach Tuesday morning along with her van, parked behind Pompidou's residence.

Police believe Ms. Minor may have unwittingly become the target of the Model Slayer after she accidentally hit Ely Wade, a 49-year-old electrician and amateur photographer behind the Sky High Club where she had been working, three weeks ago.

Earlier this week, Wade's body was exhumed for DNA testing. Tests show Wade was a match for type AB Negative blood, the rare blood type found on the bodies of each of the murdered models.

A search warrant served on Wade's residence provided a small Polaroid camera like the one used to shoot black and white photos of the women. Detectives also found additional evidence in the home suggesting both Pompidou and Wade may have known one another.

Detective Soto said, "While Wade's death was considered to be an accident, police now believe Minor was targeted by Pompidou for killing his friend, and that the two cases appear to be related."

The story went on to include information about each of the models, their bios, and photos, some of which had been taken by Pete, prior to each girl's death. Also included was a headshot of Marilynn Brewer who cops now believed to have also been one of the Model Slayers' victims.

I folded the paper under my arm. "Has Cate seen this?"

"It was on the counter when I came into the kitchen this morning. She hasn't been down since."

I glanced back up at the stairs towards Cate's room. There was nothing I could do right now. Tyler expected me at the station for the Town Hall Meeting within the hour, and I needed to get dressed and go.

"When she comes downstairs, Misty, tell her I had to go to work. I'll be back in time for dinner."

On my way to the station, I called Sam again. I had no idea if she had listened to any of my messages before or if she would even get this one, but I had to try. When her voicemail answered, I left one more message and marked it urgent.

"Sam, it's Carol. I need your help. The police arrested Pete this morning. I'm headed to the station, I've got a show at eleven. I'm free to talk after twelve. Call me."

The thing about Town Hall meetings and talk radio is that it's impossible to predict when a breaking news story or a rogue caller will sneak past a screener and derail a show. No matter how much prep time a reporter does, there's always that uncontrollable wild card out there that can take a reporter's best-laid plans and render them like a war-torn flag. That's exactly what happened Sunday afternoon. A breaking news story and a rogue caller were about to send chills down my back.

Tyler and I were seated in the studio with Papa Phil, Sergeant Lane from LAPD, and Andrew Parsons, a spokesperson from the mayor's office. The Oh Susana Fire had diverted the mayor's energies. As a result, the mayor was needed elsewhere and regrettably couldn't join us. It was a weaker lineup of city powers than we had hoped for, but Tyler was committed to the idea of Town Hall meetings, and with better than a week's worth of promo spots announcing KTLK's big push for more civic involvement, there was no changing course.

Tyler opened with a little history. While other large cities were seeing a decrease in the number of pedestrian accidents, Los Angeles was quickly becoming the pedestrian death capital of the world. Last year, 260 people were killed on L.A.'s streets, an increase of almost 43 percent from the year before, and as of June, that rate was 22 percent higher than the same time period a year ago. Sergeant Lane added the increase of pedestrian accidents was due to vehicle speed, a lack of left turn signals, and inattentive drivers, who despite laws prohibiting the use of texting while driving, continued to do so. Papa Phil and the mayor's spokesperson argued about the problems with crosswalks and the lack of funding for more.

After twenty minutes of talking heads, Tyler opened the phone lines to take a few calls. The first couple were nothing out of the ordinary. Listeners called in to complain about crosswalks and wanted to know what they could do to report a faulty traffic light. But the third call was the wild card.

Matt, our screener, said he had Mia on the line from West Hollywood. She was calling to report a hit and run.

My eyes click instantly to Sergeant Lane. "Mia, are you okay?"

"I'm fine, but I can't believe what just happened." Mia's voice sounded scratchy, like an old lady. "I was listening to the station on the way home from the market when a car came speeding past me and plowed through the crosswalk. And he...and he hit someone!"

Sergeant Lane grabbed the mic in front of him. "Mia, this is Sergeant Lane, have you pulled over?"

"Yes. Soon as I saw it happen. One of the other witnesses called the police, and the paramedics are here now. But when your screener answered, I thought I'd stay on the line and tell you what I saw. People should know what's going on."

I pictured Mia huddled next to her car with the phone pressed against her ear for security.

"Did you get a description of the car?" Lane asked.

"No. No, I'm sorry. It all happened so fast."

I pressed my headset closer to my head. "Mia, can you give me a location? Where are you?"

Mia explained she was on Santa Monica Boulevard across from the Wells Fargo building. She didn't know the cross street, but there was a partially marked crosswalk in front of her where a young man had been hit. From her explanation, I got a location and description of the scene and relayed the information to our listeners while in the background I could hear the sound of police sirens.

The relay of events, everything from Mia calling the station to Sergeant Lane taking control of the call and making sure she had pulled over, was a live example of how the news and police could work together to keep the public informed during an emergency. Best of all, before we hung up with Mia, Lane was getting updated reports from the West Hollywood PD that the driver of the vehicle had been stopped and the victim was on his way to Cedars Sinai Hospital.

I was about to wrap things up when Matt said he had another caller on the line. A woman wanted to talk to Sergeant Lane about another accident she had witnessed and was insistent Matt put her on the air. He said she wouldn't give her name, only that she was calling from West L.A.

Tyler nodded for Matt to put the caller through. Before I could welcome her to the show, she started to speak.

"I want to talk about the accident behind the Sky High Club two weeks ago. Where Ely Wade was killed. The man this morning's paper identified as the Model Slayer."

I put my hands on my headphones, the voice was Sam's. I didn't dare use her name for fear she'd hang up. But I knew why she was calling. She wanted to get her story out, and this was the only way she knew how to do it. I told her to go on.

"I was there the night Ely Wade was hit. And, Carol, I know you know my name, and I appreciate you keeping my identity a secret. You've saved my life. I'm sorry I haven't called you back, but I don't think there's anything else you can do. So I'm calling the station to let people know."

Lane interrupted. "Know what, Miss? If you know something about Ely Wade or the murders, you need to come forward."

"Sorry, Sergeant, I can't do that. You see, the woman who accidentally hit that murderous pervert was my friend. The Model Slayer's fifth victim. I'm calling to tell you, and anyone else out there listening, that the police have the wrong man in custody. Pete Pompidou wasn't Ely Wade's accomplice. He's not responsible for those girls' murders. The only possible connection Pete has to those girls is because he's a photographer."

"The police arrested him twice." Lane said, "Why do you think—"

"Because like I said, Sergeant, I was there. And if my friend hadn't called the police to report the accident and they hadn't come when they did, he would have killed her right then."

"You saw him? You're an eyewitness."

"No. I didn't see him, but I heard him. We both did. It was dark, and whoever he was, he came outside the club looking for Ely just after it happened. He must have been smoking because I remember seeing the glow of his cigarette in the dark. There're no lights behind the club, but there was enough moonlight that when he saw Ely's body, he dropped the cigarette. He would have come after Xstacy right then, except he heard the sirens and ran off. Xstacy was afraid he was following her, or us anyway. Which is why I won't give you my name. If he knew who I was, he'd find me and kill me."

Sergeant Lane put his hand on top of mine. "Miss, if you have information that's pertinent to the investigation, I urge you to come forward, we can protect you."

The phone line went dead. I turned to Sergeant Lane. "I'm afraid we've lost our caller. But if she's still out there and can hear me, please call me."

Soon as the show ended, I scooted out the door of the studio. I wanted to call Sam back. I had so many questions. So many things I wanted to ask her but couldn't. Not on the air, and certainly not with the sergeant sitting next to me. I was halfway down the hall when I heard Sergeant Lane behind me.

"Carol, you got a minute?"

I stopped and closed my eyes. Dammit. I knew before I left the studio Lane wanted to talk to me. I could feel his eyes boring into my back, and with nowhere to escape, I turned around and smiled.

"What's up?"

"I think you know what's up. You knew that last caller. Who is she?"

"A source," I said.

"A source who knows something about the murders?" Lane asked.

"I don't think she knows anything more about the murders than investigators already do," I said.

"She knows Pete Pompidou," Lane said.

"She does."

"And she knew Stacy Minor," Lane said.

"I'm sorry, Sergeant, I can't tell you any more than that."

"Can't or won't, Ms. Childs? Because if you're sitting on information vital to an investigation, I have to warn you—"

"She already knows, Sergeant. You're wasting your time." From behind Lane, Tyler approached. He and Papa Phil had been standing outside the studio, chatting and must have caught every word Sergeant Lane had said to me. Papa said goodbye and Tyler continued. "And I won't have you harassing my reporters. Carol's already been subpoenaed, and she's due before a judge tomorrow. Until then, I'm sorry, but whatever that anonymous caller reported on the air is all you're going to get."

Lane took a step closer to me. So close I could smell the stench of stale coffee on his breath. "We'll see how she feels about that after she's been sitting in a jail cell for a week." Then stepping back, he smiled, a cool, calculated parting of his lips, like a warning shot and said goodbye.

"You okay?" Tyler asked.

"I'm fine." My stomach began to knot, and I felt like I was about to be sick. "I suppose the sergeant was just a precursor of what I might face tomorrow."

"I'm afraid so." Tyler tilted his head back towards the studio. "I take it that last caller was Sam?"

"Yeah." I bit my lower lip. "I guess that was her way of trying to help Pete."

"I don't know, Carol. Sounded more to me like Sam wanted to remind you about your promise to Xstacy not to expose her."

I shrugged. "Maybe. Either way, she accomplished exactly what she wanted to do, and there's not much I can do about that now."

Tyler shook his head. "I wish I could be there for you tomorrow."

"Hey, you got a station to run. I get that."

"King will be there. I spoke with him this morning. He'll help you through any legal issues you may have. But the decision, Carol, what you decide to do. It's entirely up to you."

"Thanks, Tyler."

CHAPTER 31

I woke up Monday morning with a sense of dread. My life as I knew it—my kids, the house, my job, and friends—was about to come to a screeching halt, and there was nothing I could do about it. Last night, Chase had tried to convince me to go to dinner, one last night out before I'd be locked away in the slammer. But I couldn't. Despite the fact my daughter wasn't talking to me, I wanted to go home and spend the evening with Misty in hopes that Cate might change her mind and come out of her room. Unfortunately, that didn't happen. Misty explained while I was at the station, Cate had gone back to her dad's. Her parting message: "Mom's made her choice. It's time I made mine."

Not a great thought to wake up with, and without a lot of time to think about it, I pushed myself out of bed. I showered and dressed quickly, choosing a pair of black linen pants and a plain white cotton T-shirt with the station's logo blasted across the front of it and glanced in the mirror. I looked tired and washed-out. The circles beneath my eyes had shadows of their own from lack of sleep. I went back to my closet and grabbed the most expensive item I had in my wardrobe. A red peplum blazer with a black printed ruffled lapel and matching cuffs, a Bill Blass original Sheri had given me. As I pulled it off the hanger, I remembered Sheri quoting Blass, "When in Doubt, Wear Red."

I checked myself in the mirror one more time. Blass was right. I may not have felt confident, but Sheri's red power jacket hid a world of insecurity.

Downstairs, Misty had set the table, and the coffee maker was ready to go. When I walked into the kitchen, she asked if I'd like breakfast.

"I'm not hungry, Misty. But thanks."

"You need to eat something, Carol. You don't know how long this morning's meeting may take or when you'll eat again. How about I make you an omelet? Throw in some of my fresh veggies from the garden?"

I exhaled and squeezed my eyes shut to block the tears I could feel starting to build behind them. Was I really ready to say goodbye to all this? And for how long? And for what? To protect a girl who two weeks ago I didn't know and who if I met on the street might not even say hello to me? Why was it up to me, some local news reporter at a small radio station most people in the country would never hear about, to hold up a reporter's right to an unnamed source?

Misty sensed my angst and put her arms around me.

"Trust me, Carol, you're going to be fine."

A tear rolled down my cheek. "Prediction or wish, Misty?" I tried to laugh, and another tear escaped before I could wipe it away.

"Both." Misty took a tissue from her apron and put it to my eyes. "Chase will be here in a minute, he's going to drive us to the courthouse."

"Us?"

"You don't think I'm going to let you go alone? Besides, I want to give that judge a piece of my mind."

I laughed and wiped a tear from the corner of my eye. "He's just doing his job, Misty. We all are."

"Well, I don't like him, just the same. And I don't like this Detective Soto who arrested Pete, either, and I'm going to tell him so."

The doorbell rang. Misty patted me on the shoulder and went to answer it. It was Chase, shaved and dressed in a sports coat with a tie. I took one look at him, and my stomach sank. This was really happening. I was going to jail. There was no way out.

"You ready?" Chase stood in the doorway and tried to smile.

"Yeah." I finger brushed my hair behind my ear, then grabbed my bag off the kitchen counter. "Let's get this over with."

Misty sat in the back seat of Chase's SUV, I took the passenger seat up front. Somewhere down the 101, Chase reached over and took my hand, and I didn't let go.

"I like the red jacket by the way. Looks good on you." Chase nodded to my jacket.

"Well, don't get used to it. I understand orange is the new in color for inmates this season."

Misty put her hand on the back of my seat and leaned forward. "I wish I could help, Carol. Couple years ago, I might have had a vision and been able to give the police a description of the man they're looking for. I've done that before. You remember that missing coed?"

"I do." I smiled and put my hand on top of Misty's. I knew she was worried. About me. The kids. Herself. I had a houseful of people dependent upon me, and after today, I wasn't going to be there. At least not until the judge decided to let me out. "Misty, there's something you need to do. Charlie's coming home today, and I need you to call Cate to pick him up."

"Don't worry. We'll manage," she said.

"And Sheri, I haven't told her about any of this. She wanted us to come by for dinner and—"

"We've got it, Carol." Chase squeezed my hand. "Don't worry."

Monday mornings, things around the L.A. County Court House are usually pretty quiet. Aside from the swarm of potential jurors waiting to be selected for jury duty, the early morning business of the court is done mostly from inside a judge's solemn chambers or in one of the smaller courtrooms. Most court cases don't start until after lunch or jury selection or later in the week, leaving judges to clear their Monday morning calendar for arraignments, the filing of appeals and special hearings like mine with Judge Hensley.

On the way to the courthouse, King texted me. Today's

proceedings were scheduled to take place in the courtroom versus the judge's chamber. From the looks of things, the District Attorney hoped the ambiance of the court's bench with its high ceilings, flags, and state seal might prove to intimidate me. My red power jacket was no match for the setting. I felt a cold chill slide down my back as we entered the courtroom.

The room was empty, save for the bailiff and a court reporter who sat quietly at a table to the side of the judge's bench. Chase, Misty, and I took a seat in the general viewing area behind a short wooden partition where I had frequently sat as a journalist covering trials.

Chase leaned closer to me. "You okay?"

"I never believed it'd go this far. I mean the subpoena was kind of sobering, but I kept thinking at some point I'd have proof it wasn't Pete. That it was Scarface or Brian Evans."

Chase took my hand and squeezed it. "I did too."

Misty leaned over to me and whispered, "I thought the station would provide you with an attorney?"

"Relax, Misty." I might as well have been talking to myself. My eyes swept from a large clock above the judge's bench to the double doors at the back of the courtroom. Mr. King had five minutes to show, or I was on my own.

"Well, did they?" Misty asked again, this time her voice laced with impatience.

"Tyler asked Mr. King to come. I'm sure he'll be here any minute. But it's not like he's going to be able to do anything. I'm afraid this is going to be pretty cut and dry."

Misty folded her arms across her chest. "Well, just so you know, I still plan to give them a piece of mind."

The back doors to the courtroom opened. Soto, with the District Attorney Mr. Allen, entered, followed by two plain-clothed detectives and Eric. I felt my chest tighten and wedged myself back between Chase and Misty. The five went directly to a small table reserved for the prosecution. I glanced as they settled themselves in front of us and noticed Eric made no attempt at eye contact.

"You okay?" Chase whispered.

I swallowed hard and nodded.

Moments later, the big double doors behind us banged open, and King came through. He was out of breath and sweat ran down his brow. Holding a bulging briefcase against his chest, he waved his hand above his head. "I'm here. Damn L.A. traffic. Can't get anywhere in this town."

King spotted me in the gallery and motioned for me to join him at the defense table while he emptied his briefcase.

Before King had finished setting out his papers, the bailiff stood up from his chair in front of the judge's chamber. "His honorable Judge Hensley, presiding. Please rise."

Judge Hensley, dressed in a long black robe and carrying a copy of what I assumed was the summons, took the bench and asked us all to sit. For what felt like insufferably long, quiet moments where I could hear King's heavy breathing next to me, Hensley looked at the summons. Then put it aside and asked us all to take a seat.

"I understand, Ms. Childs, that the District Attorney believes you have information pertinent to the investigation of the murders of five women, as well as the identity of a probable witness in the vehicular death of Ely Wade."

I started to speak, but King put his hand out in front of me.

"And while given the opportunity to share this information with investigators you have refused, citing your rights as a reporter under the California Shield Law. Is this true?" Hensley looked down at me from the bench. "You may answer, Ms. Childs."

King tilted his head in my direction, his eyes met mine. We had been through this before, he knew my answer.

"I have, Your Honor."

"And has your attorney informed you that in refusing to share this information that I am within my rights to sentence you to jail?"

"He has, Your Honor."

"Then, Ms. Childs, much as I appreciate the need for reporters to maintain their right to protect unnamed sources and confidential information, I am forced today to balance that need versus the need for police to have access to information they cannot get elsewhere. For this reason, I am ordering you today to divulge your source and any information you may have concerning the murders of the five young women to the police. And since this is an open investigation, I need you to do that right now, in this courtroom, or I will be forced to sentence you to jail until such time you agree to do so. Is that understood?"

"Your Honor, if I might?" The DA was on his feet. "I'd like to make one final offer to Ms. Childs before you proceed. Give us the name of the woman you're protecting, who we believe was with Ms. Minor the night Ely Wade was killed, and you can go home."

The judge looked at me. "Ms. Childs?"

I shook my head.

"You'll need to answer verbally for the record," the judge said.

"Your Honor, before she answers, I'd like to share with Ms. Childs some photos we uncovered from Ely's home. You see our argument is not with Ms. Childs' reporting. In fact, Ms. Childs has proven to be an excellent investigator. She was very helpful early on in our investigation. It was Ms. Childs who led Detective Soto to Ms. Minor's car the day police found her body in Venice, which helped in IDing the body."

The Judge looked over at me, then back at the DA. "Would you care to expand, counselor?"

"With the first three murders, we found black and white Polaroids. Pictures of the girls posed post-mortem. We asked Carol not to go public with that information, which she agreed to do. We appreciated her professionalism and the manner in which she continued to conduct her investigations. It wasn't until Mr. Pompidou was arrested, and we learned Ms.Childs' daughter had been dating the suspect, that we began to suspect Ms. Childs' position as a reporter had been compromised in an effort to keep her daughter's name out of the news."

"I wasn't comprised." I started to stand, and King pulled me back into my seat.

"We believe Ms. Childs is protecting a witness. Someone who knows about the murders. Someone who may implicate her daughter's boyfriend if she were to talk."

"That's ridiculous," I said. "And the only reason you think I might know someone who knows anything at all about the murders is because I shared with you the location of Stacy's van. If I hadn't you might never have found it."

"Your Honor, might I point out that Ms. Childs seems to have forgotten she was on the air only yesterday when an anonymous caller phoned into the station who claimed to have known Ms. Minor. That this caller said she knew Minor had feared for her life and may have known her killer.

"And she made it very clear it wasn't Pete Pompidou, Your Honor." I wanted to scream back at the DA but didn't dare.

"An unusual statement, Your Honor. Are we really to believe Ms. Childs didn't arrange for her anonymous source to call the station in an attempt to discredit our investigation into Mr. Pompidou's suspected role in the murders?"

"Your Honor," King stood up. "It's impossible for the DA to know what was in the mind of an anonymous caller."

"Counselors!" The judge scolded both men, then turned to the DA. "Mr. Allen, let me remind you, this is not a trial. If you wish to present evidence to Ms. Childs that might persuade her to share with you what she knows about her source, you need to do so. If not, I'm prepared to announce sentencing now."

"Thank you, Your Honor." The DA opened his bag and took out a folder and placed it on the table. "If I might, I'd like to share with Ms. Childs something investigators found at the home of Ely Wade on Saturday. I believe it might ease her conscious about revealing information concerning her source and Pete Pompidou, who we believe she's been protecting."

"Protecting? Pete Pompidou?" Now I was on my feet. "Sir, I'm not protecting Pete Pompidou. I don't believe he's guilty, but I'm certainly not protecting him. I'm only interested in seeing an innocent man isn't tried and found guilty for crimes I don't believe he committed."

Hensley pounded his gavel just as King grabbed my arm and pulled me back into my chair.

"Might I remind you, Ms. Childs, while this is not a formal trial, it is a hearing, and I will have you maintain proper etiquette in my courtroom. Do you understand?"

"Yes, sir." I sat back down.

"Mr. Allen, please proceed."

"What I'd like to do Your Honor, is have Detective Soto and Agent Langdon present several photos for Ms. Childs to review. She's already aware of some of these photos. They were taken with the Polaroid camera we found at Ely Wade's home yesterday."

I scribbled a note to King and slid it under his nose. *Fingerprints?*

I hoped King might know if Soto had found Pete's prints on the camera. If he had, it was all over. If he hadn't, Pete still had a chance. King shook his head and whispered, "I don't know. First I've heard of it."

"And along with these Polaroids are several more photos. Ones I believe will convince Ms. Childs she's nothing to gain by protecting a source she's afraid would implicate her daughter's boyfriend."

King put his hand on top of mine.

The judge asked if he could see the photos first. Allen said yes, and Soto and Eric stood up and approached the bench with a handful of small Polaroids and several large eight-by-ten black and whites. After a few whispered exchanges, the judge handed the small polaroid photos back to Eric, and the others to Soto, then looked at me.

"Ms. Childs, before I ask you for the last time if you'd like to reveal your source, let me say, I agree with the District Attorney. I think you should look at these pictures."

Eric returned to the DA's table, while Soto approached me and spread the larger glossy photos out on the table in front of me.

The first photos were from inside Pete's van. Pictures of

camping gear: ropes, sleeping bags, an ice chest, pup tent, and circled and marked in yellow were plastic restraints—similar to those found on the models—and a five-inch hunting knife. The type believed to have been used to slash the models. The other photos were from the inside of Xstacy's van. A picture of a yellow sticky note attached to the dashboard with Pete's address on it, and more from the inside cargo section of the van. It looked like somebody had been living in it. Empty fast food containers, a blue blanket, like the one found in the shopping cart by the volleyball court where her body had been found, and circled in yellow marking pen, a pair of plastic restraints. Then three more photos of the murdered models. Shana Walters. Kara Stieffers. Eileen Kim. All of them taken in a studio before their murders and marked with Pete's insignia, PPP, Pete Pompidou Photography. And finally, a photo of Marilynn Brewer, a black and white full body shot of her in front of a microphone. Possibly something she'd used to promote her comedy act and another of Xstacy, also with the same insignia.

"None of this proves Pete killed those girls. He's a photographer, and he enjoys camping. So what?" I pushed the photos away from me.

"How about this?" Soto placed the last photo on the table. An eight-and-a-half-by-eleven, black and white glossy. A trump card I felt sure he had been waiting to play. A picture of three men. Two of them sitting on a tall ladder, the type used to set lighting on a soundstage. The third man, wearing a baseball cap, leaned against it as they stared into the camera. Pete was seated casually at the top, his surfer-blond hair in his eyes with a stupid grin on his face. The photo looked several years old. Halfway down the ladder was the man I knew only because I had seen his face on the internet. Soto pointed to the center of the photo. "In case you don't know, that's Ely Wade in the middle. The man on top, that's your boy, Pete Pompidou. Photo's maybe three years old."

I picked the photo up and studied it. There was no disputing Pete's identity. Soto was right, Ely and Pete had worked together. How long, I didn't know. Where the photo was taken, I had no idea.

"You see, Ms. Childs, giving up your witness doesn't hurt Pete. We already have proof Pete and Ely worked together. We just want to know what this witness of yours knows."

"She knows Pete's not the Model Slayer or his partner. And everything you've shown me, the photos of Pete's camping equipment, his address on some sticky note on the dashboard of Xstacy's van, a picture of Pete with Ely working somewhere. None of it proves he's a murderer."

I was about to toss the photo back on the table when I noticed the face of the man beneath the baseball cap. I looked closer. Maybe it was Brian or Scarface, and the cap had hidden his identity the first time I looked. But it was another face I knew, and when I realized who it was, I gasped.

"Oh my God! It's Max!" I slapped the photo back on the table and pointed to the man standing next to the ladder in the baseball cap. The same angular face and slim build as the man who had been flirting with Sheri the night I had first visited the Sky High Club. "That's Max. He's the killer!"

"Who?" Soto grabbed the photo off the table and stared at it.

"Max," I said. "The man standing next to the ladder. He was at the Sky High Club the night I went to check out the club for a story I was working on. He hit on my girlfriend. They've been dating ever since."

Soto picked up the photo and laughed. "That's impossible. You know who he is? His name's Lenny Marx. He's a world-class famous portrait photographer. He's got pictures in museums around the world."

"He may be Richard Avedon for all I care. I'm telling you if that man knew Ely Wade and Ely's the Model Slayer, then Pete is not his partner. That man is. Did you check him out?"

Soto smiled smugly. "Actually, Carol, we did. We interviewed him early on. He's no ties to any of the models, and he travels frequently for business. He wasn't in town when the murders went down. However, he did have a lot to say about Pete."

"I don't care what he said about Pete, you need to check him out. He was at the bar the night Sheri and I came in, and I don't think he was any stranger to the Sky High Club. In fact, I think he was there looking for Xstacy."

"And why would you think that, Ms. Childs?"

"Because I had gone there myself to meet with my source. She was convinced the Model Slayer's partner had been sitting up by the stage, that he was fixated on one of the dancers, and might still be there."

Soto looked at the picture again. "Those clubs are pretty dark. What makes you so sure this is your guy?"

"I was at the bar, and my girlfriend was with that man," I pointed at the photo, "maybe ten feet away. They were standing next to the cash register. There was a small light above the register so the bartender could see to make change, and it was enough light so I could see his face. Look, I'm telling you, this is your man."

"And is your girlfriend still dating this man? This Max person who you believe to be in this photo?"

"Yes," I looked back at a large clock above the court's double doors. "And if I'm right he should be at her house right now. Look, we don't have a lot of time. If you want to catch him, we have to go. If I'm wrong, you can lock me up and throw away the key, but if I'm right, my best friend may be the Model Slayer's next victim."

Soto took the picture and went back to the table and huddled with Eric and the DA while I replayed in my mind everything that had happened that first night at the Sky High Club. How I had left Sheri and went to the end of the bar and met with Sam. The way Sam was dressed and how she teased nobody would recognize her in a place like that with her clothes on. The way I was convinced Scarface was the Model Slayer's accomplice when all along it was Max, standing in the back of the bar, waiting for Xstacy and Jewels to reappear on stage.

"Your Honor," the DA looked up at the bench, "if I might have a moment."

The judge nodded and told the DA he could approach.

I whispered to King. "What's going on?"

King reached over and held my hand. "They're bargaining. Stay calm."

Seconds seemed like hours before the DA nodded to the judge, then glanced back at me and crossed back to the table with Soto and Eric and sat down. There was a mumbled exchange between Soto and the DA. Eric's eyes flashed momentarily in my direction and then back to the group. Finally, the DA stood up. "Your Honor, I believe we're in agreement."

From the bench, Judge Hensley asked me to stand. "Ms. Childs, the DA tells me there may be some doubt as to the identity of the man you've pointed out in the photo. If indeed it is Mr. Marx, I'm to understand that his current whereabouts and recent travel schedules haven't been one hundred percent verified by investigators. Because of that, and the fact that LAPD arrested Mr. Pompidou, not once but twice, and I am loath to reverse a second arrest, and that you believe your friend may be in imminent danger, I'm about to do something unusual. I am going to release you to go with Detective Soto right now so that you can go to the home of your friend. And if you're right, and this man, who you believe to be the Model Slayer, is with your friend, and the police can prove that, I'll dismiss the charges against you. But if you're wrong, I've instructed the DA to have Detective Soto return you to my courtroom without delay for sentencing. Is that clear?"

"Yes, Your Honor."

CHAPTER 32

My first clue things weren't okay when we got to Sheri's house was the security gate. It was wide open. My second, the fact Chase's car and three LAPD cruisers with their lights flashing and sirens blaring hadn't sent Sheri running to the front door, worried me even more.

Chase pulled up directly behind Detective Soto and slammed the breaks so hard the SUV skidded. Misty had to brace herself against the back of the front seat to keep from falling forward. Without waiting for us to come to a complete stop, I put my hand on the door handle and was about to jump out when Chase grabbed my arm. "Not so fast, Carol. You can't go in."

"Fat chance I can't." I pulled my arm free from Chase. "Sheri's my friend, and it's my fault Max is here." I slammed the car door behind me and sprinted toward the back of the house. I wasn't about to wait in the car with my best friend alone inside with a serial killer.

Soto spotted me and yelled for me to get back in the car, but I ignored him and scrambled up the back steps to the house and bolted into the kitchen. The room was a mess. On the center island where Sheri prepared meals like a Michelin chef, dishes were shattered, thrown about as though there had been a scuffle. On the floor lay a broken coffee cup and a blood-stained towel.

I picked up the towel. "Sheri!"

My own voice echoed back at me. The house felt empty.

Behind me, Chase, Soto, and two cops swarmed the room, their guns drawn. Misty brought up the rear.

I started to yell for Misty to get back in the car, but Soto hushed me. His index finger to his lips. Silently, he pointed for me to stay put, then nodded for his men to search the house, and went with them to check the downstairs.

Without waiting for permission, I moved toward the kitchen stairway leading to the upstairs and took the steps two at a time with Chase close behind me.

Upstairs, the double doors to Sheri's master suite were open. Whatever scuffle had started in the kitchen had continued in the bedroom. The sheets from Sheri's king-sized bed lay on the floor next to her robe and an antique clock. The clock's glass casing had shattered, the hands stopped sometime after eleven a.m. I scanned the room. My eyes went from the bed to the bay window where the mid-morning light streamed through the pane casing and shimmered off the empty dance pole.

I pointed down the hall toward the guest room and suggested Chase check there while I checked the bath. Chase refused to leave me alone and gave the bath a cursory inspection; then deciding there was nothing there, left to check the rest of the upstairs. I stood in the center of the bath. There was no sign of struggle. The towels were hung neatly by the tub, and Sheri's dressing table, littered with knickknacks and bottles of cologne, hadn't been disturbed. I was about to leave and go back downstairs when I heard a noise coming from within Sheri's closet.

"Sheri?" It was nearly impossible to see where the sound was coming from. Racks of clothing lining the closet's wall stretched the full length of the house. I started with the area closest to me, frantically pushing clothes aside as I worked my way section-by-section down the closet until I came to a group of hanging garment bags that refused to budge. Hidden behind them, a carpet runner from the hallway had been rolled up and was leaning up against the wall. I pulled it out and lay it down on the floor and quickly unrolled it. Inside, bundled like a mummy with a bedsheet from Sheri's bed and tied with a rope was a body.

"Chase! She's here." My fingers worked to untie the rope from the sheets, tearing at them until I could see Sheri's face. Her brown eyes blinked up at me as I pulled the covers from her face. "She's alive!" I pushed the sheet from her body. A sock had been forced into her mouth like a gag, and a second nylon rope had been tied around her neck with her hands tied behind her, making it almost impossible for her to move.

"Are you okay?" I removed the sock from Sheri's mouth and held her in my arms.

"I'm fine. Carol, it's Max. He's the Model Slayer. He told me everything."

Chase rushed into the room and spotted Sheri on the floor with her hands tied behind her back. In a matter of seconds, he cut the nylon rope that held her wrists with a pocket knife. Together we helped her over to a lounge chair while she explained Max was supposed to come by Sunday but had called to canceled.

"He came by this morning instead, and when he got here, he was acting strange. Different than I'd ever seen him before. He started talking about Sam, only he said her name was Jewels, and he wanted to know if she was going to be here today. When I told him I didn't know who he was talking about, he started to get mad. He said he had heard you on the air yesterday with *that girl*, and that you knew who she was, and he had to find her." Sheri rubbed her wrists as she spoke, "Oh my God, Carol, was that Sam? Is she involved in all this?

I nodded and asked Chase to bring Sheri a glass of water from the bathroom.

"You didn't give him her real name did you?"

"No. I told him I didn't know anyone named Jewels, but he didn't believe me and said he'd prove it. He got my iPhone out of my purse and started to go through it."

"Was Sam's number on your phone?"

Chase came back with the water and Sheri took a sip.

"No, but her number was, Carol. It was on my calendar where I keep all my appointments. I had listed my pole dancing lessons, without a name, and Max figured it had to be her. When I tried to grab the phone back, he picked up a knife from the kitchen counter and threatened me. He called me a spoiled brat. Said the only reason he was going out with me was because I was rich and stupid."

"Did he hurt you?"

"Not physically."

"I saw blood on a towel downstairs."

"It was his blood. We struggled, and he cut himself. But he got the phone away from me and went through all my appointments. When he saw I had you down for dinner tonight he got really excited. And then he started talking about Jewels again. He wanted to know if I knew where she might be. I told him I didn't know, and he started waving the knife below my face and threatened to stab me. I'm sorry, Carol, I lost it. I told him I thought she might be at UCLA. At the Tri-Delt House. She told me she sometimes worked there."

"That's okay. I would have done the same thing. Where is he now?"

"He made me call her, and when she didn't answer, he made me leave a message. He told me to tell her it was an emergency. That I had to talk to her. That you had given me a message for her, and I was to meet her at the Tri-Delt House. Then he tied me up and told me all the stuff he had done to those girls and stuffed me in this closet. He said if I moved, I'd choke myself to death on the rope." Sheri rubbed her neck where the rope had been.

I took out my cell phone and looked at the time. It was twelve thirty. "What time did you tell Sam you'd meet her?"

"One o'clock. Carol, you need to stop him. He said he's going there to kill her, and then he's coming back here to finish the job with you and me."

I stood up. The Tri-Delt House was the one place I hadn't thought to look again. Not since I knew Sam didn't live there. But if I called and left her a message, at least she'd know not to go there, and if I was lucky, I might be able to lead Soto to Max before he got away.

"Be careful. Carol, he's crazy."

"Don't worry. I'll be fine. Misty's downstairs. I'll send her upstairs to stay with you."

I got as far as the door to the closet and ran into Soto. His big frame filling the doorway. "And just where do you think you're going?" Soto asked.

"The Tri-Delt house. UCLA. Max is there." I said.

"How do you know?" Soto asked.

"Because he told Sheri everything. He confessed. He said he's going there to find Xstacy's friend, and he's going to kill her. If we leave now, we might catch him. Are you coming?"

CHAPTER 33

"We're too late." I could see the emergency lights up ahead as we sped behind Soto with a police escort up Hilgard. Outside the Tri-Delt house, an ambulance and a University police cruiser blocked traffic.

Chase pulled up behind Soto's unmarked car, across the street from sorority row. Up and down the boulevard, college students, girls from inside the houses and students returning from mid-morning summer classes, stood transfixed by the scene of a body lying in the street. A car, the front fender badly dented and the windshield cracked had pulled over half a block down the road in front of the Alpha Phi House.

Soto walked back to Chase's car and tapped on the window. "We'll take it from here, Ms. Childs. You need to wait in the car."

I sat long enough for Soto to cross the street, then opened the passenger door and stood up on the running board to get a better view. Officers were surveying the scene. A man's body lay prostrate in the street, his head smashed against the pavement. Sheri's pink sequined cell phone had been knocked from his hand and had skidded to the gutter and was marked with a yellow flag. Death must have been instantaneous. Blood trickled from the head and pooled around his dark hair, his eyes wide and motionless.

Down the street, a second scene played out. A patrol officer was talking to a young woman who stood in front of her parked vehicle. The officer had asked for her license. She fumbled nervously as she handed it to him. Then the officer nodded back in the direction of the body, and she looked up. For a brief second, I caught her eye as she looked at me, then back at the scene.

Sam?

I sat back down in the front seat of the car and exhaled, my heart beating like I had just run a marathon. Chase looked over at me. "You okay?"

"I think so. It all depends on what Detective Soto tells me."

Chase glanced in the review mirror. "Did you tell Cate you were here?"

"No. Why?" I turned and looked over my shoulder. Cate was running up the walk toward us. I got out of the car. "Cate, what's wrong? Are you okay?"

Cate put her arms around me. "Sheri called. She told me everything, Mom. I was at work, and when I heard the sirens, I was so scared it was you. Did they catch him?"

"I don't know yet." I brushed a strand of hair from Cate's face and pulled her to me. It felt good to hold her in my arms again. "I'm waiting to talk to Detective Soto now."

"That man who wanted to send you to jail?" Cate pulled away and looked up at me.

"The detective in charge of the case, yes. As far as his wanting to send me to jail, we'll see." I opened the car door and asked Cate to sit inside. "We need to talk."

"I know," Cate said. "I'm sorry. I shouldn't have—"

"No." I put my finger on her lips. "You did what you needed to do, Catie, and it's okay. We can talk about that later, but right now, I need to know what Pete knew about Lenny Marx."

"Lenny Marx?" Cate held my hand. "Not much. He told me he did some freelance work for him when he first came to California. Why?"

"You saw the newspaper Saturday?"

"Yeah, it's why I went back to Dad's house. I'm sorry, Mom, I didn't want to hear you say you thought Pete was innocent and that you couldn't do anything."

"Detective Soto's convinced Ely Wade was one of the model slayers and that Wade and Pete were partners."

"Soto's wrong. Pete wouldn't be friends with a freak like that."

"I believe you, but what about Lenny Marx?"

"I know they weren't friends. Pete said he worked for him for a short while when he first moved here. He told me he didn't like him. That he harassed a lot of his models. Made the girls uncomfortable. He said Lenny got a lot of good shots, but Pete didn't like what he saw and quit. Later, some of Lenny's models started using him instead. Pete thinks Lenny always had it out for him after that."

My eyes met Chase's. He didn't need to tell me we were thinking the same thing. "I think it's more than that, Cate."

"You think he set Pete up?" Cate asked.

"I think when Pete was arrested, he became a convenient scapegoat. And when Lenny found Xstacy, he either placed her car in back of Pete's house or somehow got her to go there. Either way, he made it look like she was going to meet Pete."

I glanced back out at the scene in front of us. The crowd had thinned. The coroner's van had removed the body, and we had an unobstructed view of the police as they wrapped their investigation. Soto ferried back and forth between investigators and the young woman whose car had hit Max. When Soto finished, he approached Chase's car with a notepad in hand.

"Ms. Childs? You mind getting out of the car?"

I told Chase and Cate to wait in the car and got out. Whatever Soto was about to tell me I preferred it to be just between us. I walked away from the car where we could talk privately.

"Looks like you were right, Ms. Childs. Body in the street was Lenny Marx. Even better, an eyewitness from the sorority house said Mr. Marx had knocked on the door and wanted to talk to a girl named Jewels. She said she told him they didn't have anyone named Jewels living there, and he insisted he come inside and take a look for himself. When she explained men weren't allowed in the house, he tried to push his way in and started to get aggressive. Told her he was looking for a dancer who had killed his friend. She got scared and slammed the door and called campus security. Then she ran upstairs and peeked out the window. She said she watched as Marx took out his cell phone, appeared to try to call someone, then stepped into the street and was hit by a car."

"It's really him then?" I asked.

"The Model Slayer?" Soto said. "We won't know that until we finish our investigation. But right now, we IDed him from the driver's license in his wallet. Victim's name was Leonard Marx. If what your friend told you about him confessing to being the Model Slayer checks out, I'd say we got our guy." Soto looked back down the street where Sam's car was being towed away.

"What about the driver?" I asked.

"Her name's Samantha Miller. She's a student. Pretty shaken up. She said she was leaving campus, driving south on Hilgard when a man stepped in front of her car. He was talking on his cell. Didn't appear to be looking where he was going and stepped right in front of her. She tried to stop, but it was too late. Far as I'm concerned, if this man is who we think, the girl did us all a favor."

I bit back a smile. "Then you're convinced Pete Pompidou's not involved?"

"Let's put it this way. I talked to the DA, he says you can go home. We're not interested in talking to you right now. If he needs anything else, we'll be in touch."

"Thanks." I turned around and headed back to Chase's SUV.

"Oh, and Carol." I stopped and looked back at the detective. "I assume you're planning on reporting what happened here today?"

"Any reason I shouldn't?"

"Not that I can think of. But you better hurry. Your competitors are going to want to know what happened here today. I put a temporary hold on the story, but I can't hold it for long. I wouldn't want to look like I was playing favorites."

CHAPTER 34

BREAKING NEWS. Police believe a second suspect in the recent rash of murders the press has dubbed the Model Slayings was killed this afternoon while crossing Hilgard Avenue in West Los Angeles. Witnesses say Leonard Marx, the famed portrait photographer, was struck by a passing motorist when he stepped in front of a car while talking on his cell phone. In what appears to be a bizarre twist of fate, Marx is believed to have had ties to Ely Wade, who police suspect to be responsible for the deaths of four of the five women recently murdered, and who also was hit and killed by a car three weeks ago after leaving a popular gentleman's club near LAX. While investigations continue into the connection, police report Marx's death appears to have been accidental, citing it as another indication of L.A.'s growing need for more and better crosswalks.

I filed my report live from the scene of the accident then asked Chase to drop me back at the station. I knew Tyler would be waiting for me, and I needed to debrief him on the morning activities. I explained how everything had gone down, from the courthouse to Sheri's, to the scene in front of the sorority house. When I finished, Tyler told me King had called with an update on my situation. Which at the moment was on hold. King doubted, based on what he heard back from Soto and the District Attorney, they would bother to pursue the subpoena.

In addition, King felt certain based on what had happened with Lenny Marx the DA would also drop the charges against Pete.

"That should make your daughter happy," Tyler said.

"I wish it did me," I said.

"You're not?" Tyler asked. "Pete's about to go free, you proved the cops had been pursuing the wrong man the entire time and led them to the Model Slayer and his partner. I don't understand why you're not celebrating. What more do you want?"

"That's just it, Tyler. I keep thinking how close I came to losing my best friend and what went down in front of the sorority house."

"What, are you blaming yourself?" Tyler took a tissue box from a drawer within his desk and threw it across the table at me. "You want to cry about it?"

"No. I don't feel like crying, Tyler."

"Because there's nothing you can do, Carol. Sam never told you what she planned to do. My bet is, once Sam got your message, Marx was on his way over to the sorority house, she left the house and waited for him. She knew she'd never be able to stop him. That he'd continue to hunt her down until he killed her exactly like he did Xstacy. She probably went and got her car and parked it across the street from the house. And when she saw him come up the walk and leave, she ran him over. Not your problem. You made a promise to Xstacy you wouldn't reveal Sam's identity or what happened the night she killed Ely. Far as the law goes, as long as neither girl told you she was planning to kill someone, you're in the clear."

"But what if the cops find out about Samantha? That she worked as a stripper for the Sky High Club?"

"The girl went by two names, Carol. You plan on telling them the Sky High's Crown Jewels and Samantha Miller are one and the same? Because if you do you'd be breaking your promise to Xstacy."

"I suppose you're right."

"Look, the cops ruled Marx's death an accident. My guess is they'll never know Samantha Miller is anything more than a college student. There's no reason for the cops to go looking into Sam's background, any more than they did Xstacy's when she hit Ely. The city has a skyrocketing number of pedestrian accidents every week. Both women were good citizens. They reported the accident. Stayed with the victim and cooperated with investigators. Far as the cops know, Samantha Miller is just some poor college student who accidentally hit someone on her way home from class and called the police to report the accident."

My cell phone buzzed. I looked at the screen. "It's Sheri, Tyler, I've got to take this."

I excused myself and hurried down the hall to my office with the phone pressed against my ear. "How you feeling?"

"You forgot?"

"What?" I asked.

"The boys!"

"Augh! That's right. It's Monday, I totally–"

"Don't worry. Misty and I picked them up. Charlie's in the shower, and Clint's parked himself in front of the big screen and he's playing video games. You coming for dinner?"

"You're not still planning on dinner? Not with everything that happened." I sat down at my desk. "You need to take some time."

"Maybe so, but not tonight, Carol. The boys are home after two weeks away, and I want to celebrate. Besides, the London Broil's been marinating, and the table's been set since Sunday morning. If I've any worries about what happened, I'll take it up with my therapist later. But for now, I've asked Misty to take the extra seat at the table, and I want my best friend here with me. I'm expecting you at seven. No excuses. And bring Chase."

Chase? I had been in a such a rush to get back to the station I hadn't a chance to debrief Chase on what I could or what I wanted to share with him. To thank him for not pushing me to divulge what Xstacy and Sam had told me, and for sticking with me when I needed someone. When Chase pulled up in front of the station, I was so anxious to talk with Tyler that I leaned across the seat and without thinking about it, kissed him on the side of the face. Like it was the most natural thing in the world to do. I hadn't even said goodbye.

I picked up the phone and called Chase. When he didn't answer, I left a message and told him we needed to talk. Later, I called again and left a second message. Then about four o'clock, when I still hadn't heard back from him, I began to get concerned and buzzed him back and left another message. This time, more personal.

"Hey, it's me. I'm sorry I didn't have time to tell you earlier today how much I appreciated all you did. And...well," I paused and looked back at the picture Pete had taken of the kids and me on the beach. "Look, Sheri's doing a dinner tonight. I wanted to ask if you'd like to come. I know I've been difficult–okay, inconsistent even–about keeping my personal life and my professional life separate, but I was thinking maybe I could be a little less strict about that. At least where you're concerned. Anyway, if you'd like to come, I'd love to see you there. Seven o'clock. Call me."

By the time I arrived at Sheri's, the boys were home and the place was immaculate. Sheri met me at the front door and told me once the police had left, both she and Misty had swept through the downstairs, picked up the broken pieces of china and removed any sign that anything unusual had happened. Then went and picked up the boys.

"I'd prefer if we didn't discuss anything about Max or my pole dancing in front of them. The less they know about this little incident, the better."

"What about the pole?" I asked.

"Gone," Sheri said. "Misty and I removed it this afternoon."

I hugged Sheri and told her not to worry. The boys didn't need to know what had gone down as long as Sheri was fine.

"Mom! You're back." Charlie spotted me at the door and came racing toward me. Like an overgrown puppy, he nearly knocked me down. I threw my arms around him.

"You've grown," I said. Charlie felt like he was two inches taller and ten pounds heavier. "Couple of weeks away and look at you."

"Not as much as Clint. He's playing quarterback next fall, Mom. Our team's gonna be awesome."

"I'll bet." I put my arm around Charlie, and along with Sheri, we walked down the long entry hall to the kitchen.

"Hi, Mom." Cate stood up from behind the kitchen console where she and Misty had been seated. "I hope you don't mind. Sheri asked me to come."

"Mind?" I felt relieved. "I'm just glad you came."

Sheri checked the oven. Roasted potatoes with garlic and rosemary. The smell was rich, warm and heavenly. On the counter, in a large wooden bowl, Misty had prepared a green salad and next to it, ready for the grill, was Sheri's London Broil. With a nod toward the den, Sheri asked Charlie to go tell Clint to wash up for dinner.

Charlie grabbed a roll off the counter and disappeared back to the den.

I was about to see if there was something I could do when the outside buzzer to Sheri's big security gate rang.

"You expecting someone?" I asked.

Sheri glanced out the window and buzzed the gate open. "Detective Soto. He called earlier this afternoon. Said he needed to come by." Sheri turned to Misty. "Misty, think you could let him in?"

From the kitchen, I could hear the sound of male voices.

Before I knew who it was, Cate jumped up and went running down the hall. "Pete! It's Pete. He's here."

I followed Cate down the hall and watched as Detective Soto stepped out of the way and Cate, like a cannonball, threw her arms and legs around Pete and buried her head in his chest.

Soto looked at me. "I thought since I wanted to stop by here first and check on Sheri, the least I could do was drive Pete home."

"No. No way." Cate hung on to Pete's arm and shook her head. "I'll take him home."

"You sure you don't want to ask him to stay for dinner, Cate?"

Misty asked.

Cate shook her head. "Thanks, but if it's alright with Mom, we have a lot of catching up to do."

I crossed my arms and took a step back. Cate had made up her mind about Pete. I needed to let whatever was going to happen between the two of them happen. Pete was a good kid, and Cate's future was hers, not mine to dictate. The sooner I accepted that, the sooner our relationship would get back to normal.

"It's fine," I said.

Misty put her arm around me as we watched the two of them walk hand-in-hand down the drive to Cate's car. "She's going to be alright, Carol."

"That a prediction, Misty, or are you just trying to make me feel better?"

"It's whatever you want it to be," Misty said.

I shut the door and thanked Soto for bringing Pete by.

"About Pete," Soto said. "You were right, Carol. Pete was innocent. It's not easy for me to admit, but sometimes cops get tunnel vision. I'm afraid that's what happened here. Pete was an obvious suspect. A photographer. He knew the victims and fit the profile of a serial killer. Young. White. Male. And a bit of a drifter."

"If we're confessing things, Detective, I have to admit, when you showed me all the evidence this morning, I was worried. Particularly when you showed me that photo with Pete and Ely together. If I hadn't recognized Max, I might have had a reason to doubt myself."

Soto cleared his throat. "About that photo. After the accident this morning, I went back to the jail to talk to Pete again. I showed him the picture and asked him about it. He said he'd only met Ely Wade once. The day that photo was taken. He remembered he picked up a gig on Craig's List for a lighting tech for a photo shoot at one of the big studios. That's where he met Lenny Marx. Lenny hired him after that, and according to Pete, he worked for him for a short while, but didn't care for the way he treated the girls."

"Who took the photo?" I asked.

"Marx liked to document all his shoots. Including those of the models he murdered. Detectives found more Polaroids like the ones we found at Ely's place hidden inside a safe at his studio. As for who took that particular photo of the three of them, I don't know. Only that we found that it inside Marx's safe as well."

"And you never suspected Marx?" I asked. "Even after you first talked to him about Pete?"

"Marx was Teflon. Big name. Successful. Didn't fit the profile. Which may have been why our detectives didn't spend a lot of time trying to match up his travel schedule with the murders."

"And what about Brian Evans? I thought for sure you'd think he was involved or at least responsible for Marilynn's murder."

"We did. At first anyway. Or until you identified Xstacy's van. That's when the whole case opened up for us, and quite frankly that's when we lost interest in Brian."

"I saw him at the Sky High Club one night, and I thought for sure he might be connected."

"Brian was doing his own little detective work. Too bad he didn't take more interest in what Marilynn was up to before she died. If he had, she might never have run into Ely Wade. As it was, once we started looking into Xstacy's background and realized that both Xstacy and Marilynn had connections to the Sky High Club, we got curious and started poking around. But then you already knew that, didn't you?"

"Misty knew," I said. "She suspected early on Xstacy and Marilynn were friends."

Soto raised a brow and smiled at Misty. "Psychic to the Stars, huh? I've heard a lot about you over the years. Could have used you on a couple of cases."

I nudged Misty and whispered in her ear. "You still got it, Misty."

"As it was," Soto said, "we ended up talking to a barmaid who told us the last time she saw Marilynn was the night she performed at the club."

I paused and waited to see if Soto was going to say if the

barmaid had also told him about Xstacy's friend Sam. When he didn't, I asked what he had learned.

"Barmaid said Marilynn left the club with two men. One of the men appeared to have been upset with her act. We think Marilynn was Ely and Lenny's last victim, at least that they did together. They kidnapped her from the club, drove her out to the Santa Clarita metro stop where they left her car, then took her out to Vasquez Canyon and killed her. But they botched the job. Probably because they didn't have time to plan for it, like they did the models. Ended up they had to hit her over the head and used her ex-boyfriend's dog collar to tie her to the tree. Totally different MO, which was why initially we thought Brian might have killed her and tried to make it look like a copycat murder."

"What about Xstacy? Marx had to have killed her alone. Ely was dead by then. How did he find her?"

"That same barmaid who remembered Marilynn performing at the club also remembers Xstacy coming in to pick up a check one night after she'd stopped working there. We think Marx was there, spotted her, followed her back to her van and killed her. Set it up to look like she had gone to meet Pete. By then everyone in town knew the police had arrested Pete and released him. The public was nervous, and all Marx had to do was add a little fuel to the fire."

"You mean like the Post-it note left in her van?"

"This afternoon, forensics checked the note against handwriting samples we have for Marx. It looks like a match."

"So that's it then? Brian never had anything to do with Marilynn's death or her disappearance, and it was Ely Wade and Lenny Marx all along."

"It's why I came by tonight. I wanted to check on Sheri, and when she told me you'd be here, I thought I should tell you myself, in person."

I put my hands behind me and leaned back against the door. "But why? Why does anyone do something like this?"

"I'm not a psychologist, Ms. Childs. I leave that to the shrinks and FBI profilers who would probably tell you both men had some type of childhood trauma growing up. Ely's sister said their mother walked out on them when they were kids. Cases like this the perps are usually loners and socially inept."

"I don't know about Ely Wade, but Lenny Marx was a nationally recognized portrait photographer. He was at the top of his game. He wasn't exactly socially inept."

"There's no class exclusivity on psychopaths. In fact, if Marx were alive, he'd probably even say the murders were some type of erotic performance art. It might explain the blood smiles and the mixing of their blood with their victims. But don't ask me to explain it. All I know is people are seldom what you think. A CEO is as likely to be a psychopath as a down-and-out homeless person. But that's not the reason I stopped by and wanted to talk with you."

"No?" I squeezed the door handle in my hand behind me and hoped the next words out of Soto's mouth weren't that the DA had changed his mind, and Soto was here to take me to jail.

"Don't look so worried, Carol. Much as I might have enjoyed locking you up earlier today, I'm here to tell you the DA officially dropped the case against you. You've nothing to worry about. Whoever or whatever you knew and didn't want to share with us is no longer of concern."

I breathed a deep sigh of relief.

"However, there is one more thing."

"What's that?"

Soto reached into his pocket and took out Sheri's cell phone. "I need to give this to Sheri."

I led Soto back to the kitchen where Sheri was doing her last minute prep for dinner. The boys were out of earshot in the den, playing video games.

Soto handed Sheri the phone. "I thought you might like this back."

Without bothering to look at it, Sheri thanked him and slipped the phone into her apron. "You want to stay for dinner? I can set an extra seat if you like. I'm making London Broil, and if you'll excuse the expression, it's a killer, Detective."

Soto scoffed. "Thank you, but not tonight. However, there is one more thing. Carol, I thought you might like to know Marx was scrolling through Sheri's contacts on her phone when he was hit. It looks like he had pulled up your number. If you hadn't found him, he was coming to find you."

I swallowed hard and thanked Soto for coming by, then showed him to the door.

When I got back to the kitchen, I checked my cell phone to see if Chase had called. After my invite, I had expected him to show up for dinner, but there was no message. I excused myself and told Sheri I needed to go outside and make a quick call.

I stood on the deck and rang Chase's number. The sun had set, and the lights of the city below and the stars twinkled back at me. I listened as my call went to voicemail. I wasn't about to leave another message. I already bared my soul to Chase or as much as I felt comfortable sharing. An invite to dinner, with no case looming before us, was a clear intent on my part to lower my resistance and invite him into my life. Surely he knew that.

I ended the call and slipped my phone back into my pocket. Dammit. I didn't need him anyway.

"You coming in for dinner?" My heart quickened as I recognized the voice behind me.

"You're here." I turned to see Chase standing in the doorway to the patio.

"You know me, always up for a home cooked meal."

"Me too," I said.

"However, I was hoping for something more than that." Chase took a step closer to me and put his arms around my waist.

"Like what?" I looked up into his face and put my hands on his shoulders.

"Like that last kiss we had." Chase pushed a loose strand of hair behind my ear.

"You mean...at the bar? When I was trying to avoid being seen by Brian?"

"Seemed to me there was more to it than that." Chase pulled

me closer to him.

"You're flattering yourself," I said.

"Am I?" Chase tucked his finger under my chin and pulled my face close to his. "Or are you just unsure about letting a man into your life and losing your independence? Because, lady, that's not going to happen. I like you just the way you are. Determined and stubborn as hell. My kind of woman."

My eyes met Chase's. I could feel the heat of his body next to mine. "So, are you going to kiss me or are we just going to stand here and stare into each other eyes like a couple of teenagers?"

"I've been waiting all night for you to ask," he said.

NANCY COLE SILVERMAN

Nancy Cole Silverman credits her twenty-five years in news and talk radio for helping her to develop an ear for storytelling. But it wasn't until after she retired that she was able to write fiction full-time. Much of what Silverman writes about is pulled from events that were reported on from inside some of Los Angeles' busiest newsrooms where she spent the bulk of her career. She lives in Los Angeles with her husband, Bruce, and two standard poodles.

The Carol Childs Mystery Series
by Nancy Cole Silverman

Henery Press Mystery Books

And finally, before you go...
Here are a few other mysteries
you might enjoy:

PROTOCOL

Kathleen Valenti

A Maggie O'Malley Mystery (#1)

Freshly minted college graduate Maggie O'Malley embarks on a career fueled by professional ambition and a desire to escape the past. As a pharmaceutical researcher, she's determined to save lives from the shelter of her lab. But on her very first day she's pulled into a world of uncertainty. Reminders appear on her phone for meetings she's never scheduled with people she's never met. People who end up dead.

With help from her best friend, Maggie discovers the victims on her phone are connected to each other and her new employer. She soon unearths a treacherous plot that threatens her mission—and her life. Maggie must unlock deadly secrets to stop horrific abuses of power before death comes calling for her.

Available at booksellers nationwide and online

Visit www.henerypress.com for details

MURDER ON A SILVER PLATTER

Shawn Reilly Simmons

A Red Carpet Catering Mystery (#1)

Penelope Sutherland and her Red Carpet Catering company just got their big break as the on-set caterer for an upcoming blockbuster. But when she discovers a dead body outside her house, Penelope finds herself in hot water. Things start to boil over when serious accidents threaten the lives of the cast and crew. And when the film's star, who happens to be Penelope's best friend, is poisoned, the entire production is nearly shut down.

Threats and accusations send Penelope out of the frying pan and into the fire as she struggles to keep her company afloat. Before Penelope can dish up dessert, she must find the killer or she'll be the one served up on a silver platter.

Available at booksellers nationwide and online

Visit www.henerypress.com for details

ARTIFACT

Gigi Pandian

A Jaya Jones Treasure Hunt Mystery (#1)

Historian Jaya Jones discovers the secrets of a lost Indian treasure may be hidden in a Scottish legend from the days of the British Raj. But she's not the only one on the trail...

From San Francisco to London to the Highlands of Scotland, Jaya must evade a shadowy stalker as she follows hints from the hastily scrawled note of her dead lover to a remote archaeological dig. Helping her decipher the cryptic clues are her magician best friend, a devastatingly handsome art historian with something to hide, and a charming archaeologist running for his life.

Available at booksellers nationwide and online

Visit www.henerypress.com for details

CIRCLE OF INFLUENCE

Annette Dashofy

A Zoe Chambers Mystery (#1)

Zoe Chambers, paramedic and deputy coroner in rural Pennsylvania's tight-knit Vance Township, has been privy to a number of local secrets over the years, some of them her own. But secrets become explosive when a dead body is found in the Township Board President's abandoned car.

As a January blizzard rages, Zoe and Police Chief Pete Adams launch a desperate search for the killer, even if it means uncovering secrets that could not only destroy Zoe and Pete, but also those closest to them.

Available at booksellers nationwide and online

Visit www.henerypress.com for details

Made in the USA
San Bernardino, CA
04 December 2018